ONE WISH

MICHELLE HARRISON

ONE WISH

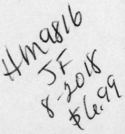

Thirteen Treasures 0.5

HM9816
JF
8-2018
£6.99

SIMON AND SCHUSTER

First published in Great Britain in 2014 by Simon and Schuster UK Ltd
A CBS COMPANY

1 3 5 7 9 10 8 6 4 2

Simon & Schuster UK Ltd
1st Floor, 222 Gray's Inn Road
London WC1X 8HB

Simon & Schuster Australia, Sydney
Simon & Schuster India, New Delhi

A CIP catalogue record for this book
is available from the British Library.

Paperback ISBN: 978-1-47112-165-4
EBook ISBN: 978-1-47112-166-1

This book is a work of fiction. Names, characters, places
and incidents are either the product of the author's imagination
or are used fictitiously. Any resemblance to actual people living or dead,
events or locales is entirely coincidental.

Printed and bound by CPI Group (UK) Ltd, Croydon, CR0 4YY

www.simonandschuster.co.uk
www.simonandschuster.com.au

For my son, Jack
A wish come true

As always, I'm grateful to my family for their support during the writing of this book, but in particular to Mum whose cooking and cleaning provided me with valuable hours to write. Thank you, my little house elf! Thanks also to Janet for talking through plotlines and making suggestions, yet again.

To my agent, Julia Churchill: you're the best. Thank you for going above and beyond, and for always believing in fairies.

Thank you to my editor, Elv Moody, whose observations and insights have made this a much better book, and to Ingrid, Elisa, Kat and the rest of the children's team at S&S whose endless enthusiasm spurred me on long after the chocolate had run out.

Finally, to every *Thirteen Treasures* fan who ~~pestered~~ asked me for another book: I'm glad you did. I know it goes backwards instead of forwards, but I hope you enjoy it nonetheless . . .

Prologue

IN A BUSY SIDE STREET OF LONDON, A hooded figure let itself into a small shop. Once inside, the person locked the door and checked that the CLOSED sign was displayed, then threw back the hood. A thin-faced, bespectacled man with shaggy grey hair, he appeared ordinary at first glance. Yet look a little closer and the tips of two pointed ears were visible beneath his hair – to those who were able to see such things at least.

Stepping over a pile of untouched letters on the doormat, the man hurried through the shop to a door at the back marked PRIVATE, a large, brown package in his gloved hands. Surrounding him on both sides were tables and shelves of the shop's wares: clocks, watches and time-keeping devices of every description. In his haste, he bumped against one of the tables, knocking a small carriage clock to the floor and shattering its glass face. He did not stop, or even pause, however. None of the items in the shop, save for the contents of the brown package, held any value to him.

Pushing through the door, he entered a little room, the

shelves of which were lined with yet more clocks in various states of repair. He set the package gently on to the table and, with trembling hands, began to unwrap it.

'Please,' he muttered. 'Let this be the one. Let the search be over.' From the brown paper wrappings, he removed an object and set it on the table. It was a golden hourglass, with two glass globes at either end, and fine, pale sand that flowed from the top to the bottom. The man peeled off his gloves and, holding his breath, laid his hands gently upon it.

Nothing.

Another dead end. This wasn't the one he was searching for after all. With a cry of rage, he flung it aside. It shattered in a flurry of sand and glass and landed on a pile of broken hourglasses he had previously checked and discarded. His face twisted in temper, the man stormed from the room and descended a narrow set of stairs to the cellar below.

He barely noticed the damp, musty smell of the place any more. At first, it had bothered him, but since taking over the shop several months ago he'd grown used to it; the cold and dark, too. He spent most of his time down here.

He stepped over a stack of books to a row of candles lined up on a shelf. With a click of his fingers, their wicks burst into flame, sending a golden glow through the dark space. Every surface was cluttered; yet more books mouldered away in damp corners; grisly ingredients glistened in glass jars. Strange apparatus occupied several tables, and scribbled notes and diagrams were scattered at every turn. And at the centre of it all stood a large, black cauldron.

The man crossed to the cauldron, treading carelessly over a balled-up note he'd long since tossed aside. From a beam above the huge, black pot, a lacy dress hung like a corpse. The man lifted his hand to caress the faded white fabric, regret and longing etched into his face.

'Some day, Helena,' he whispered. 'Some day, I'll find it. And I'll bring you back.'

Behind him, in a darkened corner of the cellar, something shifted in the shadows. Something used to being quiet and going unseen. The man half turned his head, and an unspoken question passed between them.

'I've been watching, Master.'

'And?' The man's voice was sharp.

The figure remained in the shadows, reluctant to step into the candlelight. It did not like to be seen, for good reason. Its face – if it could be called that – was terrible to behold.

'I see the boy, but not how to find him. Protection keeps him hidden; it's too strong for the vision to break through.'

The man's lips pressed into a thin line. 'Even for me.' He stared into the cauldron, brooding. There, reflected in the cauldron's depths, was the watery image of a child, but it was so blurred it was impossible to see his features or any of his surroundings clearly. The man scowled, chewing his lip. And then the scowl left his face as a thought struck him.

'Of course,' he whispered. 'Why didn't I think of it sooner?'

'Master?' the creature intoned.

The man stood up a little straighter, then scanned the cellar, looking for a particular ingredient. Once he'd located it, he plucked a small glass bottle from a shelf and dusted it off, then removed the stopper. From it, he allowed a single drop of liquid to fall into the cauldron. Then from a nearby table he took an old pocket watch and carefully wound its hands forward. Into the pot it went with a soft splash.

'I've been doing it all wrong,' he said, his eyes lit with feverish excitement. 'Wasted years trying to track the object, and months trying to trace the boy, with no luck. But now . . .'

He peered into the cauldron. 'Show me,' he commanded. 'Reveal the face of the next person the boy will meet.' The cauldron bubbled in response. In the murky depths, the water cleared and then the vision changed. As it did so, the man's expression changed also. For the first time in a very long while, he smiled. There, in the water, the face of a girl he had never seen before appeared. He watched as she walked up a path, arriving at the door of a quaint little cottage.

'The girl,' he breathed. 'This girl will lead us straight to him. She just doesn't know it.' His smile broadened, giving way to a low chuckle. 'Find the girl . . . and we find the boy.'

1

The Wishing Tree

TANYA FAIRCHILD SENSED THERE WAS something wrong with the place from the moment they walked in.

'This is it.' Her mother unlocked the door to Hawthorn Cottage and pushed it open. 'What do you think?'

Tanya followed her mother into the dark space beyond the door, dragging her suitcase and her heels. Her eyelids had begun to twitch. She rubbed at them, wondering if some dust had flown up, or if it was perhaps the effect of the darkness after coming in from outside. She wrinkled her nose. 'It smells ... *funny* in here.'

Oberon, her plump, brown Doberman, clearly agreed. His claws clicked over the wooden floor as his large, wet nose took in the scent of the unfamiliar surroundings.

'Well, of course it does.' Her mother set down her own suitcase and reached for the nearest window, throwing the shutters wide open. Bright sunshine streamed in. 'We're the first booking of the season. It's bound to smell a bit musty – the place has been closed up all through the winter.'

'No, it's not that.' Tanya looked around the holiday cottage, trying to figure out what it was that was bothering her.

Her mother continued to open all the windows, flooding the place with light and fresh air.

'Look how sweet it is,' she exclaimed, pointing to the tiny kitchenette, where an old-fashioned whistling kettle sat on a gas hob, and mismatched floral teacups, pots and pans were arranged on brightly painted shelves.

Opposite, a living-room area held an inviting blue sofa, a small coffee table and a larger, white painted table with three chairs.

'These must be the bedrooms,' her mother said, moving to two doors at the back. She opened one of them. 'Oh, Tanya, they're lovely. Come and see.'

'In a minute,' Tanya replied distractedly. It was clearer now, the sound she had picked up on as soon as she had entered the cottage: a light scuffling that seemed to be coming from underneath the floorboards. She knelt down and put her ear to the floor, trying to locate the source. It was difficult to hear, for her mother kept calling out with every new discovery. 'Mine's a four-poster bed ... and just look at the Victorian bathtub!'

Tanya covered the ear that wasn't pressed to the floor and listened harder. There it was again ... scuffle, scuffle, scratch. The smell was stronger here, too: an earthy, outdoorsy sort of smell. Oberon trotted over, his head tilted to one side, listening.

Maybe it's just a mouse, she thought, realising as she did so that her stomach was tensed into a hard knot. 'Please, please, let it be a mouse. Or even a rat. Anything but that . . .'

The scuffling paused, became a rustle. Then, alarmingly close to Tanya's ear, came another sound: a busy sniffling, snuffling noise that was far too concentrated to be coming from the nose of a mouse. Her eyelids twitched again; a warning sign. Still she hoped that she was mistaken, that it was not really one of *them* that she was about to see.

She didn't have to wait long before a crabby little voice growled up through the floorboards.

'Summer already? It must be summer, because every summer they come. Horrible, stinking humans! With their noise and their chatter, and their dirt and their disgustable, rancidious food smells!'

A sharp tap by Tanya's ear made her jump. Something had struck the underside of the floor. She shifted position, peering down through a gap in the floorboards. A tiny, bloodshot eye, half hidden beneath a bushy, grey eyebrow, glared back at her through a plume of dust. Oberon gave a yelp of surprise, then sneezed violently.

'I can see you, you little maggot!'

'Who are you calling a maggot?' Tanya said indignantly. 'We've only just arrived. We haven't done anything to you!'

'Doesn't matter.' The glare deepened. 'You're all the same. A nuisance, that's what.'

'I could say the same thing about you,' Tanya retorted. 'Always getting me into trouble for no good reason. It's not my fault I can see you – I wish I couldn't, you know!'

'Be careful what you wish for,' the horrid little voice said. 'I could easily stamp out your eyes while you sleep.'

The words sent a chill over the back of Tanya's neck, but the stubborn streak in her would not allow herself to be bullied.

'And I could easily stamp you out altogether,' she whispered. 'I should think you'd fit quite nicely under the heel of my shoe.'

She held her breath. The bloodshot eye widened, then narrowed.

'Insolent wretch!' The eye vanished from the gap and was replaced by a glimpse of jagged, yellowing teeth. 'You wait. Just you wait!'

A low growl rumbled in Oberon's throat. He couldn't understand what was being said, of course, but he knew that his beloved Tanya was being threatened – and he didn't like it one bit.

'Tanya?'

Her mother's voice nearby startled her. She sat up, banging her head on the corner of the coffee table. 'Ouch! What?'

Her mother was watching her carefully, a puzzled look on her face. It was a look Tanya had seen many times.

'What are you doing?'

Tanya rubbed the sore spot on her head. 'Nothing. I . . .' She hesitated, tempted, as she so often was, to simply tell the truth. 'I mean, I thought I saw a . . .'

Her mother's expression was changing, from puzzled to impatient.

'Tanya, please don't say "a fairy",' she said. Her voice was suddenly weary and very quiet. 'You're twelve, much too old for all that nonsense now.'

'A . . . spider,' Tanya finished, her shoulders slumping. It was no good. Her mother had never listened before. Nobody had. Why should things be any different now?

'Oooooh! A spider, am I?' crowed the voice from beneath the floorboards. 'So, the daughter can see me, but the mother can't . . . Oh, I'll have some fun with this, you see if I don't!'

Tanya got up from the floor and sank miserably on to the sofa, the fairy's gleeful laughter ringing in her ears. The relief on her mother's face did little to make her feel any better. It wouldn't last. The fairy had promised trouble, and Tanya knew only too well that she would get it. It was just a question of when.

'Why don't you make a start on unpacking and I'll put together some lunch?' her mother suggested.

Tanya nodded glumly. She got up and collected her case, then trudged to the back of the cottage. The first bedroom was larger, with the four-poster bed her mother had described, and a quaint, old-fashioned bathtub just visible through another door into the bathroom.

The second bedroom was simpler and smaller, but bright and cheerful with crisp lemon bedding and matching curtains. She heaved her suitcase on to the bed and unzipped it, pulling out her clothes and shoes into a higgledy-piggledy pile, then went over to the tiny, criss-crossed window and stared out. A rambling flower garden with a narrow stone path lay before her like something from a picture book. As she watched, a little brown hedgehog ambled across the grass and two robins perched on a crumbling birdbath. She smiled faintly, then almost tripped over Oberon who had crept in and settled on the rug behind her. He thumped his tail as she scratched his chocolate-brown head, before gathering an armful of clothes to put away. Oberon settled down for a snooze.

She worked quietly, listening out for any telltale scratches or muttering from under the floorboards, but none came. She hoped that this was the only fairy in the house. In the countryside, she knew, fairies were never very far away. Tanya had endured many a stay with her one surviving grandmother, Florence, who lived in an old country manor in Essex.

Tanya had never liked the house and dreaded it every time her mother sent her there, for it was crawling with fairies. In the kitchen alone, there were two: a funny little creature in a dishrag dress who hid behind the coalscuttle, and an ancient, grumpy brownie who lived in the tea caddy and was fond of rapping her over the knuckles with its walking stick every time she reached in for a teabag.

Then there was the unseen clan that had invaded the grandfather clock and who were the reason the blasted thing never worked. Their sly insults rang in Tanya's ears every time she passed it. Worse still, a froggy-looking creature with rotten-egg breath lived in the bathroom pipes. Much like a magpie, it stole anything it could lay its clammy little fingers on that happened to be shiny. Despite the unpleasant idea of spending her holiday sharing a cottage with whatever it was that was lurking under the floorboards, Tanya had to admit that it was better than going to her grandmother's house.

Before long, the last item had been put away and her mother was calling her for lunch. She returned to the living-room area and helped her mother carry the dishes and bowls to the table. Once seated, she poured some orange juice and helped herself to salad, bread, ham and a hard-boiled egg, munching in earnest as she suddenly realised how hungry she was.

Unsurprisingly, Oberon had awoken from his nap and was now resting his head on Tanya's knee, his long, brown nose sticking out from beneath the tablecloth. She smuggled him a piece of ham, and would have got away with it had he not wolfed it down so noisily, prompting a sigh from her mother.

'Oh, Tanya. I've told you about feeding Oberon titbits – you know he's becoming an awful scrounger. And besides, he's getting rather plump.'

'He's not plump,' Tanya muttered, but all the same she couldn't help feeling a bit guilty. Oberon *was* a dreadful beggar at the dinner table and a thief, too, when he thought he could get away with it. 'It's just . . . puppy fat.'

It was her fault, of course. It had started a few months ago, when her father had left. The first few weeks hadn't been so bad, because it didn't feel real, not at first. She could pretend that he was just away on business, like he so often was, and that soon he would be coming back. However, after a month of weekend visits and strained conversation, and the house gradually emptying of his belongings, it finally began to sink in that he really was gone. It was then that Tanya began to miss him terribly. And so did Oberon.

So when Tanya had found him curled up on a tatty, forgotten pair of her father's slippers – the last of his possessions left in the house – she'd done the only thing she could think of to cheer him up: she had given him a biscuit. In that moment, seeing him crunching happily and wagging his tail, Tanya, too, had felt better. It was an easy fix and it didn't last. She knew that, but now Oberon had come to expect it, it made it so much harder not to give in. Especially when he looked at her the way he did now, with those beseeching brown eyes of his.

She stroked the tip of his nose with her thumb. 'Good boy. Go and lie down now.' He lumbered off obediently and she pushed her plate away, her appetite gone now that thoughts of her father had crept into her mind.

'What's the matter? Not hungry?'

Tanya stared at the empty third chair at the table. 'Why are there three seats if there are only two of us?'

Her mother lowered her eyes and wiped her mouth. 'Because the cottage can take up to three people.' She hesitated. 'I know you miss him. I still do, too—'

'*You* miss him?' Tanya scoffed. She couldn't help it. 'You were the one who made him leave!'

'It will get easier.' Her mother's voice was pleading. 'I know you don't believe it now, but things are better already.'

'How?' Tanya demanded.

'Because at least the shouting and the arguments have stopped.'

Tanya got up, knocking into the table.

'I'm going for a walk,' she said stiffly.

Her mother looked crestfallen. 'Don't go far and don't be too long.'

Tanya nodded and collected Oberon's leash, along with some spare change, and zipped them into her rucksack. Oberon trotted to her heel as she opened the cottage door, passing beneath the archway that was busy with climbing roses, their scent heavy and sweet in the thick July air. She closed the door with a heavier bang than intended, then started off down the little stone path that led through the garden and away from the cottage.

Her mother was right: the arguments had stopped. She should be grateful for that, she knew she should. Yet, somehow, what the arguments had left behind was almost as bad, because it was silence. And in that silence Tanya's loneliness and anger grew and began their own ugly fight, growing louder and louder until it was all she could hear.

Soon the path came to an end and opened out on to a road. It was busier here with cars trundling along in search of somewhere to park and the cries of seagulls overhead.

Tanya lifted her nose to sniff the air and the briny scent of the sea filled her lungs. The sea wall was just a stone's throw away; she could see it from here.

At the side of the road a wooden board read: *Welcome to Spinney Wicket!* On the opposite side, a white signpost pointed in various directions: Seafront, Pier, Pavilion, Spinney Castle. She took a few steps in the direction of the pier, then paused. Faint strains of funfair music reached her ears, along with shouts of laughter. It was enough to change her mind. She knew from experience that the only thing lonelier than silence was to be alone around others who were having fun.

'Come on, Oberon,' she said. 'We'll go this way instead.' With that, she set off in the direction of the castle, Oberon's nose bumping the back of her legs as she went.

The new path took her along a little dirt road, overgrown with wildflowers and overlooked by fields of sheep and cattle. After a good five minutes of walking in solitude, she began to feel uneasy. The sounds of the seafront could no longer be heard and she hadn't seen another soul since she took the path.

Little snickering, chittering noises from the long grass caught her attention, and once or twice she thought she heard whispers from within the greenery. Tanya kept her eyes on the path; she'd had enough of fairies for one day.

Suddenly, the dirt road came to an end, bringing her to a wide-open meadow. Shielding her eyes from the sun, she gazed into the hazy distance. There, on top of a hill,

Spinney Castle sat like a crown. At the highest point, and in some of the windows, dark shapes moved; people were exploring.

From the corner of her eye, a flash of emerald light caught her attention. She turned towards it, squinting. It had come from a large, solitary tree that stood halfway between her and the castle. As she stared at it, another flash – bright blue this time – dazzled her eyes.

'What on earth are those lights?' she wondered aloud. Mesmerised, she moved towards them, quickening her pace. Oberon bounded along beside her, hardly able to control his excitement at all the new smells. As they drew nearer, Tanya watched for the mysterious lights. They seemed to go off all of a sudden in a chain: one, two, three. Silver, green, silver again. Nothing for a further minute ... perhaps the source of the mysterious lights had seen her approaching? But no, there were another two. Lilac and turquoise this time.

As she got closer still, Tanya could see the tree in greater detail. It loomed above her, almost as wide as it was tall. Its trunk was thick, gnarled and knotted. It looked very, very old. The thought struck her how odd it was for the tree to be here all alone in the meadow. There were no other trees close by; the nearest were off in the distance by the castle. Stepping beneath the cool shade of its branches, she stared up into the dense, green leaves. There she found the answer to the strange lights.

Glass bottles and jars, in their dozens – no, hundreds –

hung from the branches above. They were all shapes and sizes, and every colour she could think of. Most were coloured glass, but some were plain or had been painted. Each one contained something. She reached for one of the lower hanging ones, a small, tear-dropped bottle of pale blue. Inside, rolled tightly and bound with string, was a piece of paper with something written on it.

Are these messages? Tanya wondered. *If so, who are they for?* The harder she looked, the more she saw; it seemed that every little twig was adorned with something. And that was not all, for there were also ribbons and strips of cloth tied to the tree, too. A soft breeze rushed through the leaves, whispering over the bottle tops to create a lilting melody. The ribbons rippled and the bottles danced as though they approved, and the movement sent them swaying out into the sunshine where rays of light bounced off them in jewel-coloured flashes.

Tanya stood there, drinking it in with her eyes. She did not know what the tree was, or what all the bottles and jars were for, yet somehow it didn't matter. It was the most beautiful tree she had ever seen in her life, and it seemed to her to be curiously magical, too.

And, as she held that very thought, the knots in the gnarled tree trunk twisted and rearranged themselves. Two of the knots opened ... and blinked. Below them, a third knot puckered before opening in an enormous yawn.

Tanya stood rooted to the spot, unable to tear her eyes from the face in the tree. The tree-eyes – dewy and green –

fixed upon her and the mouth opened once more to reveal a twiggy, crooked set of teeth.

'One wish, what'll it be?' it said. 'For you have found the Wishing Tree.'

2

The Second Sight

TANYA KNEW HER MOUTH WAS OPENING and closing, but she simply couldn't find any words with which to respond. Naturally, she was used to odd things happening around her; seeing fairies meant that there was little that surprised her. But the tree had spoken. Spoken! Whoever knew there was such a thing as a talking tree, except in fairy tales? And however was one supposed to reply?

Oberon appeared equally baffled. As far as he knew, trees were for sniffing and marking territory, not talking. He cowered and pressed himself into the back of Tanya's legs. She reached down and gave his head a comforting pat, and was still searching for the right words when the tree, evidently not a patient sort, grew tired of waiting for her to answer and spoke again.

'One wish only, understood?
There are rules, so listen good.
Wish for more wishes – that's a no.
Away with nothing you will go!

No one killed or back from the dead,
And what you've wished can't be unsaid.
No changing the past, no future revealed.
Some things must remain concealed.
No exchange, no guarantees,
So make your choice responsibly.
Every wish comes at a price,
Whether it's nasty or it's nice.
So what'll it be? Tea with the Queen?
Wings for a day? Pay back someone mean?
Become stinking rich, win your true love's heart?
Grow taller, run faster, become super smart?
Talk to your dog or turn into a cat?
Eat chocolate all day and never get fat?
Find something lost, have beauty or youth?
Wish for a liar to tell the truth!
Walk on the moon, achieve instant fame?
One wish and the world could know your name.
Be sure to use your common sense,
Each wish comes with a consequence.
For wings are tricky to explain.
Fame means no peace for you again.
Riches come, but at what cost?
While magical love is easily lost.
And it's all very well scoffing chocolate all day,
Being skinny's no good if your teeth rot away!
So take your time and use your head.
There's nothing you'd rather wish instead?

Now speak it loud and speak it clear
Or write it down and hang it here.
Don't use rags or glass of red.
Choose something else, like green, instead.
Then like a little seedling planted
Your wish shall surely soon be granted.'

The tree stopped. Stared expectantly. Yawned again and then hiccuped. Tanya was still at a loss for what to say, but now her mind was racing with possibilities. One wish!

What do I wish for?

The answer came almost immediately, floating before her like one of the wish bottles on the breeze.

I wish for Dad to come back. For him and Mum to love each other again.

She opened her mouth, ready to utter the words. Her face was hot with anticipation. And then a voice, a *new* voice, sounded from somewhere within the branches above, shocking her into silence.

'Yes, yes, I heard you the first time,' it said crossly. 'You don't need to keep repeating your silly rules!'

Tanya shifted position quietly, peering up into the leafy branches. Looking this way and that, at first she could see nothing beyond the foliage and swaying glass. Then she spotted something: a boot. An extremely battered black boot, so battered that the toe had almost worn away to a hole. The boot gave way to an equally tatty trouser leg, all of which was balanced on a high, sturdy branch some way above her head. A low grumbling followed.

'. . . String, string . . . where did I put that string?'

There was a rustle in the branches and a handful of leaves floated past Tanya's head. Whoever the boot belonged to still had no idea they were not alone and was rummaging in their pockets, presumably for the lost string. Eventually, after much fumbling and several grunts of exasperation, a hand reached down to the boot and began pulling the shoelace from it.

'This'll have to do.'

Tanya hesitated, feeling like an intruder. Part of her wanted to slink away, but another more curious part wanted to find out who the person up in the tree was, because she had questions. When the tree had first spoken, she had assumed that she was witnessing another element of the fairy world. The fact that this other person could also hear the tree meant one of two things: that the person was like her and saw things most people could not, or that this tree was a different kind of magic and could be heard by anyone it chose. Given that Tanya had never met anyone, ever, who shared her strange ability, she thought the second explanation was the most likely.

She was startled from her thoughts by a loud thump in the grass and a muttered, 'Oh, heck!' from above.

She looked down. A green glass bottle with a shoe-lace looped round its neck had landed in a clump of grass just by her foot. Oberon leaped back with a yelp, giving them away.

'Who's there?' the voice demanded. An angry rustling

21

followed. Branches swished and wobbled. The mysterious tree climber was coming down.

Tanya gulped and stooped to pick up the bottle. A scrap of paper was rolled into a tight coil inside. 'You ... you dropped this,' she called eventually, not knowing what else to say.

'Well, obviously,' the voice retorted, dripping with sarcasm. Legs dangled in the air for a moment as a branch above shook, then a person not much taller than herself dropped to the leaf-scattered grass.

'Not so rough!' the tree snapped. 'I may look tough, but I'm too old for moves so bold!'

Tanya stared at the boy in front of her. The boy glared back, eyeing the bottle in her hand with suspicion. He was about her age, eleven or twelve, with skin the colour of caramel and the brightest blue eyes she had ever seen. His tousled hair was as black and shiny as liquorice, and in need of a good cut. The ends of it brushed against a grubby red neckerchief.

Tanya was aware that the tree's eyes were flitting between herself and the boy, waiting for one of them to say something. It clearly didn't like being ignored.

'How long have you been standing there?' the boy asked.

'Not very long,' Tanya answered. 'A couple of minutes.'

The boy's eyes widened.

'A-*hem!*' said the tree. Again, neither Tanya nor the boy responded.

'I heard you talking—' Tanya began, but broke off as the boy lunged towards her.

Instinctively, she leaped out of his way, only realising at the last moment that he had merely attempted to snatch the bottle from her hand, not harm her. In any case, Oberon jumped up with a warning growl, his huge paws landing squarely on the boy's scrawny chest. He went down like a skittle, landing hard on his bottom with a breathless 'Oof!' before scrambling to his feet again and taking off across the meadow.

Delighted, Oberon let out a trio of barks, as though to say, 'And don't come back!'

'Wait!' Tanya yelled after the boy. 'You forgot your wish!'

The scruffy figure, already out of hearing distance, didn't slow down. In a few seconds, he was merely a speck on the landscape, then was gone from sight. Oberon looked up at her, a ridiculously proud expression on his face. She sighed and scratched his ears. It was typical of Oberon to be afraid of a talking tree, but not hesitate to protect her if he thought she was in real danger.

She examined the glass bottle, wishing she'd had a chance to speak to the boy properly before he ran off. Now she was stuck with his wish and she didn't know what to do with it. Should she hang it up on the tree, she wondered, or was it bad luck to leave someone else's wish instead of your own? If only she could find the boy somehow. That way she could give him back his wish and ask him about the tree at the same time.

She twisted the shoelace round her fingers gloomily and stared at the ant-sized figures over at the castle. There was very little chance of bumping into the boy again in a busy seaside town such as Spinney Wicket, not unless she knew where he would be. Her only clue was the tree – if the boy had meant to leave a wish, then he would probably be back again, but Tanya couldn't wait out in the middle of a meadow for hours on end in the hope that he'd turn up. It would soon grow dark and cold.

Or was the tree her only clue? She looked back down at the bottle again.

'That's not your wish so don't dare peek,' the tree said unexpectedly, making her jump. 'Don't be a nosy little sneak.'

'I wasn't going to!' Tanya said indignantly.

Two bushy clumps of green moss furrowed over the tree's eyes in a disbelieving frown. 'Humph,' it said, before the knots in the bark rearranged themselves and the face vanished.

'I wasn't,' Tanya insisted, even though there was no one to hear her now. 'I don't need to.'

There was something on the bottle, raised lettering moulded into the glass. It read: *Pepper's Pantry* in fancy writing. Underneath, there was an address: *No. 9, The Pier, Spinney Wicket*.

Of course, there was no guarantee that the boy himself had bought the bottle of whatever it was from this place; he could have easily picked it up out of a bin. He could also,

Tanya thought grouchily, be on holiday just as she was and be returning home any day soon. But the bottle was a start at least, and it was the only clue she had to go on. She unzipped her rucksack and pushed the bottle inside, then set off towards the castle.

She had barely taken ten steps when she came across a wooden information stand that was almost entirely camou-flaged in the meadow. It was choked with bindweed, and what little wood was visible had faded to a mossy green. Tanya cleared some of the weeds. It was little wonder she hadn't seen it from the tree.

The Wishing Tree of Spinney Wicket, read the sign. *Estimated to be over two centuries old, this grand elder is Spinney Wicket's most magical resident. Legend has it that, upon buying the land from his neighbour, one Farmer Bramley and his son began cutting down a number of trees with the intention of plant-ing new crops. When they reached the tree, a small voice called out to the men, pleading with them to stop.*

The men lowered their axes, astonished to see the face of a young tree sprite taking form within the bark. The sprite informed them that elder trees, also known as fairy trees, carry vast power. This tree, it warned them, was its home and, if they should chop it down, their crops would fail and their luck would turn rotten. If they spared the tree, however, the sprite would repay them, and any human who so requested, by granting a wish.

The farmer and his son heeded the sprite's warning and, so it is said, lived long, happy lives with the most successful crops for miles around. Word of their good fortune quickly spread, and soon the tree could barely keep up with the wishes. To prevent wishes being lost or forgotten, the practice of writing them down and hanging them on the tree became common, and continues to prevail.

Today people still journey from far and wide to ask a wish from the tree, though few can claim to have seen the sprite. Those who do are believed to possess the ability to see fairies, otherwise known as the second sight.

So, what are you waiting for? Make a wish! Just be careful what you wish for . . .

'The second sight,' Tanya whispered. She had never had her ability, her oddness, described in such a way, but she found that she rather liked it. Instead of sounding peculiar and wrong, it made her feel unique. Special. So the tree could not be seen – or heard – by everyone who approached it. She felt a stir of pity; it must be lonely out here all by itself with hardly anyone to talk to. No wonder it had been so grumpy at being ignored by two people who could actually hear it. Tanya was now certain that the mysterious boy shared this 'second sight' and she was determined to find him.

Her own wish forgotten for now, she turned away from the castle and headed back to the little footpath.

'This way, Oberon,' she called. 'We're going to the pier.'

3

Ratty

THE PIER WAS A BUSTLING, JOSTLING, TOE-crushing place, accompanied by the wafting scent of candyfloss mingled with fish and chips, and the strains of carousel music from the nearby amusements. The sun, still high in the sky, beat down on the worn wooden boards beneath Tanya's feet, and through the gaps in them she could see the grey-blue seawater swirling below.

Everywhere she looked there were penny-drop machines, hook-a-duck stalls and ice-cream carts. Bags of candyfloss were strung above her head like fluffy, pink bunting. Everything was noisy and crowded; it was difficult to take it all in. She paused a moment, trying to make out the numbers on the many shopfronts. Eventually, she spotted one, number seventy-five, on a nearby souvenir shop, and groaned. Number nine, the one she was looking for, must be right at the other end of the pier.

She tried to set off, but was held in place by strong resistance at the other end of Oberon's leash. A little girl had wandered up to pat him, a sticky hand in his fur. In her other hand, she held a melting ice-cream cone, which was dripping tantalisingly on to Oberon's large, brown nose. Unable to resist, he went in for a crafty lick of the cone. The child didn't seem to mind.

'Oberon, no!' Tanya scolded, pulling him away just in time, and Oberon had to make do with licking the melted droplets from his nose.

They walked on, past tea rooms and seashell shops and toddlers having tantrums, until finally the end of the pier was in sight. There, nestled between a shop selling beach towels and buckets and spades and yet another candyfloss stall, she found Pepper's Pantry, a quaint little café. Though lunchtime was now coming to an end, it was still very busy. All the seats outside in the sun were taken, but there was one tiny table free, half inside the shop, just beneath the awning.

Tanya sat down, hooking Oberon's leash over the back of her chair. The walk in the heat had left her thirsty. Peering into the glass-fronted counter, she saw that the café boasted home-made ice cream from a nearby dairy and an array of locally sourced fruit juices in beautiful glass bottles – just like the green one she held in her rucksack. Though the contents of the red bottle, plum and raspberry, sounded especially delicious, she remembered what the tree had said:

Don't use rags or glass of red.

Choose something else, like green, instead.

And so she chose a green bottle, which was apple and pear. As she drank it, she wondered why the Wishing Tree disliked red bottles or rags; it seemed very odd. There had been a number of red bottles on the tree, no doubt left by people who were unable to see the sprite or hear its instructions. Did that mean their wishes had gone unfulfilled?

Still pondering the thought, she was peeling the label from the empty bottle when a flash of movement caught her eye. She glanced towards it – and her hand froze. A tiny girl, no taller than Tanya's knee, was edging her way over to a nearby table occupied by a family of four. Two pointed ears poked through short, messy fair hair and a single green wing stuck out through a specially made hole in the little brown waistcoat. The wing twitched and buzzed as the fairy moved, and Tanya could see that it was scarred and ragged, like something had once attacked it. She guessed that this was a grisly clue as to what had happened to the other missing wing.

As well as being unusually large, the fairy's feet were dirty and bare, and an unsightly tuft of frizzy hair sprouted from each big toe. The feet scampered over the floor, trampling over a dropped sandwich crust and squelching through a slice of tomato without a care. Then, by a chair that was tucked beneath the table, the revolting feet stopped.

Tanya's eyes travelled up in time to witness the fairy's grubby fingers delving into an expensive-looking handbag that was hanging over the back of the chair. The fingers emerged with a crisp five-pound note which was swiftly stuffed into a brown sack slung over the fairy's back. Tanya stared helplessly at the owner of the bag, a woman with a mouthful of cream scone, willing her to see. But of course she couldn't and, as the fairy skipped from table to table, pilfering pockets and helping itself to the contents of hand-bags, it was clear that nobody else could see it, either.

And the little thief didn't stop there. Right under the noses of the oblivious waitresses, it leaped on to the glass counter and slid down the other side. There it waited until every back was turned before craftily sliding the glass doors open and stealing a meat pie and an iced bun. These were carefully wrapped in napkins before joining the other stolen goods in the brown sack.

The fairy clambered back over the counter, licking icing from its fingers. The smug look on its face sent Tanya's heart pumping with rage, for now the cheeky little beast was heading right for her table. Oberon, who had fallen asleep on Tanya's feet, was given nothing more than a dismissive look before the fairy turned its attention to Tanya's ruck-sack. Before she could help herself, Tanya snatched up the bag and hugged it fiercely to her chest.

'Don't even think about it, you nasty little thief!' she whispered.

The fairy stopped dead, its eyes huge with shock. It regarded Tanya warily, then recovered itself. Its eyes narrowed to slits and its lips drew back over its teeth in an ugly snarl.

'Put it back,' Tanya said through gritted teeth, hoping her voice was low enough not to attract anyone else's attention. 'Put it all back. Now.'

'Shan't!' the fairy retorted with an infuriating smirk. 'You can't make me!'

It slunk under another table. It was right, of course. What could Tanya do? Even if she tackled it and managed to get the stolen items back, how could she return them to their owners without looking as though she herself was guilty of stealing them? Besides, she thought in disgust, she wouldn't want anyone to eat the pie or the iced bun after the fairy's dirty little fingers had mauled them.

Dimly aware that her hands had clenched into fists on the tabletop, she watched as the thieving fairy approached its next victim, a young man reading a book. Only this time the fairy did something quite unexpected. Instead of reaching for a pocket, it pored over the man's boot, scratching its chin before pulling the knot free and deftly unravelling the shoelace.

Tanya frowned in confusion. Surely the fairy wasn't going to attempt to steal the man's boots? They'd be far too difficult to make away with! This time, she realised, there *was* something she could do.

She leaned closer to the man at the table. 'Excuse me?' she began.

The man looked up. 'Yes?'

'Your shoelace is undone.' She glanced under the table. The fairy had pulled the lace completely free and was now stuffing it into the sack with everything else. *Odd*, she thought. *Perhaps it doesn't want the boot after all . . .*

The man raised his eyebrows. Clearly, he thought Tanya

was odd. Nevertheless, he gave her a polite smile. 'Uh, thanks.' He bent down, just as the end of the shoelace vanished into the sack. 'Oh . . .' He looked confused now. 'I must have lost it altogether. That's strange.'

What would it want with one shoelace? Tanya wondered.

The fairy shot a victorious look at Tanya and hissed like a threatened cat. Then it took off at remarkable speed, dragging its stolen cargo behind it. Tanya stood up quickly, jolting Oberon from his snooze. A thought had struck her, and suddenly she had a very strong feeling about what the shoelace was for – and where it would lead her.

'Well, I hope you find it,' she gabbled, grabbing her rucksack and Oberon's leash. 'I have to go now!'

With that, she took off, pushing clumsily past the other tables. She heard tuts and exclamations of, 'Well, really!' but she did not slow down or stop to apologise. This, she knew, might be her only chance. Once out of the café and back on the pier, she looked this way and that before glimpsing a brown blur headed in the direction of the pier's entrance.

She raced after it, dodging people right and left, all the while trying not to lose sight of the small, wily figure that was weaving in and out of people's legs with ease, sometimes causing them to stumble. On it went, and on, snatching a newspaper from a coffee-shop table and a bag of candyfloss from a stall as it went. Both went into the brown sack. Soon, almost at the end of the pier, Tanya could feel herself slowing. Her forehead and upper lip were wet with sweat. She couldn't keep up with it for much longer . . .

Just then, it made a sharp turn to the right, vanishing into a games arcade. Tanya stopped and waited, watching the exit closely. She didn't think the fairy knew that it had been followed, but she held back all the same, just in case this was a cunning trick to draw her into the arcade and then lose her.

Oberon gave a little whine and looked up at Tanya, as if to ask why the chase was over.

'It isn't,' she told him, stroking his nose. 'But you have to wait outside now – dogs aren't allowed in.' She tied his leash to a nearby drainpipe and stepped inside. It was dark and hot from so many people crowding round the machines or queuing at the kiosk to change notes into coins. It smelled stale: of money and old chip fat. The carpet was sticky beneath her feet. Music jangled, voices chattered and coins clattered. She edged her way around, trying to concentrate on her search for the fairy thief, but there was no sign of it.

Working her way backwards to the rear of the arcade, Tanya was beginning to think that perhaps she had been fooled after all, and that maybe the fairy had cleverly led her inside and then dodged her. She sighed, noticing a rolled up five-pound note on the floor. It must have been dropped by a tall, thin youth who was playing alone on the shooting range. She knelt to pick it up for him, then snatched her fingers back just in time as a battered black boot came out of nowhere, trapping the note in place. A brown hand flashed before her eyes, scooping it up.

Tanya leaped up, finding herself face to face with the

black-haired boy who had been climbing the Wishing Tree. He stared at her for a moment, as if trying to place her, then recognition crossed his face.

'Oh, not you again!' he said, wrinkling his nose.

'Yes, me again,' Tanya retorted. 'And don't you screw up your nose at me. Where are your manners?'

'Forgotten them.' The boy turned his back on her, but found his path barred by the youth who had dropped the money.

'What's the matter?' the black-haired boy asked, unrolling the note from its tight curl. 'Lost something?'

The older boy stared at the money, confusion spreading across his thin face. 'I thought . . . I thought I dropped something . . .'

The black-haired boy gave a cheeky grin and, still clutching the five-pound note, pretended to search the dirty carpet by his feet. 'Can't see anything here. You must be mistaken.'

The older boy nodded and scratched his head, then turned back to the machine he'd been playing. The black-haired boy slipped the money into his pocket and sauntered off, whistling.

Tanya marched after him and tapped him on the shoulder, hard. 'That's stealing!' she said.

The boy turned round and crossed his arms. 'Says who?'

'Says me,' Tanya answered, defiant.

'Really? How do you know whose money it was? Did you see him drop it?'

Tanya hesitated. 'Well, no . . . but—'

'Exactly. I was the one who dropped it. It's mine. Now go and find someone else to annoy.' He started to move away again.

Tanya's cheeks began to burn, partly from anger and partly from embarrassment. Had she made a mistake and accused a stranger of stealing without any solid proof? A stranger who was the only other person she knew who could see fairies, and to whom she desperately wanted to speak? She swallowed. 'Wait. Please. I'm sorry.' She slipped her rucksack off her shoulders and reached into it. 'I came here to look for you.'

The boy paused. 'Why?'

'To give you this.' Tanya pulled the wish bottle out of her bag. She held on to it tightly, half expecting him to grab it and run.

'You came all this way to return it?' the boy asked. 'You shouldn't have bothered. I can leave another wish, if I want to.'

Tanya watched him curiously. Despite his casual manner, the way the boy's eyes kept creeping over the bottle told her that he wanted it back. Very much indeed.

'I didn't read it, in case you were wondering,' she said.

The boy shrugged. 'Don't care if you did.' He held out his hand. 'Seeing as you're here, I might as well take it.'

Tanya held the bottle out and his hand closed round it. 'There was one other thing.'

The boy gave the bottle a light tug, but Tanya tightened her grip.

'I know you can see fairies.'

The boy snorted. 'Don't be ridiculous. You've been reading about that stupid tree, haven't you? Well, it's just a story, a legend.'

'No, it isn't,' Tanya said. 'You know it's real and so do I. I heard the tree talking. And I heard you speaking to it. I know you can see fairies, because I can see them, too.'

A sudden scurrying movement caught her eye, down by the boy's foot. She released the wish bottle into the boy's hand, a slow smile spreading across her face.

'You don't know what you're talking about,' he muttered, but he sounded less sure of himself now.

Tanya raised her eyebrows. 'I think I do,' she said. 'Because there's a fairy with very hairy toes putting a stolen shoelace into your boot right at this moment.'

The fairy thief looked up, guilt and surprise etched on to her face. She had been so intent on threading the lace into the boot that she hadn't even noticed Tanya watching. She gave a squeak and climbed, monkey-like, up the boy's clothes to sit on his shoulder, clutching her bag of loot to her tightly.

Tanya folded her arms, waiting. Finally, the boy sighed.

'Oh, all right.' He reached up and gave one of the hairy toes a prod. 'This is Turpin and I'm Henry. Henry Hanratty. Most people call me Ratty.'

'Pleased to meet you, Ratty,' she said. 'I'm Tanya. Now

what can you tell me about fairies?' She glanced at Turpin, who was chewing on a strand of Ratty's hair and glaring at her. 'Because you seem to know more than I do.'

'Plenty,' said Ratty. He took a deep breath, as though trying to make some kind of decision. 'But we shouldn't talk about it here. Follow me.'

4

Nessie Needleteeth

'THE FIRST THING YOU NEED TO KNOW about fairies,' said Ratty, 'is that they can only use magic on you if you let them.'

'If I let them?' Tanya said doubtfully. 'It's not like I tell every fairy I see that they're free to do whatever horrible things that they can think of.' She clambered over yet another stile into a deserted field, catching a splinter in her thumb as she did so. 'I ignore them—' She caught Turpin shooting her a filthy look and quickly added, '—Well, mostly.' She sucked her sore thumb and dropped to the grass, waiting for Oberon to jump over.

'What sort of horrible things do they do?' Ratty asked. He was striding ahead now, with Turpin still perched on his shoulder like a parrot.

Tanya hurried to catch up with him. They had been walking for nearly fifteen minutes, leaving the noise and bustle of the pier far behind. Already she missed the breeze from the sea. They had traded it instead for swarms of low-flying midges that kept sticking to Tanya's damp skin and

38

hair, and by now she was feeling decidedly hot and grumpy.

'Well, I know the tooth fairy is a lie.' She swatted a bug from her face. 'It stole every single one of my teeth and I never got a penny in return, just any disgusting rubbish it had picked up from the street.' She shuddered. 'It once left a chewed-up toffee that someone had spat out. I woke up with it stuck to my cheek.'

Ratty began to chuckle, then quickly turned it into a cough as she gave him a stony look. 'I was once told that the teeth are supposed to be ground into fairy forks and knives,' he said. 'But I think that's just a rumour, probably started by the fairies themselves to get parents to believe it. The truth is, you should never let a fairy have any of your teeth.'

'Why not?' Tanya asked.

'I'll explain later,' Ratty said mysteriously. 'Go on.'

'They put spells on my hairbrush all the time. It either puts tangles in my hair or makes it stand on end, like a hedgehog—'

Ratty nodded in agreement and pointed to his hair. 'That's why I don't bother combing mine very often.'

'They change my homework answers to ones that are wrong,' Tanya continued. 'That's one of their favourites – I have to check everything twice or even three times. What else . . .? They put a spell on a jam tart that I ate so that all I could say afterwards was "jam tart", until all the other jam tarts had been eaten, which was a whole day later. My father was so cross. And don't even get me started on the ones that live at my grandmother's house.' She sighed, her mood worsening. 'Which reminds me, there's something lurking under the floorboards at the holiday cottage we're staying in. I couldn't get a proper look at it, but, from what I saw, it's a really nasty one – it threatened to stamp out my eyes while I was asleep.'

Ratty frowned. 'What did you do to it?'

'Nothing,' said Tanya. 'We'd only just arrived at the cottage. We hadn't had time to do anything to upset it, but it was complaining about humans coming every summer with their noise and their mess. I don't think it would matter who we were, but the fact that I can see it definitely hasn't helped.'

'You didn't argue with it, did you?' Ratty asked.

Tanya felt sheepish. 'I might have threatened to stamp on it … but only after it was horrible to me first.'

'That wasn't a good idea.' Ratty scratched his chin. 'All the other things you've said, about the homework and the hairbrush … those sorts of things are just mischief really. Fairly harmless compared to what some fairies are willing to do to humans. I'd be careful with that one.'

'How am I supposed to be careful?' she grumbled. 'When it's there, taunting me for no reason?'

'I'll get to that in a minute,' Ratty replied. 'I want to talk about the other fairies first. Are they always the same ones you see or different?'

'The same,' said Tanya. 'I mean, I see others sometimes, too, outside of the house, but we live in London and there don't seem to be many fairies in the city. Except the ones that come to my house.'

'So the ones in your house, the ones that cause the mischief . . . do they do it for no reason?'

'No,' said Tanya. 'It's always a punishment for something I've done, like writing in my diary about them, or trying to tell my parents that they *do* exist, not that they've ever believed me. Once, when I collected frogspawn in a jar for a project at school, they turned it all into frogs overnight. They were hopping about all over the classroom, in bags and lunch boxes – it was awful. Another time I picked some bluebells from the garden and for some reason they got angry about that, too. They turned my face and hands bright blue. Said I had no business stealing them. *Stealing!* When they were in *my* garden.'

Ratty nodded seriously. 'They can be protective over plants and wildlife. Some plants are known as fairy plants: primroses, foxgloves, bluebells, elder. Stay away from them. Fairies don't like humans meddling with nature, or telling other humans about their existence.'

'There are four of them,' said Tanya. 'They've visited me ever since I was little, as far back as I can remember.'

'Four?' Ratty's eyebrows shot up into his messy hair. 'Most people only get one, like me with Turpin here.' He shrugged. 'Still, it's not unheard of to have more than one. Some fairies work in clans.'

'What do you mean, most people only get one?' Tanya asked. 'One what?'

41

'One guardian,' said Ratty. 'Everyone born with the second sight gets one. They're supposed to protect us.'

'Protect us?' Tanya snorted. 'All they seem to want to do is torment me. What exactly are they supposed to be protecting us from?'

'I'm not really sure. Other fairies, I suppose. My pa knows a lot about them. More than he tells me.'

'Your father sees fairies, too?' Tanya asked. She felt envious, wishing she had had someone to share her ability with as she'd grown up. 'What's he like?' She couldn't imagine speaking to an adult about fairies, or at least not to an adult who believed her.

'He's . . .' A small crease appeared between Ratty's eyebrows. 'He's a bit odd, I suppose,' he said at last. 'Most people seem to think so anyway. I'm used to him and his ways. You'll probably get to meet him later, if he's home.' His voice sounded strange, and Tanya wondered if perhaps he did not want to show her where he lived. Ratty's clothes, now that she was up close to him, were very worn in places and repaired with patches in others. Perhaps they didn't have much money.

'What about your mother?' she asked.

'Ma died when I was little.'

'I'm sorry.'

'I don't really remember her,' said Ratty.

'So, where exactly is home?' Tanya asked, eager to change the subject. 'It feels like we've been walking forever.' She noticed that Turpin, still balanced on Ratty's shoulder,

42

seemed restless and was drumming a beat on the top of his head with her hands.

'Not far now. We need to cross the river and then it's just a little way over the meadow.' He reached up and batted Turpin's hands away. 'Stop it, you pest.'

Turpin obeyed, but sneaked another strand of Ratty's hair into her mouth and began to chew it.

'She seems quite ... tame,' Tanya said tentatively. 'Does she ever cause trouble?'

'Not really,' said Ratty. 'She probably would, if she had any magic left—'

'She doesn't have magic?' Tanya interrupted.

'Not any more. Pa says she used to before the attack, but ever since then she's never used magic.'

'What attacked her?' Tanya asked, eyeing Turpin. 'Is that what happened to her wing?'

Ratty nodded. 'We don't know what it was, but Pa says it must have been an animal. A cat or a fox perhaps. I don't remember it happening, I was too young. Whatever it was, it almost killed her.'

'Poor thing,' Tanya murmured. Turpin's response was to stick out her tongue. She clearly didn't think much of Tanya or want her sympathy.

'Almost there,' said Ratty, motioning up ahead. They had reached the edge of the field now, and thankfully this time there was no stile to climb over, but a gate instead. Once they were through it and had fastened the bolt on the other side, a thin, shimmering silver ribbon of water divided the

43

field into two, vanishing across the horizon. A wooden bridge arched over it and Ratty led her towards it.

'There's the castle,' Tanya said in surprise. 'We're on the other side of it.'

'This is the side where the main entrance is,' Ratty explained. 'And most of the parts that are open. The dungeons and some of the towers are in ruins. They're not open to the public.'

He slowed down as they reached the river. Close up, it no longer appeared silver, but a vibrant green. Tanya peered into it, but there was no way of telling how deep it went. Long, green weeds swayed softly as the water rippled. A yellow sign nearby, however, warned of the undertow and forbade anyone to swim. Stuck to it was a missing persons' poster with a picture of a smiling young girl, probably aged eight or nine. It was yellowed and tattered around the edges, like it had been there for some time.

'Someone went missing here?'

'Lots of people,' Ratty said quietly. 'People on holiday usually. Mostly children.'

'How horrible,' she said.

'Doesn't look dangerous, does it?'

'Not at all,' Tanya agreed. She gazed at the water, longing to take her shoes off and dip her toes in. It was such a warm day and the walk through the fields had made her skin sticky. 'It looks peaceful.'

'Yes, it does,' Ratty agreed. 'And there's not really an undertow here, you know. That's further up.'

'I suppose they try to stop people going in anyway, in case they swim to where the undertow is,' said Tanya. 'But couldn't we just sit at the edge and put our feet in the water?'

'We could, but it wouldn't end well,' said Ratty.

She stared at him, confused. 'But I thought you said . . .?'

'I said there's no undertow,' Ratty answered. 'I didn't say it was safe.'

The hairs on the back of Tanya's neck stood on end. 'Why? What's in there?'

Ratty lifted Turpin from his shoulders and placed her on the ground. Then he picked up a pebble and threw it into the water. It landed with a heavy splash.

'That should wake her up,' he muttered.

'Wake who up?' Tanya scanned the surface of the water, but could only see the widening ripples. 'What are you doing?'

He reached into his pocket and pulled out several objects: a few small packets of salt, like the kind found in cafés, and a selection of rusty nails. He handed Tanya a couple of the packets and one of the nails.

'Here. Put these in your pockets.'

Tanya began to wonder whether Ratty was suffering from sunstroke. 'What on earth for?' she asked.

'They'll protect you.'

'Are you feeling . . . all right?' she asked.

'I'm fine,' Ratty snapped. 'Now stay back and watch.' He grabbed two chunky sticks from nearby and knelt by the riverside. Oberon gave an excitable yap and began capering about, waiting for the game to begin.

'He thinks you're going to throw the sticks for him,' Tanya explained.

'Don't let him chase them, whatever you do,' Ratty said. 'Put him on the leash.'

She did so, holding on tightly. Ratty nodded and then plunged the sticks into the water, moving them in small circles and making little splashes. A bit, Tanya thought, like two small legs paddling. She kept her eyes trained on the water, but all she could see were ripples. Tiny specks of green dotted the surface, making it impossible to make out anything below.

'What am I supposed to be looking for?' she whispered, half expecting a giant pike to launch itself at them, but nothing came.

'Just wait,' said Ratty. 'She's here, I know it. She's just biding her time—'

Without warning, he jerked forward, almost losing his balance. There was a soft hiss as the two sticks slipped from his grasp and slid under the water. Ratty scrambled backwards, away from the river's edge.

'What happened?' Tanya scanned the river wildly. 'Did . . . did something pull those sticks out of your hands?'

Ratty nodded silently, then pointed. A row of bubbles popped up beneath the bridge, followed by four small pieces of wood floating away downstream.

'Is that . . .?' Tanya began. 'Were they . . .?'

'My sticks,' Ratty finished. 'In four pieces. Each one bitten in two.'

Tanya swallowed hard. 'But what could do that?' By now, she knew it wasn't a pike or any other kind of fish. The sticks had been too thick for that.

A moment later, she had her answer.

A green figure rose out of the river, looming towards them. Long, matted hair choked with weeds flowed from its bony scalp. Duckweed draped its body like a webbed dress, clinging to a figure that was distinctly female. It reached out with spindly, greedy fingers that snatched wildly at the reeds on the bank, tearing them up by the roots. From its mouth came a terrible, gurgling melody that was strangely haunting.

Tanya shrieked and stumbled backwards, ready to run.

'Don't panic,' said Ratty. His voice was calm. 'She can't leave the water. As long as you're not within grabbing distance, you're safe. And with the salt and the nail you're protected from her song – that's how she lures some people in.'

The creature turned towards them, lowering itself back into the river with only its head and shoulders visible. Its weed-hair rippled across the water and, for the first time, Tanya noticed that there were objects caught in it: drinks cans, sweet wrappers ... a tiny doll. It opened its mouth – twice as wide as any human mouth – and water gushed in through silver-green teeth that jutted out in thin, spiteful spikes. Its fat tongue sat like a bloated slug. Choked, watery sounds gurgled from its throat, like it was being drowned, and then it vanished, swallowed by the water.

'And that,' said Ratty, 'is the real reason no one should go into the water here.'

It was several seconds before Tanya was able to speak. After stumbling backwards, fear had gripped her and held her to the spot. Oberon had pressed himself into her legs, but she couldn't tell which of them was shaking more.

'What . . . who is she . . . it?' she managed eventually.

'People call her Nessie Needleteeth,' said Ratty. 'Those who've heard of her anyway. She's a bit like the Wishing Tree, a legend, unless you're able to see her. And most people can't – or at least not until it's too late.' He gave a grim smile. 'You can see why there's no tourist information about her, not like the tree. Nessie Needleteeth isn't something Spinney Wicket wants to be known for.' He nodded to the undertow sign. 'Unless you have the sight, it's easier to blame the water. Not many people really know the truth.'

'But what *is* she?' Tanya said again, unable to tear her eyes from the water.

'A water hag,' Ratty said. 'You've never heard of a water hag?'

Tanya shook her head.

'It's a type of fey creature,' he explained.

She frowned at the unfamiliar word.

'Fey,' he repeated. 'It means from the fairy world. There are water hags all over the country, some more famous than others. Jenny Greenteeth is probably the most famous, but there's Peg Powler, too. Nasty pieces of work, both of them. Dragging unsuspecting people under the water to die. Not many escape, but the ones who do can't usually explain it; it's nearly always put down to the current and the weeds. But you do get some who can see, even if they don't understand. Some people say they're spirits or the ghosts of drowned women.'

'But where did she get those awful teeth?' Tanya asked.

'The story goes that her teeth rotted away,' said Ratty. 'She used to just drown people by dragging them under the water, until the day an old seamstress disappeared crossing the river. They never found her, only shreds of her clothes and her empty needlework basket. They say Nessie got her, and took all her pins and needles to use them for teeth.'

He kicked at a dandelion, sending its seeds flying through the air. 'So. Now you know to stay away from the water. And keep the dog away, too. She prefers children, but she's really not that fussy, not when it's been a while since she last fed.' He chuckled. 'Come on, let's get going. You've gone a funny colour – you're almost as green as she was!'

He headed for the bridge.

'Wait,' Tanya called after him. 'Is it safe to cross the river?' She stared at the bridge, trying to guess the distance between its bottom and the water, and remembering just how long those green, sinewy arms had been . . .

'It's safe,' Ratty replied, stepping on to the bridge. 'Many things aren't, but this is. Trust me.'

5

Protection

IT WAS ONLY WHEN SHE WAS HALFWAY across the bridge that Tanya realised that the items Ratty had given her – the salt and the rusty nail – were still clenched in her palm.

'So what are these for?' she asked, tiptoeing across the wooden boards with one eye on the water, waiting for any sudden movement, or a creeping green hand. None came. 'I know you said protection, but how do they work?'

Ratty glanced over his shoulder. 'Oh. Well, the nail is iron. Fairies hate iron – if it touches them, it burns. The same with salt. It's pure, so fairies can't bear it. Their skin will bubble up and blister if it comes into contact with them. You can even use it to stop fairies getting into a house or a room by putting a trail of salt in front of the door or on the window ledge. They can't cross it.'

Tanya stared at the nail and the little packets of salt, now slightly damp from being clamped in her hand. Such ordinary, everyday objects and yet, according to Ratty, they held great power. 'Anything else?'

Ratty reached up and gave his neckerchief a tweak. 'The colour red. Wearing it acts as camouflage and stops fairies from seeing you, but only for as long as you can keep quiet. They can still hear you, so if you speak it breaks the spell.'

'That must be why the Wishing Tree says not to use red bottles or rags,' Tanya realised. 'Where did you learn all this?' It was clearly true, for Turpin was stalking along behind Ratty with a scowl on her face and her fingers in her ears, looking disgusted at the conversation.

'Pa taught me,' said Ratty. 'He learned most of it from books, I think. Not those silly books for children, where the fairies are all kind and pink and sparkly. Books about real magic and folklore. All of this dates way back, you know. People have always believed in fairies, though not so much these days. Heck, they used to be afraid of them! They'd leave out food to keep them happy, in case the fairies ruined their crops or turned the milk sour.' He paused and leaned over the handrail at the side of the bridge, motioning to the river below.

'Don't,' Tanya said, feeling on edge. 'We should get off the bridge, it's dangerous.' She gazed across the murky water below them. Somewhere, beneath those quiet ripples, Nessie Needleteeth was waiting, flexing those murderous fingers of hers. She shuddered violently.

'Actually, we're quite safe,' said Ratty. 'Even without the iron and the salt.'

'We are?'

'Running water,' he said. 'Crossing it will break an

enchantment or lose a fairy that's chasing you. That's why Nessie moves so quickly. If someone crosses the river before she gets to them, she can't touch them.'

'Salt, running water, wearing red, iron,' Tanya muttered, committing them to memory. 'If only I'd known about this sooner.'

'There's one more thing,' said Ratty. He set off again and in a few swift steps they were off the bridge. Despite what she had just learned, Tanya couldn't help feeling relieved.

'Perhaps the most useful of all,' Ratty continued. 'Something you can always do to protect yourself from harmful magic, even if you have nothing I've just mentioned.' He gave a knowing smile. 'Turn something you're wearing inside out.'

'Inside out,' Tanya repeated. 'Right. That makes absolutely no sense, you know.'

Ratty chortled. 'Who said it had to make sense? Fairies make no sense.' He glanced at Turpin, who was sneakily listening in. 'No offence. All you need to know is that these things work.'

They were now in a wide meadow, lushly carpeted with thick, green grass. Three horses were visible a short distance away and, beyond them, a cluster of stables. As they drew nearer, one of the horses looked up with interest and began trotting towards them. Having just removed Oberon's leash, Tanya wondered whether she should put it back on.

'Why is it coming towards us?'

Ratty reached into another one of his pockets and pulled

out a carrot. 'Because she knows she'll get a treat. Don't worry, she's friendly.' He snapped the carrot into three, offering the first piece to the shimmering, black horse who had approached. She took it from him, crunching loudly, and he rubbed her nose. 'Here.' He offered Tanya a piece of carrot. 'Ever fed a horse?'

She hesitated. 'No. I rode one once at the beach when I was little, but I've never been near one since.'

'Go on, take it,' said Ratty. 'She's very gentle, I promise. Just hold your hand flat, like this, so you don't accidentally get bitten.'

Tanya took the piece of carrot and mimicked him. The horse's velvety nose tickled her palm and with a quick crunch and a swallow the carrot was gone. She stroked its nose, the way Ratty had done, and felt a surge of pleasure as the horse nuzzled her in return.

'She's a beauty, isn't she?' Ratty said, his voice full of admiration. 'I call her Morrigan. It means "great queen".' He fed her the last piece of carrot, then took a quick glance about the meadow before taking her mane and hoisting himself cleanly on to her back. He held out his hand to Tanya. 'Come on.'

'Up there?' Tanya blinked in surprise. 'But there's no saddle!'

'It's fine,' Ratty assured her. 'We'll go slowly. It's not far now.'

'Then perhaps we should just walk,' said Tanya.

'We could, but this is more fun,' Ratty persisted. 'Look,

53

there's a tree stump over there. You can use it to climb on.'
He clicked and steered Morrigan to the stump. A minute
and a scramble later, Tanya was sitting behind him. 'Hold
on,' he said.

Tanya did as he told her, but it was surprisingly calm and
steady. They set off at a walk, keeping to the edge of the
meadow in the shade of the trees. Things whispered and
shuffled in the branches above them, and Tanya knew it
wasn't just birds and squirrels. There were voices, too – fey
voices – but they were too low to make out any words
clearly. Despite the feeling of being watched, Tanya was
enjoying herself and the gentle sway and shuffle of the
horse's movements. Oberon trotted along beside them, his
nose in the grass and tail in the air.

'Who do the horses belong to?' Tanya asked.

Ratty shrugged. 'I don't know. Pa says he's seen people
mucking out the stables a few times, but it's always early.' He
patted the horse's flank and looked up, gently bringing
Morrigan to a halt. 'Here we are.'

Tanya looked around them, but could see only trees and
endless meadow. 'This is where you live?' she asked uncertainly. She peered between the trees, fairy-tale images of
gingerbread cottages and woodcutters' log cabins flashing
into her mind.

'This is the place,' Ratty confirmed. 'Hop off then.'

Tanya swung her leg back and slid off the horse, landing
lightly on the grass. Ratty dismounted, running his hand
over Morrigan's shimmering, black coat. 'Go on then, girl,'

he murmured. 'Back you go.' Morrigan gently butted his hand, then turned and headed back across the meadow, breaking into a canter.

'Right then,' said Ratty. 'Through here.' He pushed a branch back and stepped further into the little copse.

Tanya followed, dry twigs and leaves crumbling underfoot. A few steps in, she caught a glimpse of duck-egg blue through the dense greenery. They were heading towards it. A short way in there was a clearing and, finally, Tanya was able to see Ratty's mysterious home. A blue camper van stood beneath the trees. Gingham curtains were drawn across the windows, making it impossible to see inside. In front of the van, a blackened pot hung over the charred remains of a campfire. Beyond that, drying clothes dangled from a thin line strung between two trees.

'Home sweet home,' said Ratty. He reached into the neck of his shirt and pulled out a grubby-looking string with a key hanging from it, unlocking the side of the van. He heaved the sliding door open and hopped up the step, pulling back the curtains. 'Come in.'

Tanya followed, curious. She had never been in a camper van before. Inside, there was a small table with a long, cushioned bench either side of it, which she supposed doubled as beds. A tiny kitchen area was directly behind it, with a two-ring cooking hob, a kettle, toaster and a sink. Every nook was crammed with cupboards and shelves high and low, and, though a little old and shabby-looking, it was clean and tidy.

'Pa must be out,' said Ratty. He fetched a large bowl and

filled it with water, then placed it outside for Oberon, who lapped at it gratefully.

'Is that him?' Tanya asked, noticing a framed photo on a nearby shelf. It showed a slightly younger Ratty with a smiling, handsome man. Like Ratty, he had very blue, almost turquoise eyes and thick, black hair that reached his shoulders. Against his dark skin, his teeth were dazzling white. He wore a silver hoop in each ear, giving him the appearance of a gypsy or a pirate. He looked, Tanya decided, like the kind of person who would know about fairies and she wanted to meet him. Very much indeed.

'Will he be back soon?' she asked.

Ratty was clattering about in the kitchen, pouring something fizzy into two tall glasses. 'I never know with Pa. He's normally back before dark, but sometimes he stays out all night.' He placed the two glasses on the table and motioned for Tanya to take a seat. She started to slide on to one of the benches, but an angry chittering stopped her.

Turpin glowered in the doorway, stamping her feet. 'Not there, stupid girl!' she cried.

'Oh,' said Ratty apologetically. 'She likes to sit that side.' He patted the other bench. 'Best sit here.'

Tanya squeezed into the narrow seat, silently taking a sip of her drink. It tasted of elderflowers, and she gulped the rest of it quickly, thirsty after the long walk. Ratty made to sit next to her, but was interrupted by a further protest from Turpin, who pounded the side of the van with her fist.

'Whoops. Sorry, Turps.' He scrambled to the door. 'I

almost forgot.' He reached above and removed a sprig of dried red berries and leaves from a hook above the entrance. There was one, Tanya saw, in each of the windows, and Ratty quickly moved around the van, collecting them all.

'What are those?' Tanya asked.

'Rowan berries.' Ratty tossed the bunches into the driver's seat in the front of the van. 'It's another deterrent to fairies. We put them in all the entrances whenever we go out to make sure we don't have any unwelcome guests while we're not here. Unfortunately, they work on Turpin, too.'

Tanya didn't find this unfortunate at all – quite the opposite, in fact – but of course she did not say so. 'Does she live in here with you then?' she asked.

'Most of the time,' said Ratty. 'But when the weather's fine like it is now she sometimes makes a nest outside in the trees.'

Once the offending berries were out of sight, Turpin stomped into the van, nose in the air. She hopped on to the seat opposite Tanya and proceeded to empty her sack of loot on to the table. Out came the newspaper, the meat pie and iced bun, money, plus a few bits of fluff from people's pockets and bags. Ratty brushed the fluff aside and hungrily unwrapped the food.

'It was for you,' she realised. 'Turpin stole all these things for you.'

She regretted saying this immediately when Ratty lowered his eyes, embarrassed.

'Sometimes there's not much to eat,' he explained. 'Not

57

fresh food anyway. Pa isn't much of a cook – most of what we eat is out of tins.' He offered the meat pie to Tanya. 'Want some?'

She shook her head. She wasn't hungry, but, even if she had been, knowing Turpin had handled it would have been enough to put her off. Besides, as Ratty crammed the pie into his mouth, she realised just how hungry he was. He broke off a small piece for Turpin, who scoffed it noisily. The iced bun didn't last much longer. Finally, Ratty wiped his mouth and took a long drink. When he'd finished, Turpin leaned head first into his glass, lapping like a dog. Tanya watched, unable to mask her disgust, yet Ratty didn't seem to mind. When Turpin finally came up for air, she belched in Tanya's direction.

'Charming,' Tanya muttered.

Turpin grinned maliciously.

'So you've never met anyone else who can see fairies?' Ratty asked.

'No,' Tanya replied.

'That must be difficult.'

She nodded. 'I've always wished that there was someone I could talk to about them, just to know that it's not only me. That I'm not ...'

'Mad?' Ratty finished.

'Yes.' She felt her face reddening. 'Because sometimes it's easier to think you *are* mad than to have no one that believes you.'

They both fell silent. Outside, a breeze ruffled the trees

and sent whispers around the camper van. With the sunlight streaming in, it was peaceful now, but in the dark, Tanya suspected, it would feel quite different.

'Don't you get scared being out here at night?' she asked.

'Not any more,' said Ratty. 'I used to, when I was younger. But we move around a lot. We don't always stay in places like this. Sometimes it'll be on a cliff top where you can see for miles, and when it's dark all you can see are the stars. Or maybe we'll stop on a road by the beach. On those nights the only thing you can hear is the sea. It depends where we are, which town we're in.'

'How long will you be in Spinney Wicket?'

'Until Pa gets bored, I suppose,' said Ratty. 'We never stay in any place for very long.'

'You just go wherever and whenever he decides?' Tanya asked. She couldn't imagine living such a life, travelling on a whim. It sounded romantic, like something out of a fairy tale.

Ratty smiled faintly. 'He says we go wherever the wind is blowing.'

'It must be an adventure.'

'Sometimes it is,' he agreed. 'Other times, when the roof is leaking and the wind is howling all night, making the van rock, I think how nice it must be to have a proper home. To be able to keep the friends I make.'

'Do you make many?' Tanya asked. She found this difficult to believe, given how rude Ratty had been when they had first met that morning. Perhaps she had just caught him off guard. He had been speaking to a tree after all.

'A few,' said Ratty. He sounded sad all of a sudden. 'But none of them will remember me.'

She frowned. 'I'm sure they do.'

Ratty opened his mouth to reply, but was distracted by something on the shelf above their heads. He reached up behind the photograph of himself and his father, and withdrew a small, red envelope that was tucked behind it.

'This must be from Pa,' he muttered. 'I didn't see it before.'

Tanya stared again at the man in the picture, but then found her attention drawn to a glass jar next to the photograph. She hadn't paid much attention to it before as its contents were so nondescript, but now she found there was something about the jar that was bothering her. It was jammed full of odds and ends: a page torn from a book, a girl's hairslide, a ribbon, a struck match, and lots of other things that were jumbled up and which she couldn't see properly.

'What's all that stuff?' she asked.

Ratty looked up from the envelope. There was a little crease between his eyebrows. 'That? Oh, nothing. Just stuff that's been lying around the van. Pa hangs on to things in case they come in handy.'

Tanya peered at the jar. There was something about Ratty's voice she didn't believe. 'How can a struck match be useful?'

'Exactly!' Ratty laughed, but it sounded false. 'That's what I always say to him. It's just junk. It needs throwing out.'

Tanya's eyes narrowed. In such a small living space, where everything was so neat and ordered, and where space was so tight, it seemed very unlikely that a jar of such useless items would be kept. *That* was what bothered her about it. She pondered whether to voice her thoughts to Ratty, but decided against it. There didn't seem much point and, besides, something odd was happening.

Turpin had sidled across the table and was now gazing up at her. It was making Tanya nervous.

'What's the matter with her?' she asked Ratty. 'Why is she looking at me like that?'

'She likes your hair,' Ratty explained. 'She just told me.'

'She did?' Tanya stared back at Turpin doubtfully. The fairy nodded and gave a sickly sweet grin, revealing wicked little teeth.

'She wants to touch it,' Ratty said.

'Er ... all right,' said Tanya. She did not really like the idea of that at all, but, since it was the first nice thing Turpin had said or done towards her, she felt she should allow it. Perhaps she could make a friend of her after all.

The words had barely left her lips before Turpin scampered up her arm and burrowed her face into Tanya's shoulder. Tanya froze, stiff as a poker, as Turpin ran her fingers through the long, chestnut-coloured hair.

'Now you remember what I said earlier, about teeth, and never letting a fairy have them?' Ratty said.

'Yes,' Tanya said. She was distracted now, for Turpin was giving her hair a good sniff. She hoped the fairy wasn't about to start chewing on it the way she did Ratty's.

'Well, it's the same with hair,' Ratty continued. 'Hair, teeth, fingernails. They're part of you and can be used in magic. Powerful magic. Putting tangles in your hair or making it stand up on end is easy if they've stolen a bit of it.'

'But Turpin can't use magic any more, right?'

'Right.' Ratty twisted the envelope between his fingers, turning it over and over, but not opening it. He seemed troubled.

In the next instant, there was a sharp pain on the back of Tanya's neck, so piercing it felt almost like a bite. Turpin leaped back to Ratty, cackling.

'Ouch!' Tanya yelped. She rubbed at the tender spot. 'She pinched me! Why did she do that?'

'Turps!' Ratty exclaimed. 'That was a nasty trick. Say you're sorry.'

Turpin buried her face in Ratty's shoulder, her body shaking with silent laughter. 'Shan't!' she said, her voice muffled.

Ratty gave Tanya another apologetic look, then his expression became serious. He was still turning the envelope over in his hands, unopened. Tanya got the feeling he was waiting until he was alone to read it and sensed she had outstayed her welcome. She glanced at her watch. She had been out for hours now and her mother was probably starting to worry. She got to her feet.

'I should be going,' she said. 'Thank you for telling me

about fairies. I'm sure it'll be useful.' She hesitated. 'Goodbye, Turpin.'

Turpin stuck out her tongue.

'Don't take too much notice of her,' said Ratty. 'She's rotten to everyone, even Pa sometimes.' He scratched his messy, black hair and started to get up. 'I'll walk you back.'

Tanya shook her head. 'I can go by myself. I remember the way.'

The sun was still warm when she stepped outside the van. She collected Oberon, then shielded her eyes from the dazzling light coming through the trees. Ratty watched her silently, the red envelope poking out of his shirt pocket.

'Will I see you again tomorrow?' she asked.

'I'm sure you will,' Ratty answered, but again there was something about his voice that was odd. A tinge of sadness almost. 'I'll be around. By the castle or on the pier somewhere.'

'I'll look for you,' said Tanya.

She set off, heading towards the sun. She passed the stables in the distance and soon reached the river. She crossed the bridge quickly, wanting Nessie Needleteeth safely behind her. All the while she pondered the strange afternoon spent with Ratty, and wondered what the red envelope contained. She thought of Turpin and the trick she had played, pretending to like Tanya's hair just so she could be spiteful and pinch her.

Her temper flared at the memory and she found herself stamping heavily over the grass, even kicking a few dandelions when she saw them. It made her feel better. Very soon, though, the anger ebbed away and, by the time she had reached the road leading back to the holiday cottage, Tanya was finding it hard to remember what she had been angry about at all.

6

The Telltale Twitch

'RATTY?' SAID HER MOTHER, ONE EYEBROW raised. 'What kind of a name is Ratty?'

'A nickname.' Tanya ate another forkful of mushy peas and stabbed at a chip on her plate. 'I think he said his proper name was . . . Harry? Or was it Howard?' Try as she might, she simply couldn't recall what Ratty had told her when he'd first introduced himself.

'Is this Ratty another one of your imaginary friends?'

'I'm not making him up!' Tanya exploded. She put her cutlery down and pressed her hands to her forehead. 'I met him on the pier . . .' She trailed off. 'I think.'

Her mother sighed. 'You only met him this afternoon or so you say. It shouldn't be that difficult to remember, if you were telling the truth.'

'I'm not lying!' Tanya snapped. She was beginning to feel worried now. What was the matter with her? Why was she having such trouble remembering the events of the day clearly? She remembered Ratty and what he looked like . . . and there had been a fairy, too, though obviously she couldn't tell that part to her mother. *That must be it*, she thought angrily. The fairy had done something to her, muddled her memory somehow.

'The problem with being a liar, Tanya, is that you have to have a good memory.' Her mother was cross now. 'It's much harder to remember something that didn't happen than something that did.' Her voice was clipped and her cheeks and nose were starting to turn pink. 'You've been out for hours, and all I'm getting is vague, wishy-washy explanations of where you've been and who you've been with.' She eyed her daughter critically. 'You're covered in gnat bites, and don't think I haven't noticed the state of your dress. That was new on today and you've lost one of the buttons already.'

Tanya lifted her hand to the collar of her dress. There had been three daisy-shaped buttons there this morning. Now there were only two and a hanging thread where the third had been. *Strange*, she thought. *When had that happened?*

'I'm not lying,' she repeated quietly. Not this time. Lying was something she'd grown very good at over the years. She'd had to be. Being honest got her nowhere and, besides, how else could she explain some of the things the fairies had done? They were simply too bizarre. 'Really. I'm telling the truth. I can't remember.'

Her mother's expression softened. 'You do look a bit peaky. Perhaps you have a temperature; you've been in the sun all day.' She held a hand to Tanya's forehead. 'You don't feel too hot.' She looked worried suddenly. 'You didn't take anything to eat or drink from anyone, did you?'

66

Tanya shook her head. 'No. I mean, I don't think so.' Again, there was a worrying gap in her memory. 'I drank some apple juice in a café on the pier.' Strange that she could remember the earlier part of the day, and later, when she'd returned to the cottage. She and her mother had taken an evening stroll past the pier into the town centre and returned with fish and chips. She remembered all that well enough. It was just around Ratty and that horrible fairy of his that things got sketchy. She got up from the table, trying to smile. 'Don't worry. I've probably had too much sun. I'll be fine in the morning.'

Her mother nodded, looking only a little reassured.

Tanya went into the bedroom, closing the door behind her. That fairy of Ratty's must be responsible for this. It was the only explanation. She pursed her lips as she took off her dress and pulled on her bathrobe. She'd give them both a piece of her mind if she saw them again.

As she threw her dress over the back of the chair, something landed on the wooden floor with a light ping and rolled under the bed. She knelt down and picked up a rusty, brown nail. At the foot of the chair there were also two small packets of salt. They hadn't been there a minute ago. Surely these things hadn't fallen out of her pocket? Where had they come from? She shook her head in confusion and threw the items in the waste-paper basket, then headed to the bathroom, eager to wash away the day's sweat and stickiness.

Ten minutes later, she'd pulled on her pyjamas and slid

between the cool, crisp sheets, but her uneasiness wouldn't leave her. As she lay in the darkness, drifting into a doze, she thought she heard muffled muttering and scratches from beneath the bed. Several times she jerked awake, but only to a silent room and her own troubled imaginings. A sliver of yellow light was visible underneath the bedroom door and she could hear her mother moving about. It must be earlier than it felt. Eventually, a deeper sleep came. It didn't last.

When she woke again, the light beneath the door had gone. It must be late now, for her mother had gone to bed. Only a shard of moonlight lit the room through a crack in the curtains. In that thin, silver shard, dark shadows moved and, before Tanya was even properly awake, her eyelids gave a telltale twitch. It was enough to jolt her from sleep completely.

She sat up, rubbing her twitching eyes. She could smell it now, too, on the breeze from the open window: the earthy, outdoorsy smell that gave them away.

There were fairies in the room.

She pulled the bedclothes closer, her heart starting to thud. Her eyes darted around the room, seeking out every dark corner. Shadows flickered and a low, snorting snuffling sounded from underneath the bed. She half ducked as something swooped past her face, skimming the tip of her nose. When she looked up again, a large, black raven had perched on the end of the bed, its scaly claws grasping the wooden frame. Next to it stood two small figures, both male. One was dark-skinned, thin and wore a suit of leaves. The other was plump and short, with a feathered cap and an unpleasant moustache that he twirled around his fingers. They both regarded her in silence.

The raven preened its feathers briefly, then shook itself. The feathers fell away, transforming into a soft, gleaming gown. It was worn by a small woman, not much larger than the bird had been. The tips of two pointed ears poked out from her silky, black hair. Next to it, her skin was as pale as cream, glowing in the moonlight.

'What do you want?' Tanya whispered. Her body was tense, every muscle tight with dread.

'What makes you think we want anything?' Raven answered. Her voice was soft, but not exactly friendly.

'You usually want to cause trouble,' Tanya retorted. 'To punish me for something. Well, I don't know why you're here this time – I haven't done anything. I haven't written about you, spoken about you or picked any flowers that I shouldn't have '

'Actually, that's not quite true, is it?' said Raven. 'You have been talking to someone about us.'

Gredin, the dark-skinned fairy, nodded in agreement. 'We saw you,' he said. 'Speaking to that boy.' His yellow eyes were narrowed. 'We didn't like it.'

'Why?' Tanya protested, her voice rising. She racked her brains to recall what she and Ratty had spoken about, knowing that they must have discussed fairies, but not able to pinpoint anything in particular. 'If he can see fairies, too, what have I done wrong? It's not like I told him anything he didn't already know.'

Gredin's lip curled back over his teeth. 'No,' he murmured. 'Quite the opposite.'

Tanya closed her eyes, willing her memories of the afternoon to return. *Quite the opposite?* That meant Ratty had been the one with the information, telling *her* things – important things – about fairies that she didn't know. But what? The question niggled her, the answers just out of reach.

'How was I supposed to know that it's wrong to speak to someone else who can see fairies?' Tanya said, remembering to keep her voice low just in time. Indignation had chased away her fear and lent her courage. 'I've never met anyone else who can before!' She glared at the three of them. 'Why is it even wrong at all?'

Feathercap, the third fairy, stepped forward. 'It's wrong,' he hissed, 'because the less you know about us, the better.'

'Better for you, you mean?' Tanya retaliated.

Gredin's golden eyes glinted meanly, and Tanya knew she was straying into dangerous territory. 'Careful,' he said slowly. 'Be very careful.'

Tanya lowered her eyes and said nothing, but beneath the covers her fists were clenched as tightly as her jaw. It wasn't fair. How dare they bully her like this?

'How did you even find me here?' she asked.

'We can find you anywhere,' Feathercap replied. 'No matter how far from home you are. 'We're always watching.'

70

In the silence that followed, she caught another snuffling sound from under the bed. It sounded a bit like Oberon when he was eating his dinner – but Oberon wasn't in the room. The snuffle became a gulp, then was followed by a swallow.

'Feathercap, will you please see what that blasted creature is up to?' Gredin said irritably.

Feathercap gave a stroppy sigh, but hopped off the bed and vanished underneath it.

'You won't be punished,' Raven said softly. 'Not this time anyway.'

Gredin made a noise of impatience. 'How else will she learn?'

'She did not know.' Raven's voice took on a steely tone. She looked away from Gredin to Tanya. 'But now you do. You're not to speak to that boy about us, or any other fairies, ever again.'

'But I can still speak to him about other things?' Tanya said stubbornly.

Raven's voice was curt. 'It would be better if you didn't, but yes. You may, if you really must.'

Feathercap returned at that moment. For once, Tanya was glad of the interruption. The fewer rules the fairies laid out, the better. Behind him flew a strange little creature, something halfway between a hedgehog and a piglet. It looked moth-eaten and miserable, and landed clumsily on the bed, its ragged wings struggling to keep it up in the air.

'It was eating a spider,' Feathercap said, his face twisted in disgust. 'Must have sniffed it out as soon as we arrived.'

71

Tanya shuddered. She didn't mind the Mizhog much, for it never spoke or did anything unkind to her, unlike the others. It just seemed to accompany them rather like a pet, watching everything that went on with its large, gloomy brown eyes. It did, however, have a revolting diet and habits to match. As well as spiders, the Mizhog was fond of gobbling up slugs, snails, worms and woodlice. It was never quiet or discreet about it, either. Every squish, squelch, chomp and chew was plain to hear, and the remains of its grisly meals usually glistened on its whiskers for some time afterwards. It was also full of fleas and constantly scratching and licking itself.

It regarded her now, hiccuping occasionally. Something long and thin that looked suspiciously like a spider's leg dangled from its snout. Tanya looked away as her stomach gave a lurch.

Thankfully, the fairies chose that moment to leave. As usual, their departure was swift, with no goodbyes. A simple, 'Remember – we'll be watching,' was all she heard from Gredin as he leaped on to the window ledge, soon followed by Feathercap. Raven transformed once more, spreading her black wings wide and gliding to the window. As always, the Mizhog was last to depart, its hurried flaps all the more clumsy-looking compared to the grace of the creature before it. Then they were gone and Tanya could finally release the breath she had been holding on to.

She lay back in bed, willing her heart to slow. The fairies' visits normally meant bad news and a pickle she couldn't explain her way out of. It was rare, very rare, for her to escape without punishment as she had tonight, but, even so, she could not count it as a victory. They hadn't punished her, but the threat of it was still there if she spoke to Ratty again – and how could she avoid speaking about fairies to the only other person she knew who could see them?

She was wide awake now and too warm. Kicking the sheets off, she squeezed her eyes shut, wishing for sleep and morning to come. When she finally began to doze off again, it was not peaceful, for she dreamed her eyelids were still twitching and could smell that giveaway, leaf-mulch smell of fairies. Somehow, she pushed these things to the back of her mind, allowing sleep to pull her further in until she was aware of nothing.

It was not the clattering of the breakfast things that woke her, or even the sound of Oberon scratching at the bedroom door. Nor was it the sunshine streaming in on her face, the promise of another fine, scorching day ahead. Instead, Tanya woke to the unpleasant feeling of a drip sliding down her cheek. Her eyes snapped open.

Sweat. She was covered in it. At some point during the night she must have pulled the covers back over herself, but now she was unbearably hot. She turned to look at the clock on the bedside table and squealed. An ugly china doll with a chipped face and a green velvet dress stared back at her. It looked very old and there was a yellowed piece of paper pinned to it which said: EMILLIES DOLL.

Tanya frowned. Emily's doll? Who was Emily? A little girl who'd lived here once? Where had the doll come from?

She tried to throw the bedclothes off – but found she couldn't.

'What—?' she whispered.

Her arms and legs were pinned tightly to her sides, unable to move. For a moment, she thought she must have rolled herself into a cocoon of sheets, but they held fast, not giving an inch. Not only that, but her pyjamas felt . . . odd, like her hands and feet were trapped. She wriggled a hand out from under the bedclothes, then froze in shock.

Her pale blue pyjama sleeve had been sewn together at the cuff, trapping her hand inside. The stitches had been made in horrid brown wool and were ugly and frenzied, like a mad dressmaker had been sewing as if their life depended on it. She wriggled her toes and her other hand. All of them had been tightly sewn in.

In despair, she remembered the twitching in her eyelids as she had fallen back to sleep. She *hadn't* been dreaming it. This had to be the work of the fairies – though normally they stayed to watch her reaction to their punishments. Yet that didn't make sense; not after they'd made a point of telling her she wouldn't be punished this time. By now, however, Tanya knew better than to question why they treated her the way they did. It was a mystery, especially if what Ratty had said about them being guardians was true.

For now, it didn't matter why they had done it. The important thing was to get out of this mess before her mother came in and saw her. She tried again to pull the covers back, but again they would not budge. Only then did Tanya realise that things were much worse than she'd originally thought. She twisted her head to the side to find more crazed brown stitches, this time securing the blankets to the sheet underneath her. Not only had she been sewn into her nightclothes, she'd been completely sewn into the bed.

A panicky feeling rose in her chest. She forced it down, fighting to stay calm and think. Her hands – she had to get her hands free first. Luckily, her pyjamas were made of thin material and she could still grip things through it easily enough. She attempted to lift the pyjamas off over her head, only now there was another problem. They were stuck, too, because the top had been sewn to the trousers. She gave a low growl of frustration. There was only one thing for it. She brought her sleeve to her mouth and bit into the brown wool.

She gagged instantly. It tasted disgusting: damp and mildewy, like it had been forgotten in a cupboard for about a hundred years. The rough texture of it scratching against her teeth was almost as bad, but she had no choice except to gnaw and nibble at it until it broke. Eventually, it did and she was able to pull at the wool with her teeth until the stitches unravelled and her hand was free.

Immediately, she tried to unpick the other sleeve with her fingernails, but there was no obvious knot where the stitches had been tied off. She was forced again to chew her way through it, while trying not to imagine where the wool might have come from. Finally, both hands were free.

She bit back a shriek at a sudden knock at the door.

'Tanya?' her mother called. 'Are you up yet?'

'I'm awake,' she spluttered, praying her mother wouldn't come in. Thankfully, the door stayed closed, but the delicious smell of frying bacon had started to waft under it.

'Breakfast in five minutes,' Mrs Fairchild said.

'Coming!' Tanya called desperately. She waited until her mother's footsteps moved away from the door, then started to wriggle, caterpillar-like, up and out of the bedclothes. It was harder than she had imagined it would be, for the covers were sewn so tightly there was barely room to move at all. *It's a wonder I didn't suffocate*, she thought. Her anger lent her strength. A minute passed, then another. She was almost waist-high out of the sheets. From the kitchen, her mother called her again.

She wriggled harder, sweat making the sheets and her pyjamas stick to her skin. At last, her hips were free, and she was able to pull herself up and slide her legs out.

A sneaky laugh from somewhere in the room made her breath catch in her throat. She glanced about fearfully. Where had it come from?

Only then did she see what else had been left for her.

A series of large, brown woolly letters had been stitched across the beautiful lemon bedding, ruining it. Dazed, Tanya slid off the bed and crept sideways to see it better. Though the spelling was terrible, the message was unmistakable:

Leave this house.

Of course. This *wasn't* the work of the four fairies who had visited in the night after all. They had kept true to their word. No, Tanya realised. This – and the horrible doll – was the work of whatever it was that lurked under the floorboards and was in the room with her now, chuckling slyly from some unseen nook or cranny.

'Why are you doing this?' she asked in a furious whisper.

The chuckling stopped and a low muttering began. 'Leave this house,' it chanted. 'Leave this house, leave this house . . .'

'Tanya!' Her mother rapped on the door, startling her. 'I'm not calling you again – you can eat it cold!'

And then the doorknob turned and the door began to open.

7

A Jar of Odds and Ends

TANYA DID THE ONLY THING SHE COULD think of. She grabbed the pillow from behind her and threw it over the ugly brown lettering on the bed to hide it. It worked, with not a moment to spare. Her mother stood at the door, tapping her foot with impatience.

'You should be up and dressed by now, young lady.'

'Sorry,' Tanya muttered. She was well aware that the ankles of her pyjamas were still sewn together and that the top was still attached to the bottoms. She held her mother's gaze, hoping she wouldn't notice. 'I'm coming right now.'

Luckily, her mother was too busy looking at the doll. 'Where did that ghastly thing come from?'

'Oh ... I found it. In a cupboard. I thought it was ... sweet.'

Mrs Fairchild shuddered. 'It's creepy, if you ask me. Anyway, hurry up.'

Tanya nodded, watching as her mother retreated. Once she was out of sight, Tanya hobbled to the bathroom and locked the door behind her, rummaging through her mother's toiletry bag. Finally, she found what she was searching for: a small pair of nail scissors. She set to work, snipping at the wool. To her dismay, it was so thick that it left noticeable holes in her pyjamas, but there was nothing she could do about that except hope that her mother wouldn't notice.

Fat chance, she thought miserably, replacing the scissors and dumping the wool in the bin. She hurried back to the bedroom and threw the wardrobe open, ready to grab the first thing she found – but there was another shock in store.

All of her clothes had been ripped from the hangers and were strewn at the bottom of the wardrobe. She knelt down and picked up a crumpled dress, gasping sharply. The arms, neck and even the hem had all been sewn together in the same horrid brown wool. Her hand shaking, she dropped the dress and picked up her favourite jeans. Once again, the waist and ankles were tightly stitched. There was no way into them except to unpick the wool. She turned over garment after garment. Every one was the same.

Angry tears stung her eyes. She gulped them back and went to the chest of drawers, pulling it open. Once again, everything inside had been rummaged through, sewn up and savagely thrown back in. There was not a single piece of clothing untouched, not even a sock. The vicious little beast must have been sewing practically all night.

Tanya closed the door quietly and wiped her eyes. She wouldn't let it see her cry. The only thing she had to wear was what she stood in now: her pyjamas. Her mother wouldn't like that, but it was better than delaying any longer. She pulled a comb through her hair quickly and hurried to the breakfast table, ready for another scolding. Her mother gave a disapproving sniff, but said nothing as she buttered her toast.

They ate in silence, Tanya avoiding her mother's eyes. The food was lukewarm now, but it did at least take the unpleasant taste of the damp wool from Tanya's mouth. Even so, she was unable to enjoy a single mouthful. All she could think of was the work set out for her when she returned to her room. It was going to be a long morning and hers would be spent unpicking stitches.

By midday Tanya had cheered up a little. After helping to wash up and clear the breakfast things, which had softened her mother's mood, she'd hidden the horrible china doll under the bed, then managed to snip at the stitches in the bedding and most of her sewn-up clothes and return them to normal. Well, almost. Like her pyjamas, some of her things now had permanent holes in from the thickness of the wool. She had wondered how the fairy had even managed to pull the wool through some of the items, but, upon closer inspection, it looked as though the holes had been bitten. It really had gone to a lot of trouble. She'd still had a drawer of things left to do when her mother called her from the room, suggesting they use the rest of the morning to explore the castle together.

Now, as they stood at the top of the castle looking out over the ramparts, Tanya fervently hoped that when they returned to the cottage the fairy wouldn't have repeated its handiwork. She pushed the thought from her mind, determined not to let it spoil things. The sun beat down heavily on top of her head and, though a deceptive breeze whipped her dark hair around her face, the heat was stifling.

The climb to the uppermost tower had been a weary one. Most people, her mother included, were now fanning themselves and admiring the view, while listening to the tour guide's history of the castle. Tanya tried to pay attention as tales of past owners, treacherous plots and deadly battles were recounted, but her mind kept drifting as she stared into the distance. Below her, visitors flooded in and out of the castle. Beyond them, far off, she saw the Wishing Tree, its bottles sparkling in the sun.

'And like many buildings of its age,' the guide continued, 'the castle has several secret passages that have been discovered over the years.'

Tanya's ears pricked up immediately. The guide had her full attention now, for she had read about secret passages in books and always longed to discover one. There were even stories about secret passages that ran underneath her grandmother's fairy-infested manor though, after spending many hours scouring the place for them, it was looking increasingly likely that they were just that – stories.

'Three tunnels have so far been discovered,' the guide went on. 'Both were found accidentally when the castle was undergoing repairs. The first leads from a west tower bedchamber to a local pub called The Nobody Inn. The second goes from the kitchens to the site of what was once a farmhouse, and the third from the dungeons to an old well.'

'Can we see them?' someone asked.

The guide shook his head. 'I'm afraid not. The first two are only open to the public at certain times of year for special events; the next one is Hallowe'en. And the third is permanently out of bounds along with the rest of the dungeons and the west towers of the castle, for safety reasons.'

At this, Tanya let out a disappointed huff. Her mother laughed.

'Never mind. There's a tea room downstairs – how about some lunch? And an ice cream on the pier afterwards?'

But they never made it to the pier for ice cream, for Mrs Fairchild started to feel unwell during lunch. 'It's just a headache,' she said, rubbing her temples. 'Too much heat, I think. I'm going back to the cottage for a lie-down.'

'I'll come with you,' Tanya said, concerned.

'No, you stay out.' Her mother gave a weak smile and dug into her purse, producing a ten-pound note. 'Here. Why don't you go to the amusements? There's no need for your day to be spoiled by hanging around the cottage.'

Tanya took the money, feeling a little guilty, but at the same time grateful she didn't have to return to the cottage just yet. She collected Oberon from the shade of a large tree where they'd left him. He woke from his snooze when Tanya unhooked his leash, thumping his tail at her return.

Tanya stood outside the castle entrance. She didn't really feel like going to the amusements, not on her own anyway.

The heat and the visitors in the night were taking their toll and she was feeling a little sleepy. In addition to that, she needed to decide how to tackle the fairy back at the cottage before it did any lasting damage, and for this she wanted a quiet place to think.

The Wishing Tree glistened in the distance, its jewelled colours like tiny, welcoming flags dancing on the breeze. It was all the persuasion she needed. She set off, leaving the castle behind her. Oberon ran off ahead, half-heartedly chasing a rabbit which escaped him easily. Tanya found a sturdy stick and threw it a few times, but soon gave up. Oberon had never quite understood the rules of 'fetch', preferring instead to play tug of war whenever she tried to wrestle the stick from him.

He became less boisterous as they neared the tree, staying close to Tanya and eyeing it suspiciously. Sure enough, Tanya saw the tree peeking at her as she approached, and for a split second she could have sworn it looked pleased to see her. Perhaps she was right and the tree was lonely out here.

It snapped its eyes shut when it saw her looking.

'Hello,' she said quietly. She peered up into the branches, but there was no sign of Ratty or anyone else.

The tree blinked, making a great pretence of waking up. Clearly, it didn't like to appear too eager. 'You haven't left a wish here yet,' it said, its dewy-green eyes watching her closely. 'Why ever not, did you forget?'

'No,' Tanya answered, remembering how shocked she'd been after meeting Ratty. 'Not exactly. I was ... distracted.'

The tree lowered its shaggy moss eyebrows into a frown. 'It's not every day you meet a tree as wise and magical as me.'

'Oh, I know,' said Tanya earnestly, not wanting to upset it. 'You're the loveliest tree I've ever met . . .'

The tree preened, breaking out its twiggy smile.

'It's just that I was startled by the boy who was here last time,' she continued. 'You see, I've never met anyone else who can see fairies before.'

'I'm not a fairy, I'm a sprite,' said the tree a little huffily. 'I'll thank you, girl, to get it right.'

'Sorry,' she said quickly.

The tree sniffed. 'Fey's the word you're looking for. It covers fairies, sprites and more.'

'Fey?' she repeated, frowning. The word seemed almost familiar and yet she could swear she'd never heard it before.

'Hmm,' said the tree. It watched her now with something like sympathy. 'The second sight is tough to bear,' it said. 'Of that I'm sure you're quite aware.'

'Yes,' Tanya agreed.

'You could be rid of it, you know,' the tree added. 'Now that's a wish I could bestow.'

'Really?' Tanya considered it. It was very tempting. But then she remembered her exchange with the awful thing under the cottage floorboards. She had expressed her wish then to not see fairies and its reply had chilled her to the core.

Be careful what you wish for, it had said. *I could easily stamp out your eyes while you sleep . . .*

'No more mischief, no more blame,' the tree coaxed. 'Naught to lose, but lots to gain.'

'I'll need to think about it,' she said. 'Every wish has a consequence, just like you said. I need to make sure I make the right choice.' *And besides*, she thought, *I've left the blasted green bottle back in my rucksack at the cottage.*

'Very sensible you are,' said the tree. 'Brighter than you look, by far.'

'Thanks,' Tanya muttered, not sure whether the tree was deliberately insulting her or not. She became aware that Oberon had gone very still all of a sudden. At first, she thought he was unnerved by the speaking tree, but then she saw that his gaze was fixed intently on a hedgerow in the distance, his nose twitching.

'What is it, boy?' she asked. 'The rabbit you lost earlier?'

Oberon tilted his head, sniffing the air. He thumped his tail and took off towards the hedgerow.

'Oberon!' she called after him, shielding her eyes from the sun. He paid her no attention and instead sped up to a gallop. She squinted at the hedgerow in annoyance, refusing to run after him. When he reached the hedge, he halted abruptly, his tail wagging in a blur as he tugged at something, shaking his head from side to side.

'Oh, don't let it be a rabbit,' Tanya cried. She set off after him in alarm.

'Still no wish and no goodbye,' the tree grumbled after her. 'Sometimes I don't know why I try!'

'I'm sorry,' she called over her shoulder. 'I will make a

wish, I promise. Just not today!' The tree muttered something else about manners, but she was too far away by then to hear it properly. 'Oberon!' she shouted again. 'Whatever you've got there, drop it!'

Oberon did not hear or didn't care to. He continued to pull at something near the hedge. As Tanya drew closer, she caught a glimpse of red. For one horrible, shocking moment she thought it was the blood of some small animal, and a small cry lodged in her throat. Oberon liked to chase things, but he had never caught anything apart from sticks and balls. She had always convinced herself that, should he corner a creature smaller than himself, he wouldn't know what to do with it.

She braced herself for a gory sight as Oberon tunnelled further into the hedge, only his wide, wagging bottom sticking out. And then she had another shock as a brown hand poked through from the other side, trying without much success to push the excitable dog away. Tanya slowed to a walk, creeping closer.

'Will ... you ... get ... away, you ... stupid ... mutt!' a voice panted. 'Let go, I tell you! Turpin, don't just sit there chewing my hair. Do something!'

Tanya frowned to herself. 'Turpin?' she whispered.

The leaves in the hedgerow parted and a gap appeared. A small, female figure with only one wing squeezed through. Tanya recognised her immediately. This was that nasty fairy friend of Ratty's – Turpin. She did not notice Tanya, for Oberon must have blocked her view.

She launched herself at him, tugging at his tail for all she was worth.

Tanya edged closer. Through the leaves she could see the top of Ratty's dark head now, his messy, black hair falling over his face. His hands were much browner than usual, for they were covered in earth. There was a small mound of soil in front of him which he was attempting to pat into place. Unfortunately, Oberon had other ideas and, as fast as Ratty's hands were filling the hole in, Oberon's large, brown paws were digging it right back out again.

She knelt down. 'What are you doing?'

Ratty leaped back in shock. 'Heck!' he said, recovering himself. He peered through the hedgerow. His face was streaked with sweat and dirt. 'Don't sneak up on me like that!'

'Don't sneak up on him like that!' Turpin shrieked. She let go of Oberon's tail and scurried back to Ratty, giving Tanya's shin a swift kick as she passed her. Tanya gritted her teeth, but said nothing. It had been hard enough to bruise, but she wasn't going to give Turpin the satisfaction of complaining about it.

'So what *are* you doing?' she repeated, watching him closely. Was it her imagination or did Ratty look guilty?

'Nothing.' He scraped another handful of earth over the mound, avoiding her eyes. 'Just digging ... for worms. I want to go fishing, in the river.'

Tanya snorted. 'Don't treat me like an idiot. You're burying something. And Oberon is trying to dig it up.'

Oberon's ears pricked up at the sound of his name. His thumped his tail and pounced on the hole again, showering her with dirt.

'Anyway, whatever it is you're hiding, I don't care,' she said truthfully. She had enough secrets of her own to know how annoying it was when other people pried into them. She pointed at Turpin. 'That little imp of yours did something to me yesterday, some sort of spell.'

'I don't know what you mean,' Ratty said. 'She can't do magic, I told you that. Remember?'

'No, I don't,' said Tanya. She ducked her head further to better see Ratty through the twigs and leaves. 'That's just the problem. I don't remember. Whatever she did to me scrambled my memories. Most of yesterday is a blur and I want to know why,' she demanded.

Turpin flicked a beetle in Tanya's direction and glared. Ratty sighed and sat back on his heels, raking his hair out of his face. They both watched silently as Oberon thrust his nose into the hole and emerged with something wrapped in red cloth. Tanya stared at it. *This* was what she had seen, red cloth, not a bloodied animal.

'Give that here!' Ratty snatched at it, but Oberon backed away with a satisfied yap and dropped the object out of his reach on Tanya's side of the hedge. There was a soft thunk and a rattle as it landed on the grass and rolled towards her, the red cloth unravelling.

'Give it to me,' Ratty urged.

Tanya reached for the item, intending to hand it back just

88

as the last piece of cloth came away, revealing what was inside. She stared at it in confusion. It was a clear glass jar of odds and ends: a broken necklace, a couple of matches that had already been struck, a bottle top, a pen lid. All sorts of nonsense jammed in there to the brim; strange objects that seemed to hold no value. It was the sort of thing a young child might bury, pretending it was treasures perhaps, but surely Ratty was too old for such games?

'Turpin, grab it,' said Ratty. His voice was panicked.

Turpin began to squeeze back through the hedge, but Tanya was too quick. Her sharp eyes had spotted something in the jar and she snatched it away from the fairy's grasp. 'That button,' she said, pointing to a small, white daisy shape within the glass. 'That's mine. I lost it yesterday. What's it doing in this jar?'

'Nothing!' Ratty sprang to his feet and began climbing over the bush. 'It's not yours. Give it here, will you?'

'If it's not mine, then it's identical,' said Tanya. 'And I'd rather have it back on my dress than buried in some hole.' She unscrewed the jar.

'Stop – don't do that!'

She ignored him and delved her hand inside, her fingers brushing against the objects. Immediately, she felt peculiar, like a thousand forgotten dreams had returned to her at once. Voices, faces and places she did not recognise flashed into her mind. She shook herself, her fingers closing round the button.

In that instant, everything she had forgotten from the

previous day came tumbling back into her mind, filling the gaps. She gasped. 'I remember now,' she said, her hand shaking. The jar fell from her hand to the grass, some of the objects spilling out. Ratty landed next to it, his tanned face flushed. He scrabbled at the objects, shoving them all back in.

'I remember it all,' Tanya whispered. 'The pier, your father's camper van, Nessie Needleteeth ... the ways to protect yourself from fairies ...' She closed her eyes, thinking of her ruined clothes. If only she had remembered that part, it could have saved her so much bother. 'I remember it all.' She clenched her hand tightly round the button. 'And I know, somehow, that it's connected to this button.' She stared at Turpin, her eyes narrowed. 'You. You took it, when you came up on my shoulder and pretended to like my hair. And then you ... you did something, taking my memories.' Her temper flared. 'Why, you nasty, sneaky little—'

'It wasn't Turpin,' Ratty interrupted. His voice was subdued.

Tanya scoffed. 'Stop lying. Of course it was her. That dress was brand-new; the button wouldn't have fallen off by itself. She made sure she got close enough to me and then she took it!'

Ratty nodded. 'She took the button,' he admitted. 'But only ... only because I told her to.' He met her eyes finally, shamefaced. 'Turpin wasn't the one who stole your memories, though. It ... it was me.'

8

The Memory Weaver

'WHAT?' SAID TANYA. 'BUT HOW COULD you . . .? I don't understand.'

'You don't need to understand,' Ratty muttered. He wrapped the jar in the red cloth again and held on to it. 'And I didn't tell Turpin to pinch you. I just needed her to distract you while she stole the button.'

'Excuse me,' said Tanya. 'But you've just admitted to stealing my memories. I think you owe me an explanation, and not just of how you did it, but why.'

'None of your business!' hissed Turpin.

'Be quiet, you,' Tanya snapped. 'And stay back. If I find you so much as looking at any of my buttons again, you're in big trouble.' The look Turpin gave her in return made her very glad that Turpin was unable to do magic, for if she could Tanya had no doubt that she would have been transformed into a slug or something equally disgusting.

'Talk to me, Ratty,' she persisted. 'Tell me why you did this.' She tried to keep the hurt from her voice and failed.

'I mean, why tell me all those things about fairies, and how to protect myself, if you were just going to steal away the memories anyway? What was the point of giving me the salt and the iron nail if I couldn't remember what to do with them?' She shook her head. 'I found them in my pocket last night and didn't know what they were for – I threw them in the bin. *In the bin!* When I really, *really* could have done with them to help me.'

Ratty gulped. 'Did something . . . happen last night?'

'The fairy under the floorboards happened,' she said tiredly, explaining what she'd awoken to. 'I've still not finished unpicking everything.'

Ratty hung his head. 'I'm sorry.'

She stared at him, frustrated and confused. 'Why then?' she repeated. 'Is it some sort of joke you and Turpin play on people you meet?' She recalled what he had told her yesterday. 'You said you wished you could keep the friends you made, but that none of them would remember you. It makes sense now, doesn't it?'

Ratty remained silent, turning the jar over in his hands.

'Those other objects in that jar,' Tanya said. 'I felt something when my fingers touched them. Like I was remembering lots of my dreams all at once. Only they weren't mine. And they weren't dreams, were they? They were bits of other people's memories.'

Ratty's shoulders slumped in defeat. He gave a weary nod. 'I'm . . . I'm a memory weaver,' he whispered at last. The words tumbled out of him, as though he'd been bottling them up for a long time. 'I can make people forget things or I can make memories come back. I've always been able to do it, ever since I can remember.'

'But how?' Tanya asked.

'It depends on the memory,' Ratty said. 'It needs an object belonging to the person to make it work – something little for a small, unimportant memory . . .'

'Like a button,' Tanya said slowly.

Ratty nodded. 'Or something bigger, more personal, for memories that are deep and make a person who they are. If it's an object that can be undone somehow, like a thread being unpicked or a match burning out, it works better.'

'The five-pound note on the pier,' Tanya said suddenly. 'It wasn't yours, was it? It *had* belonged to that other boy after all.'

Ratty nodded again.

'So, when you picked it up and unrolled it, you made him forget and then you kept it.'

'Yes.'

'And what about me?' she asked. 'Why bother to make a friend of me at all? If you wanted me to forget you, why let me remember bits of yesterday? Why not take all my memories of you?'

'That's what I tried to do,' Ratty said unexpectedly. 'You weren't supposed to remember me or Turpin at all, none of it.' He nodded at the button in her hand. 'That wasn't enough. The memory must have been too big, too important to you, for me to take it completely. It needed something bigger.'

'Of course it was important to me,' Tanya whispered. 'You were the first person I've ever met who can see fairies, too. Not only that, you taught me ways to protect myself. It was one of the most important things that's ever happened to me.' She blinked suddenly. 'That still doesn't make sense, though. Why allow me to create a memory you didn't plan on letting me keep? You could have just brushed me off at the pier and told me to leave you alone. Instead, you brought me back to your camper van. Told me about Nessie Needleteeth.'

Ratty shoved his filthy hands in his pockets and stared at the ground, rolling a pebble under his boot. 'I don't know,' he said. 'I guess . . . for the same reasons you wanted to speak to me. I don't often meet other people with the second sight, especially not my own age. I was curious about you.'

'No.' Tanya studied him carefully, trying to untangle truth from lies. There were both here, she was sure of it. Ratty was being honest about some things, but twisting others. She had told enough lies herself to recognise the signs in other people. 'No. You've done it to other people you've met, like you said. Children you made friends with. That's why they don't remember you. But those children don't have the second sight, do they?' she guessed. 'They're just ordinary. And you make friends with them because you're lonely.'

'Not lonely!' Turpin squeaked. 'Turpin is Ratty's friend!'

She clambered up on to Ratty's shoulder, circling his neck with her arms.

Ratty smiled faintly. 'Yes, you are, Turps,' he said, patting her arm. 'But it's not quite the same.'

'You're lonely,' Tanya continued, 'because you move around all the time, never staying in one place for long. You want to make friends, but you can't keep them.' She frowned. 'But it still doesn't make sense why you'd take their memories of you.' She was missing something here, some obvious clue, but her mind jumped ahead. 'With me it was different. When you said you were curious about me, you were telling the truth. But if you had planned on taking my memory of you, you wouldn't have bothered to tell me how to protect myself or given me ways to do it.'

She knew she was on to something here, because Ratty's tanned face was suddenly looking grey.

'Something must have happened to make you change your mind about me,' she said. 'That's why you got Turpin to steal the button. You hadn't planned on it from the start, had you?'

Ratty remained silent.

Tanya cast her mind back, trying to think of things she might have said or done that could have influenced his decision, but she couldn't come up with anything. Ratty had done most of the talking anyway, and he had seemed fine up until . . .

'The envelope,' she said. 'The red one, on the shelf. After you found it, that's when you started to act strangely and then Turpin climbed up and stole my button. Something about that envelope made you decide that I had to forget you.' She paused, waiting for him to respond, but still he said nothing. He didn't need to; the expression on his face confirmed she was right.

'You're in trouble, aren't you?' said Tanya. 'That's why you and your father keep moving from place to place, and why you don't let the friends you make remember you. I'm right, aren't I?'

Ratty gave a faint nod, his face ashen, while Turpin scowled at Tanya.

'Poking its nose where it's not wanted!' she said.

Tanya ignored her. 'What was in that envelope, Ratty? What's so bad that you have to keep running from it?'

Ratty unbuttoned his top pocket, his hand shaking. From it, he pulled out the red envelope, now crumpled and grubby. He scanned the meadow, making sure they were alone before he took out a sheet of red paper. For the first time, Tanya was able to see his eyes clearly. They were bloodshot, as though he had been awake all night.

Tanya took the paper, suddenly nervous. Even though Ratty had only opened it yesterday, the paper was limp, as though it had been folded and unfolded a great many times. She opened it and began to read.

Henry,
If this letter is in your hands, it means that my worst fears have come true and that we are both in trouble. Big

trouble. You've asked me many times to tell you the truth about the reason we move around so much. That time has come.

You see, the reason we have to keep moving is you, or rather your ability. Not the second sight, the other one. Years ago, your ability was used against someone very dangerous to remove a memory, a memory which must never be recovered.

At the time, you were so young that you had no idea of the importance of what you had done, nor of the consequences. But the owner of that memory realised something had been stolen and that it was you who took it.

That person is looking for us and they want the memory back at any cost. That's why we've been running ever since it happened. Now, I believe, we've been found. If we have, it's probably me that's been recognised. We have one thing in our favour, which is that you were only a small child when it happened, and you've grown and changed over the years. Alone, you might go unnoticed.

The next part of this letter is extremely important and you must follow these instructions exactly.

1. You must not use your ability unless it's absolutely necessary. You've always known this, but now it's more important than ever – you never know who might be watching.

2. Get rid of any objects linked to memories. Hide them in a place that they're unlikely to ever be found.

3. Wait for me for one day after receiving this letter.

There's a small chance I'm wrong and that we haven't been discovered, in which case I'll come back for you. Until I've investigated further, I won't know for sure.

4. Make sure you and the van are protected at all times. This means not removing any charms from windows or doors, not even for Turpin.

5. If I don't return after one day, pack a bag with food and clothes and leave the van. Go to the place we went to on our first night in this town – the place I could tell a story about. There you'll find instructions on what to do and where to go next.

6. Trust no one and nothing, except for your instincts. Even then, question.

7. Once you've committed this letter and the instructions to memory, burn it.

I pray I'm wrong about this and that by tonight we'll be sitting by the campfire, telling stories like we always have. Of course, I'll have some explaining to do, but I knew that day would come eventually.

Remember: you must follow these instructions EXACTLY. Your life may depend on it.

Pa.

Tanya read the letter twice, then handed it back. 'Crikey, Ratty,' she said at last. 'What on earth was this memory you took?'

'That's just it,' Ratty said in a low voice. 'I don't know. It must have happened so long ago that I don't even remember myself. There's lots of things it could have been … but …' His voice trailed off. He opened the envelope again and reached into it. 'He left these, too. Four-leaf clovers and fairy coins.'

Tanya looked at the coins closely. They were silver and a mixture of sizes. She picked one up. One side showed a tree in full bloom, the other the same tree minus its leaves and fruit. 'Why has he left these and the clovers?'

'Always good to have something to bargain with,' said Turpin. 'Four-leaf clovers are very powerful. Can be used in magic.'

Tanya handed the coin back. 'Why haven't you destroyed the letter yet? You've obviously read it a hundred times.'

'I have.' Ratty put the coins and clovers into the envelope again. 'But the words won't go in.'

'What are you going to do?' she asked.

'What Pa told me to,' Ratty said, his voice dry. 'He said to wait for a day. He … he never came back last night, so, if he doesn't return tonight, then …'

'Then he's right,' Tanya finished. She frowned suddenly. 'There's just one thing I don't understand. You decided to take my memory of you before you'd even read the letter. Why?'

Ratty nodded. 'Pa's left notes for me before,' he explained. 'But never in a red envelope. We've always used it as a warning code; if something is red, it's there for protection. That's how I knew something was wrong before I'd read it.'

'And so you decided to protect yourself,' Tanya finished.

'Pa said not to trust anyone in his letter,' Ratty said miserably. 'But he's always said that anyway. That's why I stop people from remembering me.'

'Wouldn't it be easier not to make friends in the first place?' Tanya asked.

'Maybe,' he agreed. 'Pa doesn't like me to get involved with people. He tells me that we should keep ourselves to ourselves. He ... he doesn't know that I like to make friends, when I can.' He looked guilty again. 'Every time I remove a memory, I'm taking a risk. Pa would be so angry if he knew. If we've been found, then it could be my fault. Maybe I'm to blame for Pa going missing. Every time I do it, I know it's wrong, but I can't help myself.'

'I can see why,' Tanya said softly. 'I know what it's like not to have friends. People need friends. Life's not much fun without them.' She hesitated. 'And sometimes people need to trust. But I think you know that already. You want to trust me. That's why you let me read the letter.'

Ratty raked his fingers through his hair. 'You're right. I do want to, but I can't.' He stared at her. 'For all I know, you're something to do with it all. You could be a spy for whoever is looking for me.'

Tanya considered this. She could have been offended, but she wasn't. 'I see what you mean. You're right to be suspicious of me, because all this must be to do with the fairies, or someone who can see them. Otherwise, your pa wouldn't have mentioned you protecting yourself and the van, or used a red envelope. But I've got an idea. I need a knife, or something sharp, and something to tie with – a bit of string perhaps. Do you have anything?'

Ratty stared at her for a moment, then dug in his pockets. He searched several, pulling out various bits of junk before presenting her with a small penknife and a frayed piece of scarlet ribbon. 'What are they for?'

Tanya unfolded the blade. It was good and sharp. With one hand, she reached up and loosened her hair from its ponytail. Then, using the penknife, she cut off a dark lock from underneath.

'What the heck are you doing?'

She used the knife once more to slice the ribbon in two, then passed it back to Ratty. She waited until he had put it away then handed him the lock of hair. 'Hold this.' He did as she asked. Using one piece of ribbon, she secured the lock of hair tightly at one end then wove it into a deft braid before tying the second piece of ribbon at the opposite end. She released it, leaving it dangling between Ratty's fingers.

'What's this for?' he asked.

'You said you needed something bigger to erase my memory of you,' she answered. 'And you also said that hair is powerful if it's used in magic. So now you have some of mine, a braid that can be undone.'

'You're allowing me to take your memory?' Ratty asked.

Tanya rolled her eyes. 'We both know that you'd have sent Turpin to steal something from me anyway, after today, if you didn't want to be remembered.'

Ratty fidgeted uncomfortably, confirming her suspicions.

'At least this way I know you'll do it right,' she said. 'That I won't remember you at all.' She swallowed, her throat suddenly tight. 'And I'd rather that than some half-formed memory of someone who can see fairies, who might have been a friend.'

Ratty ran his thumb over the smooth lock.

'There's just one catch,' she continued.

He looked at her warily. 'And what's that?'

'That you don't take my memory straight away,' she said. 'You keep hold of the hair until you need it. Like a sort of . . . insurance. Then, if you decide you can't trust me, you can make me forget you straight away. But I hope by doing this that I'm showing that you *can* trust me. Because I'm trusting you.' She nodded to her hair, gleaming in the sun. 'I'm trusting you not to let that fall into the wrong hands. Into fairy hands.'

'Why is it so important that I trust you?' Ratty asked.

'Because you're in trouble,' said Tanya. 'And, if I can, I want to help you.'

'I don't think you can help me,' said Ratty. 'I'm not sure anyone can.'

'You've got nothing to lose by letting me try.'

Ratty gazed at her for a long moment, his eyes bluer than the sky. Finally, he slipped the lock of hair in his pocket and gave her a small smile. 'All right.'

Tanya smiled back and sat down on the grass. 'First things first. This place your pa mentioned, the place he could tell a story about. Where is he talking about?'

Ratty sat next to her, but, after a sharp tug of his shirt from a jealous Turpin, he shifted away a little.

'It's a tradition of ours,' he said, pulling up a piece of grass distractedly. 'Every time we arrive in a new town, we go exploring. No matter how boring the place might seem at first, we always manage to find somewhere, somewhere really . . . unusual. In the last town, it was this abandoned house, all boarded up. It was creepy – I didn't like it much. Before that, it was an old Roman outdoor theatre, all over-grown and forgotten. Every time we find one, Pa says, "I could tell a story about this place." And then, that evening, he does. And they're always the most amazing, unforget-table stories you could imagine. He has this way of making everything seem like an adventure, like we're real explor-ers.' He snapped the blade of grass between his fingers. 'Only, since I read that letter, I'm starting to think that we didn't find these places by chance at all.'

'You think he knew about them already?' said Tanya.

'Yes. I think he planned it. Every town, every city. They were never just places we ended up in. He took me to these places for a reason.'

They were quiet as the meaning of Ratty's words sunk in.

'He knew that some day he might have to write you that letter,' Tanya realised. 'And he always made sure there was a secret place you could go to if he did.'

Ratty chewed at his nail, deep in thought. 'Exactly. It was another one of his codes. A way he could point me to

103

somewhere only the two of us would know about if we were in danger.'

'Tricksy clever,' said Turpin, her voice full of admiration.

'Yes,' Ratty murmured. 'And he told the stories about each place so that it would stick in my mind, so I wouldn't forget it.'

'So where is the place in Spinney Wicket?' Tanya asked, aware that he had still not answered her question.

Ratty stared across the meadow, his eyes fixed on something in the distance. Tanya followed his gaze, back along the way she had come.

'The Wishing Tree?' she said.

'No. Beyond that.'

Tanya looked past the tree. Her eyes rested on the castle where she had been only a short time ago. She frowned. 'But the castle seems too open, too public. Not at all like the other places you mentioned.'

'Not all parts of the castle are public,' Ratty said darkly. 'Remember what I said about some of it being shut away?'

Despite the warmth beating down on her, Tanya felt the tiny hairs on her arms stand up. 'Which part?' Somehow, she knew what Ratty was about to say before the words were even out of his mouth.

'The dungeons.'

9
Gone

'IF THE DUNGEONS ARE OUT OF BOUNDS, how did you and your father get in?' Tanya asked. 'Surely you didn't send Turpin to steal a set of the castle keys?'

'No,' said Ratty. 'Although that might have been easier. We got in through an old well. About halfway down the shaft before you hit the water there's an entrance to a tunnel. The tunnel connects it to the dungeon.'

They had been walking for some time now, largely in silence, apart from snatches of conversation here and there as each of them gathered their thoughts. They had cut across the meadows by a faster route than before, passing the castle at a distance, and were now in sight of the bridge over Nessie Needleteeth's spot on the river.

Ratty strode quickly and stared straight ahead, his jaw clenched in determination. He had decided to go back to the van and pack a bag while waiting for his father. With little time to think about it, Tanya had followed, and Ratty had neither invited nor discouraged her. Her mind was spinning, thoughts tumbling over each other and fighting for her attention. At the forefront was everything Ratty had told her and the danger he was in. At the back, she felt a creeping sense of dread as she realised she had already, unwittingly, broken the rule about speaking to him about fairies. She pushed the thought away. It couldn't be helped. A punishment from the fairies was now unavoidable. She would just have to deal with whatever they dished up.

'How do you actually *take* a memory then?' she asked. 'I know it's connected to the object, but how is it done?'

'I'm not sure exactly,' Ratty replied. 'It's not something I can properly explain. I'll just hold the object, whatever it is, and think about what it is I want the person to forget. So, for instance, I held your button and thought about everything we did and spoke about yesterday. And then I thought about it all disappearing, like it never happened.' His eyes were still fixed in the distance, and his breath was coming in short, quick bursts. 'Some objects are much better than others. If it can be undone somehow while I'm touching it, like your lock of hair or a match being struck, or a key unlocking a door, it will work much more easily. But I just have to use whatever I can get.' He shrugged. 'A button can be undone and a coin can be spent, but not while they're loose in my hand.'

It was late afternoon by the time they reached the river's edge. The sky had clouded over, but the air was still warm and midge-infested. Without the sun playing on the water, it didn't sparkle in the same way it had before, and its true murky-green colour was much more obvious. Tanya eyed the missing persons poster of the young girl and found a lump rising in her throat. It was so faded and tattered, the image almost bleached out by the sun. She looked away as they stepped on to the bridge. Their footsteps were loud and hollow on the wooden planks.

'Careful,' Ratty said in a low voice.

'What?' Immediately, Tanya scanned the water for signs of danger, but all was calm.

'Not the river.' Ratty frowned. 'Something's been spilled on the bridge. It's slippery. I just skidded a little.'

'Oh.' Tanya looked down and saw dark splashes on the wood. At the same time, she became aware of a strange smell. It was waxy and oily. She couldn't remember it being here yesterday. She tugged at Oberon's leash, noticing Turpin making exaggerated gagging noises and holding her nose. Once they were safely across, she allowed Oberon off his leash once more and he took off eagerly, nose in the long grass.

In the distance, the three horses were visible and, within minutes, Morrigan had joined them. She trotted at Ratty's side for a while and he patted her distractedly, but did not slow his pace. 'Nothing for you today, girl,' he murmured. She bowed her great head as if she understood, yet still she accompanied them almost to the edge of the copse of trees before hanging back and then finally meandering back to her companions.

Perhaps it was the lack of light as they stepped beneath

the trees, but no sooner had they done so than Tanya began to feel uneasy. It was gloomier today than it had been before and, while yesterday it had brought fairy-tale thoughts of gingerbread cottages to mind, today all she saw were shadows and hiding places for big, bad wolves. It was not until they were well into the copse that Tanya realised why she felt so on edge.

'Ratty,' she whispered, hurrying to catch up with him. 'Does it seem very quiet to you?'

Ratty stopped suddenly and Tanya halted next to him. A second later, Oberon's wet nose bumped the back of her leg.

'It is quiet,' he answered, glancing about through the trees. 'Too quiet. I can't hear a thing. No birds singing, nothing else moving about . . .'

'No fairies whispering,' Tanya added. She shivered. 'It's like someone has already been along this way and disturbed them.'

Ratty's face lit up with hope. 'Maybe it's Pa. Maybe he's back!' He set off, faster now, pushing through the branches. Turpin scurried along behind him, her wing twitching and buzzing. Moments later, they reached the van and Ratty slowed, surveying the clearing.

The curtains were still drawn and the campfire was still ash. Tanya reached up and touched the washing, hanging as it had been yesterday. It was dry now, but no one had taken it inside.

'Doesn't mean he's not back,' Ratty muttered. He strode obstinately to the door, fumbling for the key around his neck. 'He could be sleeping.' He unlocked the door and slid it open.

Inside, the van was empty. Everything was as it had been before, neat and untouched. There was no sign that anyone had entered. Ratty hopped in, poking around on every shelf, presumably, Tanya thought, in case there was another note. It took him only seconds to find that there was nothing. He sat on one of the benches, his shoulders slumped.

'He hasn't been back.'

'That doesn't mean he's not going to,' Tanya said, but Ratty's worry was plain to see and she shared it now. 'There's still a chance.' She followed him into the van. 'I'll wait with you awhile.' She began to pull the sliding door closed again.

'Wait,' Ratty said. 'Bring Oberon inside.' He glanced out into the greenery once more. 'Even if it wasn't Pa that came through the copse before us, someone did. Best not leave him out there.' He gave Turpin a tight smile, which she returned with a doleful look. 'Sorry, Turps. You heard Pa's instructions. I can't remove the charms on the doors. Can you keep watch instead?'

'Of course she can keep watch,' Turpin scoffed. 'Turpin is the best at watching.' With that, she sprang on to a low-hanging tree branch, nimble as a monkey, and vanished into the overhead canopy of leaves.

Tanya pulled the door closed. 'What now?' she said.

'We wait, I suppose,' Ratty replied. He started to get up. 'I'll fix us something to eat.'

'Let me,' said Tanya. She went into the kitchen area and began searching the cupboards. As Ratty had described, they were full of tins and not much else. She took one down and emptied it into a small saucepan on the hob. 'I hope soup is all right?'

'Fine,' Ratty said, his voice flat.

She stirred the contents of the pan and pulled out what was left of a small loaf of bread. There was enough for a couple of slices each. She cut them thinly and spread them with butter, adding extra to make up for the dryness, and glanced over her shoulder at Ratty. He had taken out his father's note and laid it flat on the table. His lips moved soundlessly as he read it yet again.

From somewhere outside the van, a strange, high-pitched sound carried through the trees, piercing the silence. Ratty looked up from the note, his gaze locking with Tanya's. 'What was that?'

They stared at each other, straining their ears. A light wisp of steam curled past Tanya's face from the soup warming on the hob. It was the only movement in the silent stillness.

The sound came again, closer this time and longer. A desolate, miserable wail that chilled Tanya's blood. Oberon's ears went back and he gave a small, confused whine.

'Is it an animal . . . or a person?' Ratty whispered.

Tanya shook her head. She couldn't tell. All she knew was that it was the most horrible thing she had ever heard. There were a few beats of silence before it came once more.

This time it was clearer, unmistakable. Ratty stood up, creeping to the window. 'There's somebody out there,' he said. 'Someone crying!'

At last, Tanya found her feet. She put down the wooden spoon she'd been stirring the soup with and joined Ratty at the window. Slowly, Ratty reached out and drew one of the curtains back.

A loud thud sounded above them, forcing a scream into Tanya's throat. Ratty jumped, too, releasing the curtain. Something had landed on the roof of the camper van.

'It's all right,' he whispered. 'That'll be Turpin. She's probably trying to get a good look at whatever ... whoever it is.' He reached out and moved the curtain again. Tanya found that she was holding on to his other arm tightly. They both stared through the window into the clearing.

At first, they saw nothing. Then a breeze ruffled the greenery, taking the washing on the clothes line and lifting it into a gentle dance.

'Look!' Ratty pointed. 'Over there, through that gap in the laundry.'

Behind a green shirt flapping on the line, a pair of thin, pale legs were visible. They were walking slowly towards the van, as though in pain. And no wonder, for only one of the feet had a shoe on. The other was bare and caked in something brown, mud perhaps ... or congealed blood. A knee-length blue dress came into view as the figure limped closer. Its fabric was torn and muddied. Water dripped from its hem.

A small hand parted the washing on the line and then the figure slipped through. Tanya's body went rigid. Though her face was almost colourless and the blonde hair was plastered wetly to the cheeks, she recognised the girl immediately.

'It's her,' she said, her voice choked. 'The girl on the poster ... the girl who went missing by the river! Nessie Needleteeth didn't get her – she must have escaped!'

'She's soaked, poor thing,' Ratty said, his face ashen. 'We have to help her.'

He moved to the door and opened it, stepping outside.

'Are you all right?' he called to her.

The girl paused on the other side of the campfire, her face contorted with sobs. She shivered and shook, water dripping from her wet clothes and hair.

'Please help me,' she said, through stifled sobs. 'I'm so cold! I don't know where I am. I ... I fell in the river and I got lost.' Another wretched sob escaped her lips.

'Tanya, fetch a blanket,' Ratty said urgently, crossing the clearing. 'They're inside the seats. And get another soup bowl; we need to warm her up!'

Tanya rushed to the table and fumbled with one of the benches. Sure enough, the lid lifted up and inside there were piles of blankets and pillows. She dragged one out and jumped down from the van – then gasped as something held her back. She turned round, bewildered.

'Oberon, what are you doing?' she scolded. 'Let go!'

Oberon released her T-shirt from his jaws and backed

away, bumping into the table leg. His hackles were up and he shifted from side to side in agitation.

'What's wrong, boy?' she asked.

'Tanya, the blanket,' Ratty prompted. Tanya turned back towards him. He had almost reached the girl, who had stopped now and was crouched down, clutching at her foot.

'Oh, it hurts,' she moaned.

Oberon began to bark wildly as Tanya took a step towards the girl, but there was another noise, a thumping coming from above. She paused and turned back to see Turpin perched on a branch overhanging the van, whacking a stick against its roof. Her head was shaking from side to side and she was saying something – something Tanya could not hear over the girl's wails and Oberon's barking – but Tanya did not need to hear the words to know that Turpin, as well as Oberon, thought something was very wrong.

She whirled back to face Ratty, who was frozen to the spot. Whatever it was, he'd noticed it now, too. His eyes were fixed on the girl's face, and they were wide and shocked. He took a step back, towards the van.

The girl reached out her hand to him. 'Help me,' she repeated, through chattering teeth. 'I fell into the river and got lost. I'm so cold . . .'

It was the girl's colour, Tanya realised finally, that wasn't quite right. That gave it away. Her skin – lips, especially – should have been bluish if she was so cold. But they were virtually colourless, like the rest of her. Even her dress was

113

bleached and pale. *She looks . . . wrong,* Tanya thought. *Not like a real person at all, but like . . . like . . .*

Like a photograph that had once been in colour, but had been bleached out by the sun.

Ratty took another step back. The girl stopped crying and slowly stood up. And, in the gaps between Oberon's barks, Tanya could finally hear Turpin's high-pitched voice saying two words over and over again:

'Glamour! Danger!'

Ratty spun on his heels, panic etched across his face. 'Get back in the van!' he cried.

Tanya turned and dived back inside, confused and terrified. The van was now full of steam from the soup boiling away furiously on the hob, causing her to skid on the slippery floor. She hit the table hard, sending a painful jolt through her elbow. She watched the girl slowly stand up as Ratty raced towards the van. She was no longer sobbing. Instead, her face was curiously blank. The sudden change sent a ripple of fear over Tanya's skin. What on earth was going on?

Ratty was perhaps two strides away from the door when another much larger figure came crashing sideways from out of nowhere, knocking him to the ground.

'Ratty!' Tanya screamed.

Ratty grunted as he hit the dirt, rolling back in the direction of the campfire ashes. The hooded attacker scrambled after him, grabbing his leg. Ratty grabbed a handful of ash and threw it into his assailant's face, causing the person to yell – a deep, male voice – and release him.

Coughing, Ratty crawled to his feet. He staggered only a couple of steps before the man was on his feet once more. His face, thick spectacles and the iron-grey hair spilling over his shoulders were now covered with ash. He wiped it away and lunged again.

'Hurry!' Tanya urged. Above her, Turpin was still shrieking and kicking up a din in the tree. Tanya scanned her surroundings for something she could use as a weapon. Her gaze rested on the saucepan. She rushed to the hob and grabbed it, then leaped from the van towards Ratty, who was just a whisker from the man's outstretched fingers.

'Duck!' she yelled, hurling the bubbling contents of the pan. Ratty swerved just in time. As the boiling liquid met his fingers, the man's scream echoed through the clearing. He shook it from his hand, cursing, but somehow kept coming.

'Quickly!' Tanya shouted, but Ratty was not quick enough. A split second later, he was grabbed from behind and a dark rag was forced over his mouth. He struggled furiously against it, but his attacker held it firm.

'No ' Ratty began, his voice muffled.

Tanya thought quickly. The man was much taller than Ratty and wider, too. Desperate, she decided to take a risk. She threw the saucepan as hard as she could, but this time her aim was off and the man dodged it easily.

In any case, she was too late. Ratty's limbs went limp and his eyes rolled back in his head. Whatever was on the rag had rendered him unconscious, and she could only watch as he was dragged away.

'Get the fairy,' she heard the retreating man say to the dripping figure. 'We'll take care of the girl later.' With that, he vanished beyond the trees, taking Ratty with him.

'Ratty! RATTY!' Tanya yelled.

The only response she got was a low, spiteful chuckling. It was coming from the little girl from the river. The little girl who was somehow not a little girl. Tanya stared at her. She – it – had not moved. She was still, watching Tanya intently. Her face was no longer blank, but instead wore a sly, unpleasant grin. She was still dripping water, Tanya realised dimly. That wasn't right, either, for the river was some distance away. She should not be as wet as that by now.

Tanya jumped as the girl took a step in her direction. Her movements were sure and steady, like a predator. Oberon began to snarl and snap as she came nearer. She gave him a scornful look, then her eyes rested on something above the van. For the first time, Tanya became aware of a muffled sound above her, a quiet, shocked sobbing.

'Turpin,' she said hoarsely. 'She's coming for you. You have to run!'

The words had barely left her mouth before the river girl launched herself with surprising speed at the camper van, clambering up its sides like an animal before vanishing on to the roof. The van rocked and swayed, and the air was suddenly choked with growls and frightened squeals. Tanya grabbed the table to steady herself, almost tripping over Oberon. Something hit the window behind her and Tanya turned in time to see a wing flash past. It was swiftly followed by a filthy, mud-caked foot before the two figures set off into the trees. With that final jerk, the van was still.

Tanya ran to the door. The sounds of scurrying faded rapidly, leaving only the hiss of the leaves in the wind.

'Turpin?' she cried, fighting a bubble of panic that threatened to silence her. 'Turpin? Ratty?'

Nothing answered her.

They were gone.

10
A Tricksy Magic

TANYA SLAMMED THE VAN DOOR SHUT and slid the catch. She stood for a moment, unable to do anything except shake. Her eyes blurred with unshed tears. She forced herself not to give in and weep. Ratty was gone. Turpin was gone. Crying would not bring either of them back or help Tanya return to Hawthorn Cottage in safety. For that she needed a clear head.

We'll take care of the girl later. The threat echoed in her thoughts. How long did she have before they returned for her? And what did they even want with her anyway? She drew in a deep breath and blew it out slowly, trying to calm herself. A gentle movement caught her eye. The rowan berry charm in the doorway swayed lightly from where she had rushed past it. It was a reminder that she must focus.

Quickly, she moved around the van, checking behind each drawn curtain that all the protective charms were still in place. When she reached the kitchen area, it occurred to her that it was strangely warm ... until she found that the hob was still on from heating the soup. She turned it off and went to sit at the table, glad to take the weight off her jelly-like legs. Oberon laid his head on her lap, whining softly.

Ratty's letter was on the table where he had left it. She picked it up and read it again. Clearly, his father had been right about having been discovered, but what had become of him? Had he made it to the dungeon below the castle and left further instructions for Ratty? Or had he been captured, too? One thing was certain: Tanya was the only person who knew Ratty had been taken – and the only one who could help him. And, right now, she wasn't safe, either.

She folded the letter and put it into her pocket. Then she got up and checked the windows once more, this time peering past the curtains for any sign of movement. Everything looked quiet, yet it brought no comfort. Whoever had taken Ratty had been watching them without them knowing and had tricked them just as easily.

A mixture of anger and fear flooded through her. They had been so foolish to fall for it, so utterly gullible. Whoever the little girl was, it couldn't have been the *real* her that Tanya and Ratty had seen shivering in the clearing. So what was it they had seen – a ghost? She dismissed the idea as soon as it occurred, remembering the girl's cruel smile. Ghosts did not pretend to be one thing when they were another. Nor did they lure unsuspecting children away from safety to be snatched. They had seen the girl and instinctively rushed to help. Whoever – *whatever* – it had been, it had set out to trap them.

Tanya glanced around the van. She had to leave before

they returned for her, but first she had to find some way to protect herself. She guessed that Ratty's red neckerchief, and the iron and salt he'd been carrying, would have protected him from fairies. So did this mean the man who had taken him was not fey? In that case, she would need a weapon effective against humans.

She moved to the kitchen, rummaging through the drawers. There was nothing, just a little paring knife with a blunt, wobbly blade. She put it back and moved to the door.

'Here, Oberon,' she said softly. Oberon squeezed out from under the table, his tail firmly between his legs. He looked even more reluctant to go outside than Tanya felt. 'I know what you're thinking,' she told him. 'But we have to be brave. Both of us.'

She clicked open the catch and pulled the door back, wincing at the noise. In the silent surroundings, it sounded too loud. She took Oberon's leash and wrapped it tightly round her wrist. One end was leather, but the other was a fairly thick chain. It could act as a weapon if she needed it. Cautiously, she scanned the clearing, paying attention to the area behind the washing line in case something, or someone, was hidden behind the hanging clothes. All seemed still.

Tanya stepped down from the van, coaxing Oberon out after her. Her heart started to pound. She slid the door shut again. There was no key to lock it, for it had vanished with Ratty. She wondered if it mattered – whether Ratty or his father would ever again return to the van – then pushed the horrible thought away.

120

She crept past the campfire and ducked under the washing line, heading to the opening where the trees gave way to the meadow. Still there were no sounds of life, no fairies' whispers, birdsong or evidence of any other creatures. Soon she reached the edge of the trees and could see the meadow beyond, wide open and empty save for the horses in the distance. Where was she safest? In the meadow, she'd easily be able to see if anyone was chasing her, but she would also be seen herself. Here, in the tree-lined grove where she had some chance of staying hidden, it meant that others could hide, too. Either way, there was only so far she could go before the trees ended.

She decided to stick to the fringes of the grove as far as she possibly could. She'd have to make a break across the meadow to get to the river soon enough. The knowledge sat in the pit of her stomach, a tight ball of fear. She crept from tree to tree, keeping Oberon close.

Something crackled behind her. She whipped round, seeing nothing. Oberon's ears were pricked up and alert, his nose scenting the air. Then a small, brown blur hurtled towards them, flinging itself at Tanya's legs.

'Turpin!' she exclaimed. Her heart leaped; she never thought she'd be so pleased to see Ratty's grubby little friend.

'Quiet, silly girl!' Turpin hissed. Her small face was pinched and scared. She clambered up Tanya's body and stood on her shoulder, her eyes wide and watchful. 'We must go quickly.' She seized a strand of Tanya's hair and flicked it like a rein. 'Hurry now.'

Tanya moved off again, keeping close to the trees. 'Where was Ratty taken?' she asked, keeping her voice low. 'How did you get away?'

The fairy wrung her hands in distress. 'Turpin did not see where Ratty was taken. It was too fast. She was chased, by the little girl creature, until she managed to lose it in the trees.' Her eyes darted around fearfully. 'But it's still here somewhere.'

'What *was* the little girl creature?' Tanya asked, suddenly remembering something. 'When you saw it, you said something I didn't understand. You said "glamour".'

Turpin nodded vigorously. 'Yes. Is a type of fey magic – glamour. A tricksy magic, to pretend and deceive. A way of looking like something else for a little while. Is very dangerous.'

'So the girl was really a fairy in disguise,' Tanya said.

'Maybe,' said Turpin. 'Or maybe something else, using fey –magic.'

'What do you mean? If it wasn't a fairy, what was it?'

'Turpin does not know. Only that it didn't *feel* fey.'

Either way, the faded colouring made sense. Whatever it was had tried to imitate the girl, knowing that Tanya and Ratty had seen the poster and would try to help, but it had simply mimicked what it had seen on the weathered sheet of paper.

Turpin frowned suddenly, looking Tanya up and down. 'Why are you not protected? Have you learned nothing, stupid girl?'

'I . . . I didn't think I needed to be,' said Tanya. 'The man who took Ratty was human, wasn't he?'

'He looked human!' Turpin shook a fist at Tanya's nose. 'Do not trust appearances. Turn something inside out and quick about it!' She hopped off Tanya and landed on Oberon's back, watching like a miniature general.

Hurriedly, Tanya took off her T-shirt and pulled it back on again inside out. In her haste, she fumbled, putting an arm through the wrong way, but finally it was on. Turpin nodded, then resumed her position on Tanya's shoulder.

'Now here is a valuable lesson,' she said. 'You are protected, are you not?'

'Y-yes?' Tanya said uncertainly. 'If the ways Ratty told me were true.'

'Of course they're true!' Turpin said bad-temperedly. 'You are protected. I am a fairy. And yet I can still do this—' She reached out and gave Tanya's nose a painful tweak.

'Ouch!' Tanya protested, but Turpin was not finished.

'—and this.' There was a sharp tug as Turpin pulled her hair.

Tanya batted the fairy's hand away, furious. 'What is the matter with you?' she hissed. 'Why do you have to be so spiteful?'

'Shut up and listen,' said Turpin, her eyes narrowed. 'You are protected. And yet I, a fairy, can still do these things to hurt you. I can pinch, bite, kick, prod and poke you in the eye if I want to. And, if I were not so little, I could capture you and keep you prisoner. Are you understanding me yet?'

'Yes,' Tanya whispered, as Turpin's demonstration

suddenly made sense. 'You're saying that fairies can still hurt me. The protection only means they can't use magic.'

'Yes.' Turpin released Tanya's hair and patted her head. 'Not so silly after all.' She sniffed. 'Ratty was not taken by magic. He was taken by force.'

'What was on the rag?' Tanya asked. 'It made him unconscious.'

'Some kind of human medicine probably,' Turpin answered. She paused, about to say something else, then stopped and sniffed the air.

'What is it?' Tanya asked. She lifted her nose and inhaled. There was a faint scent on the air, unpleasant and harsh, but the breeze whipped it away before she could place it.

Turpin's long, pointed ears flattened to her head like a cat's. 'Something is burning,' she said. 'They're near.'

'Burning?' Immediately, Tanya thought of the camper van. She had definitely turned the hob off ... but what if someone, or something, had started a fire, thinking Tanya was still inside? Could this be what they had meant by 'taking care of her'? Or was it merely an attempt to force her outside and into their clutches?

'Maybe the trees,' said Turpin, scanning the copse around them. 'Trying to smoke us out. Hurry. We must hurry!'

They reached the end of the wooded grove, leaving nowhere to go except out into the open meadow. Turpin saw it first and gave a horrified squeak. With one hand, she jerked on a strand of Tanya's hair. The other was pointing across the meadow. 'Look!' she hissed. '*Look!*'

A plume of grey smoke rose across the horizon, billowing like the breath of a great dragon. Below it, orange and yellow flames danced at the river's edge.

'The bridge,' Tanya whispered in horror. 'The bridge is on fire! How are we going to get across now?' Desperately, she searched the length of the river for any other means of escape, but there were none.

'There's a path that leads to another road,' Turpin said. 'But is a long way away. They will find us!'

'They have to catch us first,' said Tanya. 'What if we keep hiding?'

Turpin shook her head. 'Only so long we can hide for. Soon it will be dark, and we will be cold and hungry and tired. Then they'll get us for sure. We must escape.'

Tanya remembered the strange smell she and Ratty had noticed when they crossed the bridge earlier and the wet splashes on the wood. 'Someone threw something on to the bridge,' she realised. 'Some sort of oil, to make it burn. This wasn't an accident – it's a trap! They've cut off our way across so they can hunt us down.'

Turpin nodded to the bridge. 'That is the only way.'

'But how? Even if we get there before it collapses, we'll have no chance against the flames or the smoke . . .'

'We can cross it. Turpin has an idea,' said Turpin. She climbed down from Tanya's shoulder, ready to run. 'But we must go. Now!'

There was nothing for Tanya to do except trust her. Taking a deep breath, they left the shelter of the trees and emerged into the wide-open meadow. Tanya's feet pounded the ground, her heart thudding to match. She was easily the slowest of the three; Oberon and Turpin raced ahead, the uneven grass seeming to pose no problem for either of them. They had made it only a short way from the grove when a shout sounded from somewhere behind.

Tanya glanced back over her shoulder. The river girl had appeared at the edge of the trees behind and broken into a run. Tanya turned back to the river, stumbling but managing to avoid a fall. It cost her precious seconds and she fell further behind, widening the gap between herself, Turpin and Oberon.

'Hurry!' Turpin shrieked.

'I'm trying,' Tanya panted. She forced herself not to look behind; it would only slow her down. The girl creature was not close enough for her to hear yet, but already Tanya knew it was fast. Unnaturally fast. The speed at which it had chased Turpin had taken her breath away. A movement from the corner of her eye caught her attention. A large, black shape was moving at twice her speed across the meadow towards her.

'Morrigan!' The horse drew nearer and began to slow, unsure of herself. Tanya called out again, trying to sound normal. The river girl was advancing at shocking speed. There was only one way to reach the bridge in time.

'Morrigan,' she coaxed, making the same clicking noise of encouragement she had heard Ratty use. 'Here, girl!'

The horse trotted towards her, then drew to a halt,

bowing her great head. Tanya slowed to a jog, afraid of scaring her. This had to work, for she could hear her pursuer's footfall now, thundering across the field, growing ever nearer. In less than a minute, she would be upon her. She gathered her courage and the last of her energy and took a flying leap, grabbing the horse's mane and swinging herself up on to Morrigan's back.

Ratty had made it look easy. For Tanya, it was quite the opposite. She landed with a bump, almost sliding straight off the other side of the horse's smooth coat. She clung to Morrigan's mane, pulling herself level. 'Go!' she cried, urging the horse forward. Morrigan took a few tentative steps, as though aware she was carrying an inexperienced rider. But Tanya did not have time for that. The river girl raced towards her, breathing hard. Her faded face broke into a grin as she stretched out her hand.

Tanya dug in her heels, the way she had seen Ratty do. Morrigan leaped forward. Tanya felt the brush of fingertips skim her leg as the girl lunged for her. She yelled, kicking out again, spurring Morrigan on. A triumphant laugh burst out of her as she glanced back and saw her attacker left behind, but Morrigan moved at a remarkable pace, and without a saddle or stirrups there was nothing to keep Tanya in place. She twisted her hands into the horse's mane and wrapped her legs as tightly as she could about Morrigan's huge body, clinging on for dear life.

Already she was gaining on Turpin, who had almost reached the river. Oberon was only a short distance in front of her, having stopped and doubled back to bark his encouragement. 'Come on, boy!' she cried. 'Keep going!'

Somehow, through the bumping and sliding, she managed to stay on, through sheer fright and determination. When she saw Turpin stop just short of the river, she tugged Morrigan's mane to the left to direct her before slowing her down altogether. When she finally came to a halt, Tanya's legs still felt weak as she slid off and landed, jarring her ankle. She gritted her teeth through the pain. She had at least got her breath back now, and the river girl still had ground to cover. Morrigan had bought them precious time, but moments only. She sank her fingers into the horse's silky mane, feeling the velvet nose and warm huff of horse breath on her cheek.

'Thank you,' she whispered. She ran her hand over the smooth coat and gave Morrigan's flank a firm pat, sending her on her way. There was no time for a long goodbye.

'So, what now?' she asked Turpin, coughing. Now they were up close to the bridge, the flames danced dangerously high and the wind sent gusts of choking smoke towards them. Crackles filled the air as the wood was devoured. Smaller parts had charred and broken off already, floating downstream like blackened limbs. Though most of the bridge was still intact, the heat from the flames would prevent them going anywhere near it.

'We wait,' said Turpin. She ducked as a shimmering orange flake of wood floated past her, then surveyed the meadow.

'Wait?' Tanya said incredulously. 'We don't have time to wait! She'll be here before we know it!'

'She will not make it in time,' said Turpin. 'The bridge will not hold.' She sniffed the air. 'This fire was started by magic.'

As she spoke, a chunk of the bridge's handrail fell away, landing in the water with a hiss. It drifted a couple of feet then came to rest, prevented from going further by rocks either side of the river. The fire roared higher and the bridge creaked in protest. A supporting beam underneath was next to depart, crashing into the water.

'It's going,' Turpin said, shielding her face from the heat. 'Get ready.'

A terrible groaning rose above the crackling flames. The bridge began to lean to one side, sinking low, like a creature in pain.

There was a moment where it seemed to resist and hung suspended for a couple of seconds before finally collapsing with a mighty crash into the pea-green water, sending up clouds of ash and smoke. The broken bridge lay in a mound, most of the flames now extinguished. Finally, Tanya could see what Turpin had planned.

'Come on,' the fairy said. Nimbly, she edged down the sloping mud and began to pick her way across the smoking pile. Tentatively, Tanya followed, moving carefully on her jarred ankle. There were still enough pieces of the bridge left for them to clamber across without having to venture into the water and risk facing Nessie Needleteeth, but they would have to be fast. Though it was still holding together, the fire had weakened it, and chunks were breaking away and being swept off by the current.

Tanya stepped on to the wrecked bridge, watchful for any movement in the water. Even though she was protected, the thought of seeing Nessie Needleteeth was enough to put her on edge. However, the thought of being caught by their pursuer was somehow worse and, as the sound of ragged breathing reached her ears, she knew that they were almost out of time. She shooed Oberon ahead, testing the charred wood beneath her feet. The air was thick with smoke and ash, and she brought her sleeve up to cover her mouth and nose.

Something snapped behind. Tanya looked back, fearing the bridge was about to collapse further, but it was worse. The river girl was climbing down the bank towards the bridge, clawing through the charred debris. Brushing away splinters of wood, she looked up at them through matted blonde hair and stepped on to the bridge.

At the sound of Tanya's horrified gasp, Turpin looked back. Her eyes widened.

'Run!' she squeaked.

The thing pretending to be the little river girl gave a hideous grin . . . then lunged straight for them.

11
The Chase

TANYA SCRAMBLED OVER THE BROKEN wood, desperate to put distance between herself and the thing behind. Splintered wood tore at her clothing and scraped her skin, slowing her down. Holding her back. Just ahead of her, Turpin was faring slightly better, but not by much. Her small face was streaked with ash and her wing was quivering helplessly, a segment of it torn and fluttering.

Behind them, the girl creature grunted and cursed in its efforts to reach them. Tanya glanced back again. Fear lent her fresh strength and she surged forward, finding herself almost level with Turpin. The fairy's breath came in short rasps. The race across the meadow had sapped her energy, making her movements clumsy and slow.

Tanya took another quick look over her shoulder. The girl was making quick progress towards them, not seeming to care that her skin was becoming cut and bloodied as she crawled on hands and knees over the wood.

'If Turpin still had magic, she would send it into the

water,' Turpin panted. Her face twisted viciously. 'Leaving Nessie Needleteeth to crunch its bones.'

'She could just as easily crunch ours if we fall in,' Tanya said. She freed Turpin's wing from yet another spike of wood. 'Jump on to my shoulder, I'll take you across.'

Turpin shook her head and struggled on. 'No. It will slow us down and make us easier to catch. Go, fast as you can. Don't wait!'

'It's no use running.' The eerie voice rose up from behind. It had changed now. It was no longer the voice of a little girl, but instead deeper and older ... and much more cunning. 'There's nowhere for you to go.'

Tanya turned back, coughing. Anger made her bold.

'What have you done with Ratty?' she yelled. Another bout of coughing almost cost her her balance. A plank of wood cracked beneath her. She wobbled, then managed to right herself, hopping to another sturdier piece. She was ahead of Turpin now, but Oberon had beaten them both to the other side and was waiting patiently. More lumps of wood broke away and were sucked into the green water rushing past them.

'Don't worry about the boy,' said the creature. 'He's safe. He won't be harmed as long as he gives us what we want.'

'Lies!' Turpin hissed. 'All lies!'

'Then why are you chasing us?' Tanya demanded. 'If Ratty's the one you want?'

The thing smiled. 'To make sure you understand we don't mean any harm to your friend.'

'Close your ears,' said Turpin. 'It says these things only to slow you down!'

Tanya knew Turpin was right; the creature was trying to distract her, but at the same time the urge to find out what was going on was too strong to ignore.

'What is it that you want from Ratty?' she demanded.

The creature's eyes narrowed craftily. 'He stole something long ago. A memory. Now he must give it back.'

Tanya thought of the letter from Ratty's father. It had only mentioned a dangerous 'someone', not *two* people, and Ratty hadn't known what the memory was at all. 'Then you're wasting your time,' she said. 'He doesn't know where it is or even *what* it is!'

'Perhaps not,' said the thing. 'But *somebody* does . . .'

Tanya was almost at the riverbank, with only a few dangerous steps left to take. She knew she had to keep moving, but found herself unable to tear her eyes away from its face. Something odd was happening. Its face was bubbling and rippling, becoming longer and losing the childlike plumpness. Things shifted – bones, Tanya realised – under the surface of the skin, and the hair thinned and fell out in clumps leaving a bald, scabbed head. The cheeks hollowed and the eyes became sunken. It was awful, grotesque, and yet Tanya couldn't look away.

'What's happening to it?' Her voice shook, thin and scared.

'The running water,' said Turpin. 'It cannot cross the river without breaking the tricksy glamour. Whatever it really is, we shall soon see.'

'But why is it still chasing us?' Tanya said, panicked. 'Ratty said running water would stop a fairy.'

'Only if it *is* a fairy,' Turpin squeaked. 'And only then from chasing a human.' She dodged a flame that had begun to singe her wing. 'It can still chase other fairies – like Turpin.'

The thing edged closer. Its body was changing now, too. The shoulders widened, ripping through the blue dress and leaving it in tatters. Underneath it, the pale skin hung in doughy folds, as though it had been stretched and strained many, many times.

On the riverbank Oberon began to growl. Tanya looked up. His hackles were raised and his teeth bared, his brown eyes fixed intently on something in the water. She followed his stare to the murky-green river, seeing nothing except broken wood and bubbles. Then something shifted just under the surface, and she thought she saw a strand of hair floating on the surface before it vanished in an eye blink.

The bridge shook dangerously, and the sounds of splintering wood rose above the creaks and groans. It collapsed further, sinking deeper into the bubbling water. With no time to hesitate, Tanya took a flying leap at the riverbank, clearing the last of the wood. She landed ankle deep in water, not quite making the bank first time. She gasped as the cold water and mud sucked at her feet, but managed to squelch her way out to safety. Anxious, she turned and scanned the bridge for Turpin – and froze.

The bridge was now almost entirely underwater. Huge pieces of it were breaking away and floating off with the swirling current. Between two huge planks, partially underwater, Turpin floundered, watching the creature. Her expression was one of horror mixed with something else that Tanya could have sworn was recognition.

Frozen, Turpin was whispering something, a word Tanya didn't recognise: 'Morghul ... Morghul.' It made no sense. Was it another type of fey creature ... or could it be a name?

Behind her, the scab-headed creature grinned, reaching out.

'Turpin, move!' Tanya yelled.

'Can't!' Turpin struggled in vain, getting nowhere. She was trapped.

Tanya cast her eyes about for anything that could help. If only she had something she could throw to Turpin, to help pull her free ...

Oberon's leash! It was still wrapped tightly round her wrist. If she went back on to the bridge a little way and threw it, it should be long enough to reach Turpin.

Swallowing hard, she stood at the river's edge. The last thing she wanted was to climb back on to the sinking bridge, but if Turpin was to have any chance she had no choice. Screwing up her courage, she leaped back across the water, landing badly on a smoking lump of wood and jolting her ankle painfully once more. She gritted her teeth and began to unwind the leash.

'No!' Turpin shouted, seeing what she was about to do. 'Go back. You must escape!'

'I'm not leaving without you!' Tanya shouted.

'How touching,' the scab-headed thing crooned. Its bony fingers wrapped round Turpin's arm and tugged, hard. Turpin's screech of pain made the hair on the back of Tanya's neck stand on end.

'Let her go!' she yelled, shaking the leash free. 'Take your hands off her!'

The creature grinned and tugged again, the movement forcing them deeper into the water. Now only Turpin's head and shoulders were visible. The river weed rippled around them . . . then erupted in a green fountain of hair, teeth and long, lean arms. Nessie Needleteeth rose out of the water and loomed over them, her wide, gurgling mouth open and her hideous teeth glinting. This time, Turpin's screams were joined by those of the other creature as the river hag sank her teeth into its droopy white flesh, dragging it backwards. Something snapped beneath the water and Turpin bobbed to the surface. She tried to lift herself on to a piece of nearby wood, but her face twisted in pain and she fell back into the water again. Just inches from her face, violent thrashing movements disturbed the water and horrible gargling noises filled the air. Things crunched and bubbled below the water. Shreds of faded blue fabric rose to the surface, floating eerily downstream. The water stilled.

Then, further along, the pale-skinned creature broke the surface of the water, gasping. It fought the current, but whatever injuries it had sustained had weakened it, and it thrashed and drifted away from Nessie's clutches and out of sight.

'Turpin!' Tanya shouted. 'Grab this!' Clipping one end of the leash to her belt, she threw the looped leather end in Turpin's direction. It hit the water just out of her reach and sank. Quickly, Tanya gathered it in and threw again. This time it slipped through Turpin's fingers and vanished beneath the water once more. Growling in frustration, Tanya hauled it in a second time.

'Please catch it this time,' she murmured, for she could see that Turpin was losing strength. She threw a third time and it seemed to work ... until a green hand shot out of the water and seized the leather loop. It tugged, pulling Tanya to her knees. She cried out as she landed, splinters piercing the palms of her hands. The river hag lurched out of the water again, Oberon's leash clenched firmly in her fist. Her other hand reached for Turpin, encircling the fairy's wrist. She smiled a terrible smile, water leaking from her teeth. White shards of bone were tangled in her hair. She yanked the chain again, pulling Tanya flat against the sinking wood.

Tanya spat river water out of her mouth. She struggled, trying to unclip the leash from her belt, but succeeded only in grazing her knuckles against the wood. Another pull from Nessie took her out further. Thinking fast, she grabbed the chain with both hands and tugged with all her might, pulling Nessie towards her. The river hag's mouth opened in surprise and she toppled forward with a screech, spraying foul water into the air. Tanya used the distraction to unhook the leash from her belt and yanked it again violently. It was enough to wrench it free from Nessie's fingers – but not enough to make her release Turpin.

The river hag rose up in fury, her eyes blazing. Her mouth opened and the song began, a watery, lilting gurgle that Tanya knew would sound very different if she were not protected. She staggered backwards, sliding on the damp wood. Nessie cut through the water like an eel, still clutching Turpin.

Tanya twisted away from the water, hauling herself over the wreckage of the bridge. Like a shepherd, Nessie was herding her to the middle of the river, where the centre of the bridge was now completely underwater. Tanya was all out of ideas. Not only had she failed to save Turpin, but it now looked unlikely that she would escape the river hag, either. She considered jumping off the bridge and trying to swim for the bank, but having seen Nessie move so quickly she knew she would never make it in time. Besides, she would never forgive herself if she abandoned Turpin now. There had to be something she could do . . .

She caught sight of the poster of the missing girl on the board nearby. Its tattered corners flapped in the breeze like a trapped bird trying to fly away. A horrid thought forced its way into Tanya's mind: would it be her own face on that board in a few days' or weeks' time? Would she be just another missing person, like that poor little girl? Even though she was protected from Nessie's song, she knew that the river hag did not really need magic to kill her. All she would have to do was hold her under the water until Tanya could no longer fight. Or perhaps a slow roll in the mud at the bottom of the river like crocodiles did, until their prey stopped struggling. And then those teeth ...

Stop it! she told herself. She had to focus. Nessie hadn't won yet and Tanya had surprised her once. Perhaps she could do it again. On the riverbank, Oberon began to bark. Tanya looked down at the leash still clenched in her hand, pulling herself on to a piece of wood that was higher up as Nessie loomed closer.

'Come to me, child,' she croaked. Her voice was wet and rasping, like something that had drowned long ago. 'I'll make it quick.' She ran her fat, grey tongue over her terrible teeth, eyeing Tanya's arm. 'Juicy, juicy, tender ...'

'Never!' Tanya hissed. 'You'll have to catch me.'

Nessie threw back her head and laughed, spurting green water from her mouth. Her eyes flashed with excitement. 'My pleasure.' She lunged through the water again, dragging a shivering, choking Turpin with her, and grabbed on to a piece of wood near Tanya's foot that was hanging like a thread. She ripped it away easily and flung it into the water like it was no more than a matchstick, then seized another. 'If I have to,' she gurgled, 'I'll tear this bridge apart piece by piece until there's nothing left.'

Tanya glanced desperately to either side of the river, hoping to spot someone who could help her. There was no one, not even a dog walker in sight. She backed away further, stumbling over slippery, crooked wood. She loosened the leash, wrapping the leather strap round her wrist, and allowed the heavy chain end to fall free at her side. As the river hag's hand took hold of another piece of wood and began wrenching it apart, Tanya swung the leash as hard as she could.

It snapped down on the gnarled, green fingers with a satisfying *thwack*. With a violent scream, Nessie snatched back her hand like she had been stung, releasing Turpin from her grasp.

'Turpin, swim!' Tanya cried. 'Swim for the riverbank!'

Coughing and spluttering, Turpin obeyed. Her movements were slow and jerky. Nessie could have caught her in a heartbeat. The river hag cast a dismissive glance at Turpin escaping then turned back to Tanya with a cruel smile. 'Small bones,' she said. 'Hardly worth picking my teeth with. But you ...' She smacked her lips. 'There's enough meat on you to keep my belly full for weeks. A leg here ... an arm there. Ten scrumptious little toes to snack on ...'

'Do not listen!' Turpin squeaked, coughing through mouthfuls of water.

Tanya clutched at the broken handrail, weak with horror. She knew Turpin was right; Nessie was now trying to overpower her with words, to cripple her with fear. She drew the leash through the water, ready to strike again. The river hag sank lower into the water, then vanished beneath the murky-green surface. Tanya's head whipped this way and that, her eyes finding every bubble, every ripple. The water stilled and became eerily silent, the only sounds and movement from Turpin's clumsy doggy-paddle as she neared the river's edge.

Tentatively, Tanya made for the bank along the burnt bridge, still grasping the broken rail for support. She could not remember a time when her heart had ever hammered so hard; every thud seemed to rattle her ribcage. She stepped over a space where a board was missing, testing the next one for safety.

A green hand shot through the gap and grabbed her ankle. Tanya shrieked, trying to shake herself free, but a swift tug pulled her off balance. She slid across the slimy wood, crashing through what was left of the handrail. Turpin's scream and Oberon's frenzied barks were the last things she heard before she hit the water.

She crashed into the icy-cold depths, her feet thrashing out, searching for the bottom. It seemed endless. Her toes struck something in the deep, a hard structure: a piece of the bridge, maybe, or a bicycle? Her hands snagged on long strands of slimy weeds ... or hair. Bony fingers wrapped themselves round her wrists, tugging her down deeper. She lashed out, kicking anywhere, her feet finding soft flesh, freeing herself and buying valuable seconds. Her head broke the surface, submerged in green duckweed. She managed one grateful breath before Nessie surfaced with her, her hands clawing for Tanya's face.

Tanya rolled, the sky above flashing past her eyes. A dark shadow swooped overhead, skimming the water. Tanya took another choking breath, brushing duckweed out of her eyes. A whirlwind of leaves had blown up from nowhere and was whipping across the river. She saw Nessie's hands coming for her again, heard Turpin shouting from somewhere behind her . . . and above that a strange, rasping noise, a familiar cawing sound . . .

Through the thick storm of leaves she could just make out black wings beating the air, shielding her from the water hag. There was a flurry of feathers in front of Tanya's face, a scrape of scaly talons against green skin. Nessie's scream rang out. Something was attacking her. Tanya pushed back, kicking for the riverbank with all her remaining strength. She could only hope that it did not come for her after it had finished with Nessie.

Her lungs burned with each breath as she flung out her arms for the bank. On the sloping grass she could see Turpin standing on Oberon's back, hopping up and down as she shouted Tanya's encouragement. Her foot struck the bottom, finding the squelching mud for the second time. On hands and knees she dragged herself out, coughing and exhausted, landing at Oberon's paws. He covered her in wet licks, not seeming to mind the mud and specks of duckweed. Turpin jumped on to her shoulder, wringing out her dripping hair, which she then flapped like a rein.

'We must go,' she urged. 'No time to waste.'

Tanya nodded, too exhausted to speak. She hauled herself to her feet and looked back at the river. Swamped by the tornado of leaves, Nessie Needleteeth was screaming curses at the sky while a large, black bird clawed and gouged at her. Her face was covered in scratches and, where her eyes had once been, two red pits streamed. Her hands batted at the leaves and snatched for the bird, but her attempts were now blind and futile.

As Tanya watched in amazement, the bird soared higher with a victorious caw, halting its attack. The swirling leaves spiralled after it into the air, following the flow of the river until both were out of sight.

Turpin's eyes narrowed. 'More tricksy magic,' she said. 'But this time good.' She eyed Tanya with relief, but there was wariness, too. 'Most do not live to tell the tale after a tussle with Nessie Needleteeth. Something came to protect you.'

Tanya stared at the water, shivering. Nessie Needleteeth screamed into the air, empty fists pounding the water. She sank down into the green depths, gurgling through her jagged teeth, then vanished. The ripples grew fainter until the river looked almost peaceful, the only sign of what had happened being the fallen bridge.

'Come on,' said Turpin. 'We must leave this place.'

Tanya nodded again, turning from the river. As they began to walk, a cool breeze sent icy prickles over her wet skin and flapped her hair into her face. There was something caught in it: a tiny, green leaf.

Tanya pulled it from her hair. Like the black bird, the leaf was very familiar. It looked just like the ones that Gredin's clothes were made of. She clenched it in her cold fingers,

Turpin's words replaying in her head: *Something came to protect you.*

For the first time, she wondered if Ratty had been right about the fairies after all.

Was it really possible that they could be guardians who were looking out for her? That all their cruelty was really trying to keep her away from terrible dangers like the river girl, like Nessie – dangers that Tanya hadn't even been aware of?

She checked behind them once more, fearful that the strange, doughy creature could have climbed out of the river once more, but there was no sign of it.

'Turpin, what *was* that thing?' she asked. 'For a moment, you almost seemed to recognise it. And you said a strange word . . . Morghul?'

Turpin looked uncomfortable. 'It looked like something,' she admitted finally. 'A . . . creature Turpin once knew from long ago. But it cannot be.'

'And what about the man who took Ratty?' Tanya asked. 'Did you recognise him?'

Turpin hesitated, then nodded.

'Who was he?'

But Turpin's mouth clamped into a tight line and she refused to say a thing more.

12

Brussel Sprouts and Baths

B Y THE TIME THEY REACHED THE ROAD which led to the seafront, Tanya and Turpin had stopped dripping, but their clothes still clung damply to their skin. For Turpin, this wasn't much of a problem as there was only one person who could see her, but, as they wandered along the road and encountered people returning from the pier, Tanya received some very strange looks indeed. Not only was she wet and smeared in river mud, but the mud had a very unpleasant smell to it; rather like stewed cabbage and week-old fish soup.

Turpin was perched on Tanya's shoulder, and the smell was so close to her nose that it was making her eyes water. However, she hadn't the heart to tell Turpin to get off, for the cold little body was still trembling into her neck and her damaged wing was quivering.

'That's going to need looking at,' Tanya said. 'It's singed and torn in a few places. And please,' she continued, lowering her voice and trying to speak without moving her lips, 'stop chewing my hair.'

Turpin spat out the hair sulkily. 'Tastes like mud anyway.'

Finally, they reached the little path that led to Hawthorn Cottage. Tanya paused and took a breath before starting down it. She had still not figured out what she was going to say to her mother about the mess she was in. Not only that, but in the struggle with Nessie Needleteeth she had lost Oberon's leash in the river. And, as she neared the cottage, she saw that she had even less time to prepare, for her mother was reading on a chair beside the porch, soaking up the last of the afternoon sun.

She looked up from her book as they approached. Her mouth dropped open and she jumped to her feet, dropping the book on the floor.

'What on earth . . . what happened to you? Are you hurt?'

Tanya shook her head, with difficulty, as Turpin was still huddled into her neck. 'No, I'm not hurt. But there was an accident. A bridge behind the castle collapsed into the river. We . . . I fell in.'

'Come inside quickly, before you catch a chill.' Mrs Fairchild bundled her through the cottage door. 'You need a warm bath and a hot drink. That's right, Oberon, I did say "bath", and that includes you, too.'

Oberon skulked under the table and hid. A bath was his least favourite thing, even higher on his list of least favourite things than the vet.

'Stand there and don't touch anything,' Tanya's mother said. She filled the kettle and put it on the stove, then hurried into the bathroom. A moment later, Tanya heard the

146

rush of water as the taps were turned on. She returned with a blanket, which she wrapped round her daughter, almost smothering Turpin in the process. 'Whatever were you doing behind the castle anyway? It's lonely over on those fields, and that river is dangerous. Someone at the tea room told me people have drowned in there.'

'They have,' Tanya said in a small voice. She adjusted the blanket so Turpin could breathe.

'Any other girl would be content to stick to the pier,' her mother continued. 'They'd be happy to come somewhere like this, but not you. You have to wander off by yourself – or were you with that boy again ... what's his name? Ferret?'

'Ratty,' Tanya muttered.

'Yes, Ratty.' Her mother wrinkled her nose, as though the word tasted unpleasant. She sniffed suddenly. 'Speaking of which, you smell a bit ratty yourself. What is that revolting stench?'

'The river mud,' said Tanya, hanging her head. Turpin squeezed out of the blanket and hopped on to the table, helping herself to a grape from the fruit bowl.

'Well, I just hope we can get the smell out of that blanket.'

Turpin rolled her eyes and stuffed the grape into her mouth. 'Grumbly, grumbly grumble,' she said. 'Does it ever stop moaning?'

'Shush,' said Tanya.

'Don't tell me to shush, young lady,' her mother snapped.

'I've had a horrible morning with all sorts of problems and the last thing I needed was you coming back half drowned and being checky.'

'No . . . I mean, I wasn't,' Tanya said helplessly. She threw Turpin an exasperated look, but the fairy was too busy scoffing the grapes to notice. 'Wait, what do you mean? What problems?'

'Oh, everything,' her mother replied. Her expression was sour. 'First of all I couldn't find my headache pills. I looked everywhere and then they turned up in the bin – goodness knows how they got there. Then the toaster blew up. Turned out the wire was frayed – it looked like something had chewed through it.' She shuddered. 'I telephoned the owner and he insists there aren't any mice. Then the bottle of milk I opened only yesterday somehow managed to go off. It's very odd.'

'Very odd,' Tanya repeated, frowning.

'Sounds like fey mischief to me,' said Turpin, between slurps of grape.

'That's just what I was thinking,' Tanya murmured.

'Pardon?' her mother enquired.

'Nothing.' Tanya pulled the blanket tighter around herself. 'Is the bath ready yet?'

'I'll go and check.' Her mother scuttled off, returning a moment later. 'It's full. Go and jump in . . .' Her voice tailed off and she sniffed the air again, making a face.

'All right, I'm going,' Tanya said in a huff. 'You don't need to keep on sniffing me!'

'No,' said her mother. 'Not you. There's something else. Can you smell . . . burning?'

Tanya followed her mother into the kitchen, sniffing hard. 'All I can smell is river mud.'

'Whatever can it . . . oh, no!' her mother cried. She rushed to the stove, snatching the little kettle away from the flame. She lifted it up to reveal the bottom. It was blackened and buckled, and a shake revealed it was empty. 'I must have forgotten to put water into it!' she said in distress. 'It's ruined! I'll have to buy another one.'

Tanya bit her lip. Her mother hadn't forgotten at all – Tanya had watched her fill it at the sink with her very own eyes, and it hadn't been on the stove for long enough to boil dry. Something must have sneaked it off and emptied it, and she had a very good idea of what that something was. Her fists clenched under the blanket as a spiteful voice echoed up through the floorboards.

'Mother put the kettle on,
Daughter stinks, oh, what a pong!
Mother put the kettle on,
We'll all have tea!
Thingy took it off again,
And tipped the water down the drain,
Kettle's ruined – what a pain!
Now all GO AWAY!'

Turpin giggled, then hastily stopped as Tanya shot her a disapproving look.

She swallowed down her anger. *Thingy?* she thought. *Is*

149

that what the beastly creature calls itself? She reached out and touched her mother's arm. 'Don't worry, Mum,' she said. 'It could have happened to anyone. Sit down. I'll make the tea when I've had a bath.'

Mrs Fairchild smiled faintly and patted her daughter's hand. 'It's all right, love. I'll make it. Go and have your bath.' She turned away, reaching into a cupboard for a saucepan.

With her mother's back turned, Tanya beckoned to Turpin. 'This way,' she whispered. Turpin followed, looking puzzled. 'You need a bath, too,' Tanya explained, once they were safely in the bathroom.

Turpin shook her head. 'Turpin doesn't like baths.'

'I can tell,' Tanya muttered, remembering the fairy's grubby hands when she had first met her. 'But that's tough. I don't like Brussel sprouts, but I still have to eat them.'

Turpin stared at her in confusion. 'Brussel sprouts?'

'What I mean is, we all have to do things we don't like doing,' Tanya argued. 'Look, never mind. I'll run you a little bath in the sink—'

Turpin stuck out her bottom lip and folded her arms. 'No. Nope. No way.'

'Turpin,' Tanya said sternly. 'There are all sorts of germs in that river water. Your wing is cut and bleeding, and you need to wash the dirt off it. Otherwise, it could get infected and then it'll hurt even more. And you might . . .' She hesitated. 'You might even lose it.' She went to the sink and

150

turned the taps on. 'Come on. You'll feel much better afterwards.'

Turpin scowled, but Tanya sensed she was winning. She picked a bottle out of her mother's toiletry bag. 'You can even have some of this lovely bubble bath,' she coaxed. 'It smells like honey.' She poured a little into the running water. It foamed up nicely.

Reluctantly, Turpin clambered up beside the sink, staring at the frothing water.

'No peeking,' she growled finally. She turned her back on Tanya and peeled off her little waistcoat.

Tanya suppressed a smile. 'No peeking,' she agreed, shrugging off the muddy blanket. 'That goes for you, too.'

'Huh,' Turpin scoffed.

Fifteen minutes later, Tanya clambered out of the bathtub, freshly scrubbed and mud-free. She wrapped herself in a fluffy bathrobe and pulled the plug, watching as the dull water drained away. Now she was safely back at the cottage, the shock of the day's events was starting to catch up with her. Her thoughts turned to Ratty. Where was he? Was he safe? She imagined him being held, in a cell somewhere, while shadowy figures demanded information from him. A cold feeling crept into the pit of her stomach.

Splashes from the sink brought her back to the present. Turpin was humming away to herself, even gargling with the soapy water. Tanya also noticed that she had helped herself to her mother's toothbrush and was using it to scrub her back. She sighed, making a mental note to give it a good

151

rinse later, and to try and replace it without her mother noticing.

She picked up a small towel and offered it to the fairy. 'Time to get out now, Turpin.'

Turpin gave another splash, sending foam into the air. 'Don't want to. Turpin likes having a bath.'

'I thought you *didn't* like baths,' Tanya said, trying to hide her impatience. 'You didn't want to get in and now you don't want to get out?'

Turpin shrugged. 'Turpin never had a bath before. How was she to know she would like them?'

'Never? Then how do you clean yourself?'

'Like this.' Turpin licked her arm like a cat washing its paw.

'I see.' Tanya rolled her eyes. 'Come on, out. The water must be getting cold by now, and your toes will be all wrinkled up if you stay in there much longer.'

Turpin stopped splashing. 'Wrinkled up?'

Tanya nodded. 'Like raisins.'

The fairy leaped out of the sink, grabbing the towel out of Tanya's hands. 'You said Turpin would feel better after a bath!' she wailed. She bundled herself up in the towel and peered at her feet anxiously. 'You tricked her! You wanted her to have ugly feet! Turpin does *not* like baths.'

'I didn't trick you,' Tanya said crossly, looking at the fairy's feet. They were far less ugly now they were clean. The hairy toes even looked rather sweet. 'The wrinkles will go in a little while. Stop squawking.'

'Oh.' Turpin blinked. 'Then Turpin does like baths.'

'Good,' said Tanya, rubbing at her damp hair with a towel. 'You can have another one tomorrow.'

Turpin looked at the sink in delight. 'I can?'

'Well, yes. Most people have them every day.' Tanya emptied the sink. 'Now hold still while I comb your hair.'

The fairy obliged, sitting meekly as Tanya teased out the tangles. By the time she had finished, Turpin's hair was almost dry and now gleamed like honey. Tanya held up a small mirror. 'Look how pretty you are underneath all that dirt,' she said.

Turpin snatched the mirror and preened, pleased with herself. 'Very.'

'Ratty won't recognise you,' said Tanya. She put the comb down and filled the sink again, rinsing out Turpin's filthy clothes before wringing them out clean. 'It's a warm night. These should be almost dry by the morning—'

She stopped abruptly. Turpin was hunched over the mirror, her shoulders shaking. Her wing had escaped from the towel and was twitching pitifully, and a choked sob emerged from behind her hands.

'What's wrong?' Tanya asked in alarm. 'Did I hurt you?'

'No,' Turpin wept. Her voice was muffled. 'You said that Ratty wouldn't recognise Turpin . . .'

'Oh, I didn't mean it, silly,' said Tanya. She patted Turpin's shoulder awkwardly. 'Not really. I only meant that he'd be surprised, that's all—'

The fairy lowered her hands and glared at her through

red-rimmed eyes. 'Turpin knows what you meant,' she said. 'Ratty will always recognise his Turpin.' Her face crumpled again. 'But what if . . . what if Turpin never finds him?' She buried her face in the towel again and howled.

Tanya watched her in silence, feeling wretched. 'Don't cry, Turps,' she said eventually. 'You'll see Ratty again, I'm sure of it.'

'How can you be sure?' Turpin said, sniffling.

'Because I'm going to help you find him.' The words came out more forcefully than intended, sounding much more confident than she felt.

Turpin looked up at her, eyes lit with hope. 'But how? We don't know where he's been taken!'

'I know,' said Tanya. 'But don't forget, we've been left a clue.' She picked up the wet clothes and pulled the red envelope out of her pocket. It was now soggy and smudged in places, but still readable. 'We have Ratty's letter.' She skimmed through it again until she came across the part she was looking for. '*Go to the place we went to on our first night in this town – the place I could tell a story about. There you'll find instructions on what to do and where to go next.*'

She placed the letter on top of the dresser to dry out. 'Now I know that doesn't exactly take us straight to him, but if his father did manage to leave those instructions before he vanished then maybe we can find them. It might help us to figure out what's going on and where Ratty might have been taken.'

Turpin nodded slowly.

'But I'm going to need your help,' Tanya continued. 'I know this secret place is the castle dungeon, but it's going to be tricky to get in. Ratty mentioned something about a passage leading into it from an old well. Do you know it?'

'Yes.' Turpin nodded vigorously. 'Yes, Turpin knows it. She went there with Ratty on the first night in Spinney Wicket.'

'Good,' said Tanya. 'Is it easy to get in without being seen?'

Turpin's face fell. 'No. Is in a very busy place near the pier. Lots of people.'

'So you went when it was dark then?' Tanya guessed. 'When everything was closed?'

'At night, yes,' said Turpin. 'When no one was around.'

Tanya nodded. 'Then that means we'll have to do the same, you and I. We'll do it tonight. We'll sneak out and find the well.' A chill ran its icy fingers up her spine at the thought of the dangers that lay ahead. She pushed her fears to the back of her mind. Ratty was depending on her, and being afraid wasn't going to help him. 'Now dry your eyes,' she told Turpin. 'We need to fix your wing.'

13

The Grudge-keeper

TURPIN WIPED HER EYES AND BLEW HER nose into the towel with a great, trumpeting honk. Tanya politely looked the other way, poking through the toiletry bag. At the bottom she found a travel sewing kit and some antiseptic cream.

'I could try to sew the torn bits,' she said. 'But it's going to hurt.'

'No, silly!' Turpin squeaked. 'Needles are steel, which has iron in. It will burn.'

'Oh.' Tanya's face fell. 'Then it'll have to be the cream. It might sting a little at first.' She unscrewed the cap and dabbed some on.

Turpin's eyes watered, but she managed not to squirm too much. 'What we need,' she said through gritted teeth, 'is Spidertwine.'

'What's that?'

'Is a magical thread,' said Turpin. 'Made by the fairies. Almost invisible, but unbreakable to humans. Very, very strong and can stitch cuts together to heal perfectly.'

'And do you have any?' Tanya asked.

'No,' the fairy said gloomily.

'Then we'll just have to hope for the best,' said Tanya. She replaced the lid on the tube of cream and put it back. They left the bathroom and went into the bedroom, where Tanya spread Turpin's damp clothes on the windowsill to dry. Shortly after, Mrs Fairchild called Tanya to the kitchen.

'Wait here,' she told Turpin.

Turpin pouted. 'Why?'

'Because I can't talk to two people at once,' said Tanya. 'Not when one is a fairy. It's too confusing.' She tugged on some fresh clothes and hung her bathrobe on the chair. 'We'll need to find you something to wear, too.'

She went to the kitchen, where a pot of tea and a loaf of apple cake awaited her. Oberon slunk out from under the table, looking sorry for himself. While Tanya had been in the bath, her mother must have hosed him down outside. Though he was clean, there was still a strong whiff of wet dog about him. She smuggled him a small piece of cake, which her mother chose to ignore, then made her excuses and took a second cup of tea and a smaller slice of cake back to the bedroom.

'Don't eat too much of that,' her mother called. 'I thought it'd be nice for us to eat out this evening – you don't want to be full of cake.'

'I won't,' Tanya mumbled. She shut the door behind her, then gasped, almost dropping the tea. The china doll was back, sitting boldly on the bed. Only this time it had been

157

stripped down to its frilly undergarments. They had been white once, but were now faded and yellow with age.

'Ta-dah!' said Turpin. She stepped out from behind the doll, giving a proud twirl. The green velvet dress flared out, a perfect fit. 'Turpin found some nice new clothes to wear.'

'So I see.' Tanya put the tea and cake on the bedside table and stuffed the doll back under the bed. 'Somehow, I don't think Thingy is going to be very happy about it.' She stiffened as a light scuffle sounded from under the bed. Clearly, Thingy was listening. Even so, she couldn't help but smirk. There was something comical about seeing Turpin neat as a pin and dressed in dolls' clothes. 'Here,' she said. 'I brought you some tea and cake.'

Turpin hopped over to the bedside table and thrust her head into the cup, lapping thirstily before breaking off a fistful of cake. 'Turpin thinks,' she said, through a crumbly mouthful, 'that Thingy is not very happy about anything.'

'It seems happy enough to make trouble,' Tanya retorted before she could help herself. She waited for a muttered threat from under the floorboards, but heard only silence.

Turpin crammed more cake into her mouth. 'Many fey creatures like to make mischief. But trouble, nasty trouble, this is different. Not without a good reason.'

'But that's just it,' Tanya protested. 'There is no reason! It terrorised us from the moment we walked in – we didn't have time to upset it. It seems to dislike all humans.'

Turpin gave a thoughtful nod. 'Turpin once knew a fairy like this. Long time ago, before Ratty was born. This fairy –

158

Nipkin was its name – was the guardian of a little girl. Its name was Delia. Not a very nice little girl, Turpin always thought, but Nipkin was a good and loyal guardian.

'Of course, all little children must grow up one day. Nipkin knew this as well as anyone, but when Delia became a woman and got married, things changed. Her husband did not see fairies and neither did their children. Very soon, it seemed that Delia did not want to see fairies, either, and wanted to forget all about them. Even Nipkin.'

Turpin took another bite of cake, momentarily distracted as she caught sight of her reflection in the mirror. She smoothed her hair vainly. Tanya poked her.

'Go on.'

'It started very slowly. Delia would seem to not hear things that Nipkin said and, when she did, Nipkin did not always get an answer. Its answers became shorter and quieter and, whenever Delia's husband or children asked who it was talking to, Delia began to say, "Nothing."

'Months and years passed like this, and soon Nipkin forgot its name was Nipkin and instead started to think it was called "Nothing". But Nothing did not want to be a Nothing. It became resenting and ugly. It did things to upset Delia and her family so that Delia would pay attention to it, but of course this only made Delia unhappy and resentful, too. With every unkindness, Delia began to show unkindness, too: dressing in red so she could not be seen by Nothing, and keeping her doors and windows blocked with lines of salt so that Nothing could not follow her.

'So, Nothing took to living under the floorboards in the dark where it could roam the house freely, coming up only to cause trouble. And every bit of trouble, every grudge, began to weigh on Nothing's shoulders, even grudges that were not its own, but that came into the house with other people. It kept them all and grew uglier and uglier and meaner and meaner until one day the family went to live somewhere else, leaving Nothing alone with only its grudges for company.'

'Then what happened?' Tanya asked.

'The house became Nothing's house,' Turpin said. 'An unhappy, grudge-keeping house full of arguments and tears. Families came, families left. All with their own grudges. Nothing collected them all, feeding off them. Until one day, when a new family came, a family that was different to many of the others. In this family was a small boy who, like Delia, had the second sight, but whose guardian had died protecting him.

'The boy knew Nothing was there and he was often blamed for the tricksy things Nothing did. At first, he was angry. The boy often felt alone and sad because of his ability and Nothing was making things worse. But then the boy realised how sad Nothing must be, too, to do the things it did. Now, being a kind and special boy, he decided that the next time Nothing did something naughty, he would not hold a grudge. Instead, he told Nothing, "I forgive you."

'Nothing was confused. It had been such a long time since it had experienced forgiveness that it had forgotten all about it. But the same thing happened the next time. The boy forgave it and even left it a small gift of food. And, when the boy shared his forgiveness not only with Nothing, but with his family, too, for blaming him for the things Nothing did, a strange thing happened: Nothing began to let go of the grudges. And the more grudges it let go of, the more it remembered its old self, and soon it no longer wanted to cause misery. Nothing and the boy began to talk, and soon became friends. And, when all the grudges were gone, Nothing became Nipkin once more.'

Turpin paused, brushing cake crumbs from the front of her dress. 'Turpin thinks Thingy is like Nothing.'

'You mean a grudge-keeper?' Tanya asked. 'That it – I mean, Thingy – was a guardian once, with a proper name?'

The room was very quiet, like everything in it was holding its breath. Thingy was still there, listening, Tanya was sure of it. Could she find it within herself to forgive the trouble it had made? She was still angry, but the tale of Nothing had reduced it from a boil to a simmer. How long had Thingy been lurking in the cottage by itself, growing more and more bitter? She thought of all the people who must have passed through on their holidays, and all the different grudges building up one by one.

She knelt by the side of the bed, lifting the blankets, and peered underneath. The scratching sound had come from somewhere under here.

'Thingy?' she said to the dark, empty space. 'I'm sorry I don't know your real name, but I know you must have one.

161

Anyway, I wanted to tell you that even though what you did was horrible when you sewed all my clothes up, and sewed me into the bed, I'm going to try to forgive you.' She paused. 'If I said it now, it wouldn't be true and I don't think either of us would believe it, but in a few days I think I might be able to manage it.'

She reached for the cake on the bedside table and broke off a small piece. 'In the meantime, I'm going to leave this for you. As a sort of ... peace offering.' She leaned under the bed and placed the nugget of cake on one of the floorboards, then got up, allowing the bedclothes to fall back into place. The bed creaked as she sank down on it, then all was quiet. In the silence that followed, there came the faintest of wooden scrapes, like a floorboard being lifted very carefully. A moment passed, then it came again as the floorboard was lowered back into place.

Tanya climbed off the bed once more and peeked beneath it. Save for a few small crumbs, the space where she had left the piece of apple cake was empty.

14

In the Dungeons

'WAKE UP!'

Tanya forced her eyes open with difficulty. They were gritty through lack of sleep, for she had not long dropped off. The room was dark, with just a sliver of moonlight cutting through the curtains.

'What time is it?' she mumbled.

'After midnight,' Turpin replied. She tugged impatiently on Tanya's hair, so close that her breath hissed across her nose in a soft whisper. 'Turpin has been trying to wake you for minutes and many more minutes. Time to go, silly girl. Get up!'

Tanya sat up, pushing the warm bedclothes back with great reluctance. Though she had gone to bed early, it had taken her a long time to fall sleep, firstly because her thoughts were alive with the dungeon and what awaited them there, and secondly because Turpin had crawled on to Tanya's pillow and made some sort of nest in her hair. Tanya's attempts to extract herself had been unsuccessful; Turpin had simply burrowed closer and even let out a few little snores.

Tanya stood up, shivering, wriggling out of her pyjamas to change into the clothes she had placed on the chair before getting into bed. She dressed by moonlight, pulling on jeans and a thin sweater – making sure it was inside out first – then lost her balance, hopping clumsily as she tugged on a sock. She hit the chest of drawers with a thump, finally managing to steady herself, much to Turpin's disgust.

'Stupid oaf!' she hissed.

'Sorry,' Tanya mouthed helplessly. She held her breath, listening hard. From the room next door, she heard her mother mutter something, then an ominous creak of the bed. Was her mother getting up or had she simply stirred and rolled over? Tanya remained still, ready to spring back into bed, but all stayed silent. She sat down to put on her other sock, then tied her shoelaces. Then, using her pillows and an extra blanket, she padded out the bedclothes to make a convincing sleeping figure, should her mother wake up and check on her. As an afterthought, she collected the china doll from under the bed and tucked it under, too, spreading some of its dark hair across the pillow.

'Good,' Turpin whispered approvingly. 'Very tricksy.' She had jumped on to the windowsill and was inspecting her clothes which Tanya had laid out to dry. 'Still soggy,' she said, poking them. 'Turpin shall have to wear the pretty clothes a little longer.' She sounded disappointed at this, but as she gently smoothed down the dress it became clear why: Turpin liked the dress and didn't want to ruin it in the dungeon. 'Hurry,' she said to Tanya impatiently.

'I am,' Tanya whispered. She knelt by the bed, and from underneath it pulled out her rucksack, which she had hidden there earlier in the evening. Inside it were a couple of things she'd managed to sneak past her mother's watchful eyes: a pocket torch, a small bottle of water, plus Ratty's letter. She also had the money her mother had given her earlier to spend on the pier and, though she thought it unlikely that she would need it, she took it anyway. From the waste-paper bin, she retrieved the packets of salt and the iron nail that Ratty had given her, tucking them away in a pocket. Then she beckoned to Turpin with a whisper.

'Let's go.'

They crept through the cottage to the front door, with Oberon padding behind them. Tanya knelt down and kissed his nose. 'You have to stay here, boy, and not make a fuss,' she told him. 'There's no way you can climb down a well.'

From a hook above a kitchen shelf, she took a spare cottage key. The door gave a faint click as she unlocked it, and then she and Turpin slipped out into the night.

The sky was overcast, with the moon just a blurry glow behind thick cloud. The path away from the cottage was dark, but Tanya didn't dare to switch the torch on yet for fear of being seen. Instead, she kept her eyes fixed on Turpin, who scampered ahead as confidently as a fox. She seemed quite at home in her nocturnal surroundings, and none the worse for how little rest they'd had.

By the time they reached the main road, Tanya felt properly awake. It was well-lit here. The night air was fresh on

165

her cheeks and the scent of sea salt invigorating, but the emptiness and quietness of the street niggled at her like a gnat. During the day, the road was jam-packed with cars, tooting horns, voices and seagulls pecking at discarded chips. Now there was nothing; no cars and no noise apart from the faint sounds of waves breaking over the sea wall. She hoisted her rucksack higher on her shoulder and wrapped her arms round herself.

Soon they reached the pier entrance, gated and locked for the night. Turpin led her past it, kicking through chip papers littering the ground and occasionally helping herself to the odd chip here and there. Further on there was a small amusement funfair, with dodgems and waltzers and a big wheel. Tanya eyed the carousel, where the painted wooden horses were frozen mid-gallop. Everything about it looked wrong in the dark: the bright colours washed to grey, the teeth that were now grimaces instead of grins. She averted her eyes and hurried on.

'Almost there,' Turpin whispered, leading her across the road opposite the seafront into a narrow cobbled street. She recognised the street from the previous night; she and her mother had bought their fish and chips from a little shop on the corner. Turpin scuttled on. The end of the street broadened where it came to meet several others in a crossroads. Beyond the crossroads stood a weathered, grey stone well.

'This is the place,' Turpin hissed.

Tanya followed her. The well was covered with a little slated steeple, and on top of the steeple was a weathervane perched on a tall rod. Turpin scrambled up the sides as Tanya approached. She stopped next to Turpin, resting her hands on the stone rim. Its surface was rough and as cold as a tombstone. The top of the well was covered with a metal grate, presumably for safety and to prevent people from throwing litter in.

Tanya set her rucksack on the edge and took out the torch. She flicked it on and shone it into the well. The reflection of the torchlight bounced back from the water far below. She flashed the beam at the curved walls. They were green and furred with moss. A short way down, thin metal rungs were built into the brickwork.

'That's it,' Turpin whispered. 'That's the way down to the secret passage entrance.'

'But how do we get past the grate?' Tanya asked. 'It's fixed in place.' She gave it a tug, but it held firm.

'No,' said Turpin. 'Is only held in place weakly since Ratty and Don visited.' She edged round the rim, pointing. 'See here? There are two bolts, but both are rattly loose, loose enough for you to undo with your hands.'

Tanya reached through one of the metal squares. Her fingers brushed against damp, spongy moss. Then they found something cold, circular and hard. 'Got it,' she said, starting to unscrew it. 'You get the other one.'

'Can't,' Turpin said. 'Is made of some kind of iron and would burn Turpin. Same for the steps. Turpin will have to be carried.'

Tanya continued to work her fingers until the nut was

free. She pulled it through the grate and put it in her pocket, then began to work on the other one. Less than a minute later, it too was safely in her pocket.

'Now lift here,' Turpin instructed.

Tanya took the grate in a firm grasp and pulled. For a moment, she feared it was too heavy for her, but slowly it began to lift. There was a scrape of rusty hinges as it swung back and came to rest heavily on the opposite side of the well.

'Now down, down we go,' whispered Turpin, glancing about warily.

Tanya handed the torch to Turpin and unzipped her rucksack again. 'Hold the torch and get in the bag.' She waited as Turpin obediently climbed in, leaving only her head and shoulders and the hand holding the torch free, then hoisted the bag on to her shoulders before climbing on to the side of the well. It suddenly looked even deeper and darker than it had before.

She gripped the top rung and lowered her legs into the black space, reaching out with her toes until she found another rung lower down. Once she was sure it was secure, she eased herself down.

'Now you must close it behind us,' said Turpin.

Tanya gaped at the mouth of the well. 'Do I have to?'

'You has to,' Turpin replied. 'We cannot leave any clue that we came down here. Too risky.'

Tanya's heart sank. She knew Turpin was right, but the idea of shutting themselves in filled her with dread. Still gripping the rung with one hand, she reached for the grate with the other and heaved it over, ducking as it crashed into place.

'Careful!' Turpin hissed in her ear. The sound of the crash echoed in the depths of the well.

'I'm trying,' Tanya retorted. 'It was lucky I could lift it by myself at all.' She clung to the metal rung, staring up at the sealed grate above her head. She felt trapped, like she'd been thrown in a prison cell. Never, ever would she have believed herself to be capable of doing anything like this. Especially not at night, with only a fairy for company.

Something hard rapped her on the back of her head, and the light from the torch flickered crazily.

'Chop-chop,' said Turpin.

'Did you just hit me with that torch?' Tanya exploded.

'Shh,' Turpin whispered. 'Wasn't a hit anyway. Just a little nudge.'

'I'll nudge you with it in a minute,' Tanya hissed. 'See how you like it.'

'Grumbly, grumbly.' Turpin patted the back of her head. 'Just like its mother. Giddy up. We must hurry. Turpin does not like this place.'

'I'm not exactly thrilled to be here, either,' Tanya muttered. She lowered herself further down the well shaft, hand by hand, foot by foot, testing each rung before allowing her weight fully on to it. 'Keep that torch steady.'

The air grew colder and damper the further down they went. The rungs were slick with condensation, emitting a

169

metallic smell. They were so chilled that they numbed Tanya's fingers.

'How much further?' she asked.

'Little way yet,' Turpin said in a subdued voice.

'What's the matter?'

'The smell,' Turpin muttered.

'I know,' Tanya said, wrinkling her nose. 'It's so stale and rotten.'

'Not just that. Turpin can smell the iron in the ladder. It makes her feel sick.'

'I'll try to hurry.' Tanya shuddered as her fingernails caught the side of the well, dragging up green slime. She carried on, deeper and damper. 'What am I looking for? A door or something?'

'A very small door,' Turpin whispered. 'When you reach the end of the ladder.' She buried her nose in Tanya's hair and let out a little moan. 'Oh, it burns. Hurry.'

The torch hung from Turpin's fingers, its light flickering crazily, making Tanya feel a little dizzy, but she said nothing. She knew Turpin couldn't help it. Instead, she focused on finding each rung with her feet and tried to ignore the increasing numbness in her fingers. She had to keep going, for Ratty's sake.

Finally, her foot found only air. There were no more rungs. She glanced down, seeing the glint of water a short distance away. Holding the ladder with one hand, she reached out and patted the slimy walls, first on one side, then the other. Her fingers brushed wood. It was a small, square panel, set back a little way into the stone. There was a metal ring in the centre. She pulled it, bringing the panel open with a creak. It came to rest just above her knees, forming a small platform that was supported by a heavy chain either side. A gaping square of black in the well wall stared back at her.

She took the torch from a shivering Turpin and shone it into the dark space. It was narrow, but wide enough to allow a slim man through. Tanya would fit easily. She took off her rucksack and helped Turpin on to the platform, watching as the fairy crawled weakly into the small tunnel.

She pushed her rucksack through, then pulled herself on to the platform, gripping one of the chains for support. On hands and knees she crawled into the cramped space, feeling cold, hard stone against her palms.

'Don't go too far ahead, Turpin,' she said. 'The light from the torch is too dim.'

Turpin paused, waiting as Tanya pulled the hatch closed after them, sealing them in the tunnel. In the flickering torchlight, the fairy's small, pinched face was horribly pale. Tanya was beginning to feel queasy, too. Now that the fresh-air supply had been cut off, all that remained was the horrid, musty scent that reminded her of a damp cellar.

'Let's get moving,' she said, holding on to her rucksack and crawling along. 'Is it this narrow the whole way?' It would make for a long, unpleasant journey if that was the case. Thankfully, Turpin shook her head.

'No. Just narrow for a little longer. Then opens into a wider tunnel further up, until we reach the castle.'

'And how long will that take?' Tanya asked. The castle was visible from the seafront and even looked quite near. Yet appearances, she knew, could be deceptive.

'Not so long,' said Turpin. 'We shall be back before the dawn.'

'I should hope so,' Tanya muttered. She was uncomfortable now, not just from being hunched over, but from the very feeling of the place: cold, trapped and claustrophobic. The thought that they were venturing into a dungeon wasn't helping matters.

She crawled onwards, the worn stone digging into her knees and hands. She felt the air change, growing colder and a little fresher.

'Here,' said Turpin. 'You can stand up now.'

Tanya lifted her head and saw that the tunnel had opened out to become wider and taller. She got to her feet, blowing into her cold hands for warmth.

'Give me the torch,' she whispered.

Turpin handed it over. Tanya shone it at their surroundings. The tunnel was still fairly low; a tall adult might have to stoop. The walls were constructed of the same ancient cobbled stone, with iron sconces set in every so often. The waxy remains of long burnt-out candles clung to the walls below them. Tanya wished they were still alight, for the torchlight didn't stretch very far ahead. The ground was uneven beneath her feet, with some stones jutting and others missing.

'Let's try to be quick,' said Tanya, upping her pace. She wrapped her arms round herself. The castle and the escape tunnel were hundreds of years old. She could not help but imagine who might have used the tunnel in the past; inhabitants of the castle under attack? Or perhaps even prisoners that had discovered the secret exit and used it to escape. She held those thoughts in mind, trying not to allow her fears to manifest themselves, but every so often the reality of what she was doing crept in and sent a cold shiver of fear rippling over her skin.

It's for Ratty, she told herself. *I'm doing this for Ratty.* And though she tried not to think it a horrid little thought came into her mind anyway.

'What do we do if there's nothing there?' she blurted out.

Turpin stopped walking. 'Nothing there?'

'In the dungeon. What if Ratty's pa never made it this far and there's no clue about what to do next?' Her voice rose. 'How will we find Ratty?'

The fairy wrung her hands. 'Turpin does not know what we will do. Only that we must try.'

They began walking again in silence, each keeping to their own thoughts. On they walked, and on, with only the flickering torchlight for company. Now and then there were small changes in the air, the stale sluggishness sometimes giving way to chilly draughts, and in one part the tunnel even grew wet and green. Thick slime coated the walls like ruined fabric.

173

'Careful,' said Tanya. 'It's slippery here. We must be passing near water of some kind.'

'Yes.' Turpin nodded, lifting the hem of her dress away from the slick ground. 'Turpin remembers this from last time. We are close now.' She scampered ahead.

Once again, the ground became drier and the air cooler. It was fresher here, too; a gust of cool air snaked round Tanya's ankles as she hurried after Turpin. The fairy's footsteps halted suddenly.

'What is it?' Tanya asked, lifting the torch. A huge, rusted gate came into view.

'The dungeons,' Turpin whispered, covering her nose. 'More iron. Oh, the smell . . .'

Tanya drew closer. The gate was unlocked and stood ajar. She reached out and pulled it open wider. Turpin rushed through first and stood on the other side, panting. Tanya slipped in after her. They now stood in another underground tunnel. This one ran the opposite way to the one they had just left, and was both wider and higher.

Turpin led her to the left. 'This is the way. Other way leads up into the castle, but is all blocked off.'

Tanya followed her along the tunnel. It was plain to see why the place was off-limits to the public. Underfoot it was extremely uneven, and the jolt Tanya had taken to her ankle in the meadow began to throb as she stepped in the dips and crevices. A short way along they came upon a row of cells, each one a tiny, empty space. Tanya shone the torch into each one, seeing nothing but hard stone floor and dark corners. In one a squeaking rat fled the torchlight and hid behind an old wooden bucket.

The tunnel ended, bleeding into another containing more cells. Again, Tanya checked each one, hoping to spot another red envelope or some kind of clue that someone had been down here. There was nothing.

They turned into a third tunnel. This was wider still, with a large area full of strange instruments, with more cells set further back. Tanya approached one of the devices. It was ancient and wooden, with leather straps attached in four places. It looked strangely familiar, like something she had seen in a book once.

'What is this?' she wondered aloud.

'Wicked things,' said Turpin, cringing away from the instrument. 'Made by humans to hurt each other.'

'A torture chamber,' Tanya realised. She flashed the torch around, picking out more wood, more restraining straps and spiteful-looking spikes. She lowered the torch, not wanting to see any more, and moved away to the cells. They were as dark and gloomy as the others, and each one empty, until . . .

Tanya stiffened. 'What's that?'

There was something in the corner of the third cell, a dark shape. She moved closer. Could this be the mysterious clue left for Ratty?

Turpin crept into the cell and approached the object. She reached out and gave it an experimental prod.

A terrible sound sent them both stumbling back, shrieking. Turpin grabbed Tanya's leg in panic, making her jump again and drop the torch. It spun in circles, flickering madly. The noise came again, a wretched groan that gave way to a bout of coughing.

And then a voice cut through the silence, a dry, croaking rasp.

'Who's there?'

15

The Prisoner

TANYA BACKED INTO THE WALL OPPOSITE
the cell, her breath caught in her throat like a chunk
of poisoned apple. Turpin released her leg and clambered up her body, burrowing into Tanya's neck. The torch
continued to spin in circles, highlighting the cell one
moment and the wall the next. Finally, it slowed and went
into a sluggish roll, stopping just short of the cell's entrance.
Cautiously, Tanya bent down and reached out for it.

Her hand shook as she shone it into the cell once again.
Except for the rumpled sacking on the floor that Turpin had
poked, the cell was empty. There was nowhere for a person
to hide, and yet Tanya was sure the voice had come from
here.

A dry, hacking coughing began, startling them both once
more. Tanya froze, the torch beam resting on the sacking.
Something small was twitching beneath it with jerky movements. It had to be another rat. She shuddered, shining the
torch this way and that, but there was no one else in sight.
Yet, when the coughing subsided, the voice came again.

'Who's there, I say?'

Tanya gulped. Had they accidentally disturbed a criminal or a vagrant hiding out here? The voice sounded particularly hoarse, as though its owner had swallowed a boot full of broken glass.

'I— I'm sorry,' she began. 'We didn't mean to disturb you, whoever you are. We were just leaving.'

'No!' The word came out in a rasp. 'Don't go – please! I need help.'

'Where are you?' she asked uncertainly. The voice sounded so close, and yet . . .

'Over here,' it croaked.

'Careful,' Turpin whispered. 'Something tricksy is afoot here. Turpin can sniff it in the air.'

'Where?' Tanya repeated, poised to run. This was feeling increasingly suspicious, like they were about to walk into a trap.

'Here.' The sacking jiggled again.

Tanya's eyes narrowed. 'You're under that scrap of cloth?'

'Yes.' The voice was weak now. 'I have a . . . a problem. It's a little embarrassing.'

'Maybe it's a fey,' Turpin said in Tanya's ear. 'Stay here. Turpin will investigate.' She clambered off Tanya's shoulder and slid down her body, approaching the cell like a cat preying on an unsuspecting mouse. She crept inside, stealthy and silent. Tanya aimed the torch at the sacking. There was a small bump in the centre of it. With her face screwed up in determination, Turpin reached over and poked it – hard.

'Ouch!' the voice complained. 'I wish you'd stop doing that!'

Turpin squeaked and grabbed the cloth, throwing it clear to reveal the owner of the mysterious voice.

There, squatting on the cell floor, was a fat, warty toad. It blinked furiously and coughed, the same horrible hacking cough they had heard before.

'Will you please get that light out of my face?' it complained.

Tanya's mouth dropped open. 'You're a ... you're a toad!'

'Well spotted,' the toad answered sarcastically. 'And, by the way, you're still shining—'

'But you're a talking toad,' Tanya said in confusion.

'And you're continuing to blind me with that torch,' it snapped, weakly lifting its clammy toad fingers to shield its eyes, then elapsing into another fit of coughing.

'Sorry.' Tanya lowered the torch and aimed the beam away from the toad, waiting for the coughing to stop. She crept closer to the cell, still wary. Turpin stood a little way back, also watchful. Once the coughing had subsided once more, the toad blinked repeatedly as its eyes adjusted. There was something unusual about them, Tanya thought. They were such a beautiful, familiar blue. And then ...

'Turpin?' the toad croaked. It craned its warty head closer to the fairy. 'Is that—? It is you!'

Turpin peered at the toad, seemingly as confused as Tanya was. Then a frown spread across her brow, and her eyes went

179

huge and wide. 'Oh, yikes,' she said. 'Tricksy, tricksy, *tricksy* magic ...'

'What's going on?' Tanya demanded. 'Do you know this toad, Turpin? Because it seems to know you.'

Turpin nodded dumbly, clearly too stunned to speak. Tanya turned to the toad, waiting for some kind of explanation. Already she had a premonition of what she was about to hear.

'Pleased to meet you,' the toad said. 'My name is Don. And I'm not actually a toad, I'm—'

'Ratty's father,' Tanya interrupted. She stared at it in shock. No wonder those blue eyes were familiar – she had seen them in the photograph in the camper van, and they were so very like Ratty's. For a moment, she had hoped that the search for her friend was over.

'Oh, dear, oh, dear, oh, dear,' Turpin muttered, finding her voice at last. 'This is bad. This is very, very bad ...'

'It could be worse,' said Don. 'I'm alive at least.' He coughed again. 'Just about. Say ... you don't have any water, do you? I'm parched.'

'Yes.' Tanya hurried into the cell and dropped to her knees, rummaging through her rucksack for the water bottle. She unscrewed the cap and tipped a little water into it, then set it before the toad.

'I'm afraid that won't work,' Don said. 'Toads don't drink the way humans do. They absorb water through their skin.' He crawled forward. 'You'll have to pour it over me.'

'Oh,' said Tanya. 'All right.' She tilted the bottle, trickling the water over the mottled green skin.

'Ahh,' the toad breathed, pressing itself into a little dip in the ground where the water was collecting. 'Oooh. Keep going.'

'Better?' Tanya asked, when the bottle was half empty.

'Much,' Don agreed, sounding far less croaky now. 'Two days I've been down here, without food or water.'

'What happened to you?' Turpin squeaked.

'I'll get to that,' Don answered. His expression was suddenly grave, even for a toad. 'After you tell me where my son is and,' he nodded at Tanya, 'who this young lady might be.'

'Its name is Tanya,' said Turpin, still staring at the toad, aghast. 'It has the second sight. Ratty made friends with it on the pier.'

At the word 'friends', the toad's mouth pressed into a disapproving line. 'Go on.'

'Ratty tried to take its memory of him, but it didn't completely work,' Turpin said, getting flustered. 'And then things happened very quickly. There was tricksy magic to lure Ratty away, and then he was snatched by—'

'I can guess who,' Don cut in. 'Solomon. But how? Henry should have been protected!'

Turpin nodded fervently. 'There was something else, using a glamour. Turpin thinks it was not fey.'

'Then what kind of something?'

'Morghul,' Turpin said hoarsely.

There was a silence as they exchanged a long look that Tanya could not interpret. Again, she wondered about the unfamiliar word, but sensed she might learn more from listening rather than asking questions just yet.

'That's not possible,' Don whispered. 'We both know that.'

'They tried to catch Turpin and Tanya, too, but we escaped.'

'Only thanks to Nessie Needleteeth,' said Tanya. 'And we nearly got eaten in the process.'

Don studied Tanya, his blue eyes shrewd in his toad-face. 'Well, Turpin clearly trusts you,' he said at last. 'And Henry must have, too, or you wouldn't be here.'

Tanya nodded. 'I have Ratty's letter,' she said. 'That's how I knew to come here, after you went missing. I was hoping to find whatever clue you meant to leave, and then perhaps bring Turpin to you, and . . .' She faltered.

'And then I would know what to do?' Don said. 'And take over from there?'

She nodded. 'Yes.'

Don sighed. 'That's understandable. You should never have become mixed up in all this – it's why I've always discouraged Henry from making friends. It was simply too dangerous.'

'But I *am* mixed up in this,' Tanya said. 'Ratty is gone, and you're a toad, and Turpin is a fairy who can't do magic. Which means . . .'

'Which means that we need you,' Don finished. 'Will you help us?'

'I'll try,' said Tanya doubtfully. 'But what can I do? I'm ... I'm just a girl. There's nothing special about me, except maybe for the seeing fairies part.'

'You're not just a girl with the second sight,' Don said. 'You're a girl who escaped kidnap and clambered down a well into a dungeon to help someone. That makes you extremely brave, in my book.'

'I'm not brave,' Tanya said in a small voice. 'I've been scared the whole time.'

'That's exactly why you *are* brave,' Don insisted. 'To do something you're afraid of, especially for the sake of somebody else, is the very definition of courage.' He lifted a webbed foot up and studied it glumly. 'And besides, the real question is what can *I* do, in my present form?'

Tanya fell silent, pondering his words. 'You still haven't told us how you ended up as a ... well, like that.'

Don scowled. For obvious reasons, Tanya had never seen a toad scowl before. It was a spectacularly ugly thing to behold.

'I got the feeling we were being watched,' he said. 'On the evening before I left, I saw someone on the bridge, just standing and staring at the thicket of trees where the van was hidden. I told myself it was probably nothing, but the next morning, before Henry was awake, I left the letter for him to find and went out. It wasn't long before my suspicions were confirmed. I was being followed. I didn't want to lead anyone to Henry, so instead I took a bus to the next town and collected several items that I'd hidden in various places.

'By late afternoon I thought I'd shaken them off. I came back and stayed on the pier until it closed, then spent the rest of the evening in a tavern. While I was there, I wrote more instructions for Henry, then, once it was dark and the streets were empty, I came here.' He closed his blue eyes for a moment before continuing. 'I'd only been down here for a few minutes when I realised I wasn't alone. I tried to hide and sneak back out through the well, but I was caught.' He shook his head. 'By Solomon and an accomplice. Whoever – whatever – it was it was strong. I never saw the face, for it wore a mask. But it wasn't fey because it stripped me of my protection.

'I just had time to swallow the note I'd written for Henry so they couldn't get their hands on it before it overpowered me. Then Solomon threatened me, tried to get me to take him to Henry. When I refused, he turned me into this.' He looked down at himself in disgust. 'There was no way I could climb out through the well. I've been trapped ever since.'

'The items you'd collected,' said Tanya. 'Were any of them linked to the memory that Ratty stole?'

'No.' For the first time, Don looked relieved. 'They were worthless. A mere trick to encourage anyone following me to reveal themselves.'

'But who is Solomon, and why did he come after *you* when it was Ratty that stole the memory?' said Tanya.

'Because he suspects I'm the one who knows where the object is hidden,' said Don. 'And he's right. Now he has Henry, he'll be back to bargain with me.'

'Except you won't be here,' said Tanya. 'Not if I get you out.'

'But then that means I'll stay as a toad,' said Don, looking suddenly greener than even a toad should look. 'I can't stay like this forever, I just can't!'

'What about if I took you across the river?' Tanya asked. 'Would crossing running water break the spell?'

Don looked to Turpin, who wrinkled her nose.

'Turpin does not think so.' She leaned forward and gave the toad a good sniff. 'Is a very strong magic, stronger than a glamour. Meant to last, until it is undone.'

'There may be another way,' said Don, but he looked somewhat troubled.

'We'll figure something out,' said Tanya. 'But for now we should get out of here. This place has a horrible feel to it and, like Don says, we could be expecting company at any moment.' She unzipped a side pocket of her rucksack and motioned to Don. 'Hop in.'

The toad's blue eyes narrowed. 'Is that meant to be funny?'

'Oh,' said Tanya, realising what she'd said. Clearly, Don was a little sensitive about his new appearance. She couldn't blame him. 'No. Sorry.'

With as much dignity as he could summon, Don shuffled to the pocket and climbed in clumsily. Tanya zipped it half closed again, allowing a space for him to see out. Then she lifted the bag on to her shoulder and nodded to Turpin. 'Let's go.'

They left the cell, navigating the dank tunnels once more. Tanya took the lead, with Turpin a couple of steps behind, holding her nose and muttering to herself about the smell every time they passed one of the iron wall sconces.

'Young lady?' Don croaked from the depths of the rucksack.

'Its name is Tanya,' Turpin reminded him.

'Right. Beg your pardon – Tanya. Where is it we're going? I forgot to ask.'

'We'll have to go back to my holiday cottage,' Tanya said. 'It's the safest place I can think of. Besides, if I'm not there when my mother wakes up, I'll be in trouble. Big trouble.' Already thoughts of her mother were giving her a headache. She chewed her lip. 'You haven't said exactly what we need to do next to help Ratty.'

'That's because I haven't figured it out yet,' said Don. 'Why?'

'Because my mother could be a problem,' said Tanya. 'Or rather, doing things without her noticing could be a problem.'

'No problem,' Turpin piped up.

Tanya looked at her. 'What do you mean?'

The fairy grinned slyly. 'Turpin knows of ways to make problems go away. Sneaky ways up her sleeves. Oh, yes.'

'But you won't hurt her,' Tanya said in alarm. 'You must promise me ...'

'Of course not hurt!' Turpin was indignant. 'Just tricksy and clever ways.'

'Like what?'

'You shall see,' was all Turpin would say.

They continued through the darkened tunnel in silence, the only sounds their footsteps and an occasional croak from the rucksack every now and then when Tanya stumbled on some uneven part of the passage. Underground draughts snaked round her ankles, making her shiver. This place, never touched by the sunlight, was so very cold. Bone-chillingly cold. It would take her ages to warm up again.

Finally, the air became stale and sluggish as the passageway narrowed. Tanya took off the rucksack and bent down, dragging it along beside her as she began to crawl. 'We're nearly at the well,' she told Don. 'Only a little way further now.'

When the torch beam picked out the outline of the trapdoor in the wall, she paused, waiting for Turpin. Wordlessly, the fairy clambered into the rucksack once more, and Tanya pushed the trapdoor open and crawled out on to it, gulping in the cool night air. Once she was safely on the iron ladder with the rucksack over her shoulder, she secured the trapdoor and began to climb.

Going up was somehow easier than going down, though perhaps, Tanya thought to herself, it had more to do with the relief she felt at escaping the dungeon. Soon she reached the top of the well, handing the torch to Turpin while she grappled with the iron grate. This part, pushing and not pulling and with only one hand to do so, was definitely not easier, especially not with Turpin's groans about the smell ringing in her ears. Yet somehow she mustered the strength to heave the grate back on itself. It landed with a resounding clang against the stone rim.

Tentatively, she poked her head out of the well entrance. The only sign of life was a startled fox that had been scavenging in a bin. It took off as she clambered out, setting the rucksack aside as she lowered the grate back in place as quietly as she could. Her fingers touched something cold and slimy on the rim of the well.

'Yuck,' she said, wiping her hand on her jeans. 'Slug.'

No sooner had she uttered the word when something thin and sticky lashed out past her arm, whipping the slug away. There was a wet chomp followed by a croaky belch, and then Don's voice trembled from the pocket of the rucksack.

'Oh, please tell me I didn't just . . .'

Tanya stared at the damp spot where the slug had been. 'I'm afraid you did,' she said. 'You just ate a slug.'

Turpin emerged from the rucksack, shaking her head. 'Yikes.'

Don stared at them both, his wide eyes full of disgust. 'Oh, this is wretched. I didn't mean to, I really didn't. But when you said "slug" I couldn't help it.' He gave a little moan. 'What's worse is that it was actually . . . delicious.'

Tanya's stomach lurched. 'I'll let you know if I see any more.'

'No,' Don begged. 'Please . . . don't. That squelchy mouthful is going to haunt me for the rest of my days.'

'Well, it's not really your fault,' said Tanya. 'Until you're turned back to your real self, it's just your nature.' She turned off the torch and put it away. 'And you have to eat something.'

'Wait until Ratty hears about this,' Turpin said, her eyes glinting. She made a sloppy chomping noise. 'Squish, squish, swallow!'

'He won't,' Don said sharply. 'Because you're not going to tell him.'

Turpin grinned and hopped off the side of the well.

They set off through the deserted town. The clouds had cleared a little now, allowing sprays of stars to pepper the sky. When they eventually reached the little path that led to the cottage, Tanya paused, rooting in her bag for the key. Her fingers closed round it, yet she stayed still on the path, her mind awash with questions, one in particular.

'What are we waiting for?' Turpin murmured, looking towards the cottage longingly. She yawned. 'Is sleepy time.'

Tanya hesitated. 'This memory,' she said. 'The memory Ratty took. He said he doesn't remember what it is.' She studied Don carefully. 'But, if you know where the object attached to the memory is, then you must know about the memory itself. What was it? And who is Solomon?'

Don fidgeted. 'Somebody dangerous,' he said, in a hushed voice. 'A fey man. A worker of dark magic.'

A chill ran over the back of Tanya's neck. Suddenly, the shadows surrounding the cottage had all grown a little bit darker. 'And the memory?'

'A spell,' Don said. 'One that, if remembered, could wreak havoc. That's why it must remain hidden.'

'What ... what kind of spell?'

But Don shook his head. 'I think it's best I say nothing more, for now. The fewer people who know the truth, the less dangerous things will be.' He glanced in Turpin's direction, then looked away just as quickly. Tanya pretended not to notice. Instead, she approached the cottage and inserted the key into the door as quietly as she could, but all the while she was aware of a small movement on the edge of her vision. Turpin's wing was trembling very slightly.

As they entered the cottage and crept to the bedroom, Tanya stole a look at the fairy's face. She was wide-eyed now, all traces of sleepiness gone. Her expression was one that was haunted.

Turpin knows, too, Tanya realised. *She knows everything Don knows about the stolen memory. And, whatever it is, she's afraid.*

16
The Rift

TANYA WOKE FROM A TROUBLED DREAM in which she was being smothered to find that Turpin's foot was up her nose. After removing it, she yawned, stretched and sat up. Turpin stirred a little before snuggling back down on the pillow. Cautiously, Tanya looked around the room. There was no sign that Thingy had been up to any mischief. She got out of bed and pulled her dressing gown on over her pyjamas.

'Good morning,' a voice croaked.

She knelt down and peered beneath the bed. Next to a bowl of water, Don squatted on a handful of leaves she had brought in from outside.

'Morning,' she replied. 'Did you sleep well?'

'No.' The blue eyes looked a little pink around the edges. 'I'm hungry. And you have a horrible snore.'

Tanya stood up again, insulted. 'That's what happens when you sleep with a fairy's foot up your nose.' She glanced at the clock. It was still early; she hadn't yet heard her mother get up. 'Stay here. I'll go and find something for you to eat.'

She left the bedroom and went into the dining area, padding across the floor. With the curtains drawn, the room was still dark. Oberon got up from under the table, wagging his tail in greeting. Evidently, he had forgiven her for leaving him behind on her night-time walk. She began to make a fuss of him, then paused mid-stroke. There was something stuck to her bare foot. Something grainy. She frowned, slowly moving away from the table and into the kitchen. With each footstep came a light crunch. She reached out and switched the light on.

The kitchen floor was covered with cornflakes. For the briefest of moments, Tanya wondered if perhaps Oberon had pulled the box off the counter and managed to tip them out, but she quickly dismissed this idea. The cornflakes were so neatly arranged and evenly placed that this could be no accident. They covered the entire kitchen floor, except for several carefully spaced gaps. And not just any gaps; these were letters, again displaying a misspelled message: GETT OWT.

Dismayed, she crunched through the cereal to the cupboard under the sink in search of a dustpan. That was when she noticed a second message stamped into spilled sugar on the counter. This one said HOOMANS STINK.

'I thought we'd discussed this, Thingy,' Tanya said in a low voice. She found the dustpan and brush, first sweeping up the sugar, then setting to work on the floor. 'I'm trying to be patient, I really am, but you're such a troublemaker.'

There was no reply. Even so, Tanya got the feeling she

was being watched and listened to. She swept everything into the bin, trying to focus on remembering Turpin's tale of Nothing rather than allowing herself to get angry, but it was difficult. Supposing Tanya hadn't woken early and her mother had found all this? She sighed, opening the fridge. There was a punnet of strawberries on the top shelf. She helped herself to a handful, wrapping a few in kitchen paper and putting them into the pocket of her dressing gown for Turpin. The remaining ones she left on the kitchen counter.

'These are for you, Thingy,' she said. 'I hope they put you in a better mood.'

Unfortunately, there was nothing in the kitchen that was suitable for Don. Tanya remembered the slug from the night before and, grimacing, opened the front door of the cottage. She did not have to go much further than the porch to find a couple of woodlice and a slimy, pink worm. 'Sorry,' she told them, sweeping all three into another sheet of kitchen paper and returning inside. As she closed the door, her mother's voice made her jump.

'What were you doing out there?'

Tanya stuffed the twist of paper into her other pocket. 'Just . . . seeing how warm it is outside,' she said lamely. 'So I can decide what to wear today.'

Her mother filled the saucepan with water and put it on the stove to boil. 'I take it those are yours?' she asked, pointing to the kitchen counter.

Tanya glanced at the spot where she had left the

strawberries for Thingy. Several chewed green stalks displaying teeth marks were all that remained.

'Oh . . . yes,' she muttered, picking them up and dumping them in the bin. 'Sorry.'

Her mother put two teabags in the pot, then peered into the sugar bowl. 'Where's all the sugar?' she exclaimed. 'That was full last night!'

Tanya cringed. There was no other option but to take the blame. 'I spilled it. The cornflakes, too. I'm sorry,' she repeated.

Mrs Fairchild shook her head. 'What's got into you?' she said grumpily. 'Butterfingers.'

'Butterfingers!' a voice hissed from under the floor.

Tanya clenched her teeth. Clearly, it would take more than cake and a few strawberries to change Thingy's grudge-keeping ways. She slouched back to the bedroom. Turpin was awake now, sitting expectantly on the pillow, and had changed into her ordinary clothes which were now dry. Tanya removed the kitchen paper from her pocket and presented it to her, then knelt to push the other sheet beneath the bed for Don.

Turpin gave a little shriek and scrambled back. 'Yikes!' She glared at Tanya. 'Turpin does not eat disgusting squelchings!'

'Whoops.' Tanya switched the papers over. 'Wrong one.' She slid the woodlice and worm under the bed. The tip of the toad's tongue flickered at the edge of his mouth in anticipation.

'Stop looking at me!' he said haughtily. 'I don't need an audience.'

'Right, sorry.' She retreated and sat down on the bed, trying not to listen to the inevitable gulps and soggy chewing noises coming from under the bed. When they finally stopped, Don waddled out, looking less hungry but thoroughly shamefaced.

'I've been thinking all night,' he announced. 'And I believe I have a plan.'

'A plan to save Ratty?' Turpin asked. Her fingers and chin were sticky with strawberry juice, some of which had dripped on to Tanya's pillow. 'Turpin likes plans.'

'Yes,' said Don. 'A plan to save Henry. And possibly return me to my human state.' He looked at Tanya. 'But it's going to be dangerous. And, as you're the largest and most capable of the three of us, much of that danger will be directed towards you.'

Tanya swallowed, remembering her guardians saving her from Nessie Needleteeth. Should she really walk straight back into danger? There wasn't much choice if Ratty was to be saved. 'What do we have to do?'

Don took a deep breath. 'The only thing we have to trade in return for Henry is the object linked to the missing memory.'

Tanya frowned. 'But last night you said the spell is so dangerous that the memory can never be returned.'

'Yes,' Don admitted. 'I did. But I've been over and over it in my head all night, and I can't see any other way to get

Henry back. The fact is, without it, he'll never be released. His power makes him too special. Too valuable. Especially to a worker of magic. Even without the memory, his ability could be used. It's why I've worked so hard to protect him all his life from being discovered.'

'I have another idea,' said Tanya. 'If you know where the object is hidden, then that makes you just as valuable as Ratty is. What if you bargained with him – your knowledge in exchange for Ratty?'

'I already tried that,' said Don. 'Down in the dungeon. I begged Solomon to release him. Said if he did I'd take him to the object myself. He refused. And that's how I knew that he has no intention of letting Henry go.'

'So Solomon means to keep him and use his power even after they have the memory,' Tanya said in dismay.

'I believe so.' Don hung his head. 'So you see, if I had simply told them the location of the object, I would no longer have been of any use to them. That's why the only solution I can see is to take them the object in person.' His blue eyes looked watery all of a sudden. 'It's all I can think of to get close enough to Henry to try and get him back.'

'So we need to collect the object,' Tanya said. 'Is it far? And can you be sure it's still there?'

'Oh, it's still there all right. And no, it's not far at all.' Don gave a smug smile. 'You see, Henry was too young to remember, but this isn't the first time we've been to this town. We came here once before, soon after the memory was taken.'

'You mean . . .?'

'Yes,' said Don. 'The object is hidden right here, in Spinney Wicket. It's been so long, I had to make sure it was still here. Still hidden.'

Tanya gaped. 'Wasn't it a risk, coming back? What if someone had seen you? Followed you?'

'Even if they had, they would never have known what they were looking at,' said Don. 'This hiding place was a particular stroke of brilliance on my part, even if I do say so myself.'

'So where—?' Tanya began.

Don cut her off. 'All in good time, my dear. First things first. We have to break this wretched spell. And to do that we need to pay a little visit.' His expression was devoid of smugness now. In fact, Tanya thought he looked rather worried.

'Who are we visiting?' she asked.

'Two people,' said Don, glancing sideways at Turpin. 'Sisters actually. They happen to be fey and rather powerful.'

'Oh, yikes,' Turpin breathed. 'Not that loony pair!'

'Loony?' Tanya echoed.

'They are somewhat, um . . . eccentric,' Don said. 'As you'll come to see.'

'And where exactly do we need to get to?' Tanya asked. 'Only my mother—'

'Not far,' said Don. 'Well, as far as travelling goes anyway.'

'You're talking in riddles,' said Tanya. 'Is it a long way or not?'

'It's difficult to explain,' said Don. 'But in our world, no, it's not far at all. We simply need to go to the seafront.'

'Glad we cleared that up,' Tanya muttered, as confused as ever.

'Is an in-between place,' said Turpin. 'A mixed-up, magicky place most humans don't notice, unless they know what they are looking for. There are lots of them. You just need to know where to look.'

'A mixed-up, magicky place,' Tanya repeated. Even though she was afraid for Ratty, she could not help but feel a thrill of excitement. What was on the seafront that she had never noticed? And who exactly was it that Don was planning to visit?

'We'll need those coins that I left for Henry,' Don said. 'The four-leaf clovers, too.'

'What for?' Tanya asked.

'You'll see when we get there,' Don said infuriatingly. 'So, when can we go?'

'Well, I think—' she began, then stopped as something long, sticky and pink lashed past her foot into the space under the bed. She felt her toes curl in revulsion. The long, pink something had been Don's tongue.

'Spider,' he muttered apologetically. 'So, when?'

'As soon as possible,' Tanya answered with a shudder.

It wasn't difficult to get out of her mother's way for the morning. After clearing away the breakfast things and offering to replace the spilled cornflakes and sugar, Tanya left the cottage, with Turpin and Oberon trotting along beside her and Don tucked out of sight in the pocket of her rucksack.

It was an overcast day, but still warm and muggy and, with it being the holidays, it made little difference to the number of visitors on the seafront.

'Good,' Don croaked over the cacophony of voices. 'It's busy. That's very good. We don't want to stand out.'

'Where exactly are we going?' Tanya asked, as they neared the pier.

'Keep going,' Don replied. 'Turpin knows where it is. Just follow her.'

They passed the bustling pier, arriving at the funfair. As they squeezed through the throng of people on to the promenade, Tanya eyed the carousel, recalling how sinister the motionless wooden horses had seemed when she had passed them in the darkness the night before. Now, as they galloped to the cheerful music with squealing children on their backs, it felt like a different place entirely.

Turpin led her past various rides. They blurred into a mix of colour and whirring noise; the dodgems, the waltzers and a helter-skelter, and even a big wheel. At the very edge, overlooking the sea, was a roller coaster and, next to it, a brightly painted ride that looked a little like a ghost train.

'This one,' Turpin announced.

Tanya stared up at the rickety-looking cars that were rattling along the track, bursting out of one set of wooden doors and whizzing down a slope before vanishing into another. On a wooden board that arched across the width of the ride, the words 'THE RIFT' flickered in silver lights. Surrounding it was a painted ring of bright red, spotted toadstools with small, winged figures dancing around them and playing strange instruments. At the centre of the fairy ring, two children danced, too. Though their mouths were smiling, their painted eyes were glazed over, as though they were each in a dream.

'The Rift?' Tanya murmured. 'What is this?'

'Something that isn't what it seems,' said Don's muffled voice. 'Get in the queue. We're going to buy a ticket. Only our ticket won't be quite the same as everyone else's.'

'And why is that?' Tanya asked.

'Because we're going to pay using one of the coins I left for Henry.'

Tanya took a step towards the ticket booth, where a surly-looking man sat hunched over a till. He was very old, with a face as wrinkled as an elephant skin and fuzzy white hair. He also happened to be a dwarf, for as Tanya got closer she saw that he had a large head and hands that seemed out of proportion to the rest of his body.

'No dogs,' he said flatly, motioning to a gap in the side of the booth. 'Leave him here, with me.'

Tanya nodded mutely, coaxing Oberon into the tiny booth where the little man sat high up on a stool, his feet dangling in the air. She gave Oberon a pat, then moved round to the front of the booth, reaching into the rucksack. Her hand brushed against clammy toad fingers offering her a cold, silver coin. She took it, enfolding it in her palm. There were people behind them in the queue now, impatient to get on. She quickly slid the coin through the gap in the glass window, not meeting the little man's eyes.

There was a slight pause before his crinkled, brown hand closed over it. Wordlessly, he pressed a button on the till and the drawer sprang open, but Tanya noticed that he did not put the coin into the tray. Instead, he slipped it slyly into his shirt pocket and slid a green ticket back through the narrow gap. Tanya took it, daring to look up at the last minute. The little man's eyes were trained upon her intently, far more alert than they had been moments before. For the briefest of moments, Tanya thought she saw the tips of two pointed ears protruding from the white hair on either side of his face. She blinked and they were gone.

She pushed through the barrier to the entrance, waiting for a cart to become free. From behind the painted doors, she could hear screams, laughter and music, and she wondered what else lay behind them. A moment later, a cart burst through the lower set of doors and came to a juddering halt before her. She stepped aside to allow the passengers off, noticing as they exited the cart that there was a purse on the seat.

Turpin squeaked in delight, but Tanya pounced first, snatching it out of her grasp.

'You just can't help yourself, can you?' she scolded, after handing it back to the lady who had dropped it.

Turpin hopped into the cart, huffing bad-temperedly.

Tanya clambered in beside her, resting the rucksack on the seat between them. There was a click and a safety bar lowered into place across her lap. Then the cart jerked forward, rattling towards a set of painted wooden doors with the sun on one side and the moon on the other. The doors flew open, plunging Tanya into the darkness beyond.

17
Gretchen and Griselda

TANYA'S EYES HAD BARELY BEGUN TO adjust to the darkness when a cloud of blue smoke puffed out from above, enveloping the cart as it rattled over the tracks. It emerged on the other side of the cloud in a dimly-lit tunnel, where a huge, silver moon and twinkling stars glowed above her head.

'Welcome to The Rift,' said a deep voice. 'A wondrous interstice where a glimpse of magic is possible! Hold tight on your journey through the inbetween of night and day, of land and sea, of life and death, and prepare yourself for sights you only ever imagined ...'

As the stars faded to black, the moon changed into a giant, luminous clock face, its hands fixed on midnight. It began to strike in deep booms that echoed around the tunnel. The cart swept past it and turned a corner. The lights overhead changed to green and, ahead, a large, black cauldron rose out of a swirling mist. Three waxwork figures in pointed hats surrounded it, stirring, chanting and cackling. As the cart drew nearer, a frog popped up out of the cauldron, followed by a skeleton hand, before sinking slowly back in.

The cart took another turn and Tanya felt her weight shift back as it began to climb higher on a slope. The witches' cackling subsided, and she felt her hair ruffle as a growling, glittering trio of dragons billowing smoke swooped above their heads.

'Nothing like real dragons,' said Turpin, sounding bored. 'Real ones are much uglier.'

Tanya leaned over the rucksack. 'Are you sure we've come to the right place? This just seems like a typical fairground ride.'

'Of course I'm sure,' Don replied. 'Be patient. We're nearly there.'

They were on some upper level of the ride now. The tunnel turned to blue, with silvery lights playing across every surface to give the impression they were underwater. Melodic singing had begun somewhere nearby, but underneath it Tanya could hear the rattles and clanks of another cart behind them.

'I don't understand,' she began. 'How ...?'

Something moved in the shadows up ahead. Not a waxwork this time, but a real figure, not quite the size of a child nor an adult. A dwarf, Tanya realised. Though she could not see its face, the straggly outline of the hair was very familiar. Could it be the same little man she had given the fairy coin to?

Before she had a chance to wonder further, the figure

reached out and pulled on a lever. There was a loud creak and suddenly a section of the track ahead lifted up and swung to the left, taking the cart with it straight towards a brick wall. Instinctively, Tanya clenched her eyes shut and threw up her hands in front of herself, waiting for the collision ... but it never came. She opened her eyes in time to see the section of wall still bafflingly close before they took another abrupt turn and she realised that the entire thing was a cleverly painted illusion which masked another secret part of the track. Behind them there was a grinding clank as the track slotted back into its original place.

They were rolling down now, gathering speed and whipping through another thick fog, only this was not the artificial stuff they had experienced on the other parts of the ride. Instead, it was dense and grey with a salty taste, leaving a damp stickiness on Tanya's cheeks and lips. Bubbles flew through the air around them and the singing grew louder, the lone voice merging into several. Still they plunged down, down, down, and the thought struck her that this was impossible, for they must surely be way below the promenade by now, if not below sea level.

Glass cases loomed through the mist either side of the cart and, as Tanya peered closer, she saw scaled limbs, fins and long, flowing hair swirling in sea-green water.

'Mermaids,' she breathed, watching as the figures flipped and pressed their webbed fingers up against the glass.

'The merfolk are another inbetween,' said Turpin. 'Not for us.' She huddled closer to Tanya. 'Careful. Do not listen

205

too closely to their song. It can bewitch, even if they do not mean to.'

The cart hurtled on and the glass cases receded into the sea mist. The scent of the air changed to something that Tanya recognised well: the earthy, damp smell that had invaded her room so many times. As if on cue, her eyelids began to twitch.

Greenery sprang up around them and whispering filled Tanya's head. A ring of red toadstools, much like the one painted on the ride's sign, rose slowly up through the grass. Figures danced within it to a strange melody, most of them fey and playing instruments that Tanya had never seen before, but one of them – a small boy – was human. Round and round he danced, smiling at first and dancing the jig with enthusiasm, but as he passed her for the third time Tanya noticed that he was changing, becoming taller. Older. His shoes and socks became worn and full of holes, and a saddened, hungry look overtook his face, yet still he danced, gripped by whatever spell the music held over him.

'A fairy ring,' Turpin whispered. 'Most magical traps for unsuspecting humans. They are lured by the music, but, once they step in, is very hard to get out again. Only way is to throw something inside out into the circle to break the dance, or to be pulled out by someone with one foot firmly outside the ring. Otherwise, the dance can go on for many years, even a century, though it may only seem to last a night.'

The fairy ring faded, but the greenery remained, thickening and growing denser. Winged creatures buzzed in the air, some of them swooping low over the cart to inspect its passengers curiously. Tanya felt a couple of spiteful tugs to her hair and a pinch on her arm, and gritted her teeth through the fairies' tittering laughter.

The cart continued to gather speed, whipping her hair up around her face and snatching the fairies away on the wind. She gripped the sides tighter, squeezing her eyes shut until, with a scrape and a bang, they jerked to a stop. Tentatively, she opened her eyes and blinked. They appeared to be in some kind of potting shed. Various garden tools surrounded them, and the only source of light was from a broken, cobwebbed window.

'I believe we have arrived,' Don announced. 'Could someone please get me out?'

Turpin lifted the toad out of the rucksack and placed him on the ground, where he stretched out one slimy leg, then the other.

'Where are we?' Tanya asked.

'I told you,' Don said impatiently. 'We're in an inbetween. It's a sort of . . . pocket, if you like. Not quite our world and not quite the fairy realm, either, but somewhere, well . . . in between the two. Discreet and tucked away, for those who don't want to be easily found. They can only be reached by certain portals which are also inbetweens.'

'So the ride is a portal,' said Tanya. 'Because it's built right between the land and the sea?'

'Correct,' said Don. 'Of course, there are lots of in-between places like that. But not everybody knows how to use them, so they are wasted.'

'You still haven't told me who it is we're here to see,' said Tanya.

At this, Turpin tittered with laughter. Don scowled.

'Two sisters,' he said at last. 'And fey, although they grew up in our world, along with their older brother.'

'Why did they grow up in our world?' Tanya asked.

'It happens more often than you think,' said Don. 'Most commonly with changelings—'

'What are changelings?'

'Fairy children that are exchanged with human children,' said Don. 'If fairy children are born sick, or even if they are very ugly, the fairies will often choose to switch them with a healthy or pretty human child.'

'That's terrible!' Tanya burst out.

'We don't like ugly ones,' Turpin muttered.

Don nodded. 'Sometimes it's even done out of mischief or revenge. But these children were not changelings. The entire family was fey, though they used glamour to disguise their fairy traits. Whether they were banished from the fairy realm as a punishment, or came here of their own accord, I never found out. But all three of them, the brother especially, were brilliant.'

'You knew them as children?' Tanya asked.

'I lived next door to them,' Don replied. 'We played together and went to the same school. And, although I couldn't see through the glamour that made them look human, they couldn't disguise the fact that they were magical. When they were around, animals developed the ability to talk, sweets grew on trees, toys would come to life.' He paused, smiling. 'Best of all, our enemies never went unpunished. Whether they were made to bark like a dog, or plagued by a stench no one else could smell, they always got their comeuppance.'

'So what went wrong?' Tanya asked. 'I know something must have, because you don't look very happy at having to come here.'

Don sighed. 'Everything was fine until we grew up. And then the sisters had a falling-out.'

'About what?'

Don looked uncomfortable now. 'They both fell in love with the same man. After that, everything changed. They grew very . . . competitive, each casting spells on the other to make them less appealing to this man. The more outrageous these spells became, the more difficult it was for them to hide their true natures. Things got very . . . ugly, shall we say. And that's how they ended up here, out of the way where they can curse each other to their heart's content.'

'But surely, if they hate each other, they'd want to live apart?' said Tanya.

'Oh, no,' said Don. 'They might hate each other, but they can't live without each other. Living together is the only way they can keep an eye on each other – to make sure neither of them tries to pursue the man in question.'

'Sounds very odd,' said Tanya. 'What are these spells they cast on each other?'

'You'll see,' said Don. 'Just . . . try not to stare too much. Oh, and don't eat or drink anything they offer you. They don't get many visitors, so when they do they try not to let them leave.'

'Great,' Tanya muttered. 'So where are they?'

'This way.' Don hopped towards the shed door. It was not locked or even closed properly. Tanya clambered out of the cart and followed, with Turpin at her side. She pushed the door and it opened silently, into a very ordinary little yard with high walls and a gate a short distance away.

Don took the lead, hopping quickly to the gate. This led out into a narrow alleyway much like the ones at home, only there was an air of something that didn't feel entirely normal. Looking up, Tanya saw a strange sight. The sky was the colour of a pale, purple bruise. It was impossible to tell whether it was dawn or twilight, for both a sun and a crescent moon floated overhead. But it was more than that. It was the silence of the place. It felt like they were in a bubble, cushioned from all the sounds of real life.

'I don't think it's too far,' said Don.

'You don't *think*?' said Tanya. 'You mean you don't know?'

'I do know,' Don snapped. 'But it's been a while since I last came here, and it doesn't help that the blasted portal brings you out somewhere different every time. I just need to get my bearings.'

He hopped off ahead at a surprising speed, turning into

another little side alley that opened on to what at first appeared to be an ordinary-looking street. Rows upon rows of terraced houses stretched as far as the eye could see, all lit by the strange, purple dawn-twilight. It looked very much like an average street in London, Tanya thought ... but, as she looked closer, she saw things were slightly askew and didn't make sense.

'There are daffodils growing in that garden,' she said in surprise.

Turpin looked at the flowers, uninterested. 'So?'

Tanya pointed to a tree on the other side of the road. 'So, that tree has plums growing on it. We've got a plum tree in our garden and it doesn't get fruit until late summer. But daffodils are spring flowers. And look there – blackberries! They shouldn't be out until September.'

'Things are higgledy-piggledy here,' said Turpin. 'Is a topsy-turvy place where all the seasons are mixed up.'

'That's why witches and fey folk like it here,' said Don, who had stopped in front of a little wooden gate. 'They can always get their spell ingredients at any time of the year.' He gestured to the gate. 'This is the place.'

Tanya looked up at the house beyond the gate. It was extremely narrow, with only two windows that were squeezed in one on top of the other above the front door. 'People actually live here?' she asked. It seemed too small to be possible.

'Nothing is what it seems,' said Don. 'Now ring the bell and let me do the talking.' He lowered his voice. 'And remember, don't eat or drink anything they offer you – hide it if you have to, but don't let a crumb pass your lips.'

Nervous, Tanya reached out and jangled the large, silver bell on the door. It was opened almost immediately by a tall, thin man whose cheekbones jutted from his cheeks. He had grey hair and was dressed in a tattered black suit, and would otherwise have been very nondescript were it not for the fact that he was both slightly see-through and hovered a few inches above ground level.

'You rang?' he inquired.

'Er, yes,' said Don. 'Good morning. I mean, good evening.' He looked at the sky in confusion. 'I mean, oh . . . never mind. I'd like to see the ladies of the house, if I may.'

'Certainly, sir,' said the butler, who did not seem surprised in the slightest to be talking to a toad. 'And whom should I say is calling?'

'D-Donald.' Don swallowed, visibly nervous. 'Donald Hanratty. And this is Tanya . . .?'

'Fairchild,' Tanya put in.

The butler looked at Turpin expectantly.

'Turpin,' she announced. 'The Terrible.'

'Very good.' The butler vanished, quite literally, leaving the three of them silent on the doorstep.

Tanya stared at the space where he had been standing. 'Was that . . . I mean, is he a . . .?'

'Ghost,' Don finished. 'Yes, poor chap. He's been here for some years now. Had a heart attack on a train halfway between London and Birmingham and ended up in the wrong inbetween. Or maybe he didn't like the one he was supposed to be in. Who knows?'

'And you,' said Tanya, raising an eyebrow at Turpin. 'Turpin the Terrible?'

Turpin shrugged. 'Made it up.'

Tanya peered into the gloomy hallway beyond the door. It stretched back into shadows, with nothing to see except for plain white walls and spotless chequered tiles. A moment passed, then a high-pitched shriek of excitement echoed from the depths of the house.

'I told you the sisters get excited when they have visitors,' Don said. His voice sounded strained all of a sudden.

'How sure are you that they can turn you back?' Tanya asked.

'Fairly sure,' he answered. His voice had thinned out to a croak once more. 'Just don't leave without me.'

Tanya frowned. 'Why would we—?'

She never got to finish the sentence for the ghostly butler reappeared just then, beckoning to them.

'This way, please,' he said grandly, sweeping through the hallway. Tanya and Turpin followed, with Don's hops behind them sounding like wet slaps on the tiles. Two high-pitched voices having some kind of heated conversation drifted to them in snatches, but Tanya was unable to make out any specific words. They were shown to an imposing, black door at the end of the hall, beyond which the voices were rising to screeches.

'Where are they? Where are they?' The voice was like

fingernails clawing a blackboard. 'I know you've hidden them, you sneaky old stoat! Where are my pearls?'

A second voice cackled. 'You think pearls will make a difference with a face like that?'

The butler cleared his throat. The two voices hushed immediately, then one called out in a sugary but scratchy tone:

'Come in!'

The butler stood aside. As Tanya pushed the door open, she felt a rush of cold air as she passed him, and got the distinct feeling that, if she tried to walk through him, she would be able to. The door swung back to reveal a busy, brightly-lit room. There was something peculiar about it, but Tanya could not take it in straight away for, despite Don's warnings not to stare, her eyes became fixed on the two figures who stood at the centre.

Though Don had described them as sisters, there was very little about them that was recognisable as female. Nor, Tanya thought, did they look much alike. The one standing nearest wore what looked like a wig, piled high in black ringlets that were like fat little sausages. What at first looked like streaks of grey were actually cobwebs, and there were things crawling and jumping within the curls. *Fleas*, Tanya realised with a barely suppressed shiver. The woman wore a sickly lavender dress that could once have been a ballgown, but now it was faded and stained and full of holes. However, her most disturbing feature was her face. Her nose was a wet, pink pig's snout and, below it, a coarse, black beard which had been woven into a neat plait dangled almost to her waist and was secured by a purple bow.

The other sister had not fared much better in the looks department. She wore a similarly hideous dress in faded yellow and her hair was a matted, mustard-coloured mess in which things also nested – only this time it wasn't fleas. It was mice. She had a large, quivering grey nose like that of a cow or a bull, complete with a silver ring through it. She too had a beard: long, orange and parted in the middle and thrown back over her shoulders.

Tanya's eyes darted from one to the other. According to Don, this was what they had done to each other. *No wonder they'd had to come to an inbetween*, she thought. There was no way they would be able to lead normal lives in the real world.

The sisters stared back at her with expressions of delight. The pig-snouted sister was the first to speak. 'A girl! A girl has come to see us, Gretchen. How lovely!' She lifted an eyeglass hanging around her neck and peered through it first at Turpin, then at Don, then at the door they had just come through. 'But where is Donald?' she asked anxiously.

'He's . . . er—' Tanya began, then looked sideways at the toad.

'Yes, where?' Gretchen squawked. 'Where?'

'I'm here, my dears,' Don announced. 'Down here.'

The sisters gaped at the toad, their faces frozen in horror.

'Gretchen,' Don continued politely. 'Griselda. It's so lovely to see you again.'

215

18

The Bearded Sisters

GRISELDA TOOK A TINY STEP FORWARD, her snout twitching. 'Donald?' she said in a faint voice. 'My Donald? Is that really you?'

'What do you mean, *your* Donald?' Gretchen said sharply. 'He's not your Donald and never was!'

'Now, ladies ...' Don began.

'Oh, no ...' Tanya looked at Turpin, beginning to understand. 'When he said they'd both fallen in love with the same man ... it was *him*, wasn't it? They did all ... all that to each other because of Don?'

Turpin nodded, her face glum. 'They say love. Turpin says madness.'

'Maybe there's not much difference,' Tanya murmured.

Griselda knelt down before Don. 'It *is*, Gretchen,' she said in a wobbly voice. 'It's him! Come and look at the eyes. It's all in the eyes!'

Gretchen hurried to her sister's side and bent down to inspect the toad. 'Oh!' she wailed. 'Oh, Griselda, you're quite right – I'd recognise those dreamy sapphires anywhere!'

'Dreamy sapphires?' Tanya whispered. Turpin made a gagging noise.

Griselda scooped up the toad, pressing him against her ample chest, and whisked him away to the back of the room. Gretchen ran after her, protesting. 'Put him down! You'll smother him with those things!'

Tanya and Turpin followed them. There were cauldrons of various sizes everywhere; some stacked in piles and others bubbling up sweet or noxious fumes. Books lined the walls, most of them large and grand and very old-looking, and there were strange objects dotted about; things that looked like instruments from the science laboratory at school. At the back, where the sisters had taken Don, shelves were crammed with jars of weird and sinister-looking ingredients. As they drew closer, Tanya saw one grisly jar marked FLIGHT that was half full of small, glittering wings of all colours and sizes. Some looked like they were from butter-flies or bugs; others were similar to ones she had seen on fairies. At the bottom of the jar several smaller insects such as flies and ladybirds lay motionless and belly up.

Tanya moved on, skimming labels and contents, unable to take everything in. 'Bad girls' curls,' she read. 'Bog beans. Cornish brownie. Dragon's drool ... madman's beard, poison ivy, skunk spray. Warts – assorted sizes.' She paused, going back to the Cornish brownie. The red-faced creature in the jar was banging the sides of the glass with his fists. An extra label smeared with something dark had been hastily stuck on at the bottom: WARNING! BITES! As she stepped away from the shelves, she finally realised what else was strange about the room. It was perfectly round, with the ceiling sloping up into a domed shape like the inside of a witch's hat.

'That doesn't make sense,' she said, nudging Turpin who had clambered up on the shelves and was pulling faces at the brownie. 'Look at this room. Not only is it huge, but it's round. There's no way all this would fit in that tiny, cramped house we saw from the outside.'

'The outside is just an illusion,' said Turpin. 'Sometimes people who should not be here get into the inbetween by accident. Things are disguised to look normal. As normal as they can anyway.' She leaped off the shelf and landed neatly on a nearby table, where Griselda had placed Don. Both sisters had pulled up stools and were gazing into his eyes.

'. . . And so,' Don was saying, 'I really need to get back to my proper form. I'm no use to Henry like this and time is running out. And you two marvellous magic makers are my best chance of help.'

Griselda wiped a tear from her snout and sniffed. 'It's an outrage,' she said at last. 'Turning a beautiful creature into this!'

'An outrage,' Gretchen agreed.

Don looked up at them hopefully. 'So, do you think you can undo it?'

Griselda scoffed. 'Do we think we can undo it? Of course we can! It's just a matter of figuring out the right way. We shall have to consult the books.'

218

'I've got an idea,' Gretchen announced. Without warning, she grabbed Don and planted a huge kiss on his wide mouth.

'Gretchen!' Griselda screeched, snatching Don out of her sister's hands. 'You filthy sneak! You shameless floozy! You know that old wives' tale doesn't work! It's any excuse with you, isn't it?'

Gretchen licked her lips, looking pleased with herself. 'It was worth a try.'

'I thought it had to be a princess who could turn a toad back with a kiss,' said Tanya.

Griselda waved a hand dismissively, still glaring at her sister. 'Another myth. And anyway that's for frogs. But it does have to be true love, which is why *I* should try it!' She seized poor Don and pressed her lips against his, hard.

'You cheat!' Gretchen yelped. She jumped up so suddenly that one of the mice fell out of her hair and ran off across the table. She ignored it, batting Griselda's hands to force her to put Don down. 'Your love is no truer than mine! You just wanted to kiss him!'

'Well, so did you!' Griselda snapped.

Needless to say, it hadn't worked. Poor Don was still very much a toad, only now he was breathless and half smothered and looked plain terrified. Tanya shot him a sympathetic look and a worried one at Turpin. It was quite clear that when it came to Don – no matter what form he took – the sisters were completely crazed.

'So, what could we try next?' Tanya asked. 'If the kiss didn't work?'

'Lots of things.' Griselda scratched her head, showering the table with fleas. 'We need to have a good think.' She glanced at her sister slyly. 'Gretchen, dear? Would you make some tea?'

'Why do I always have to make the tea?' Gretchen snapped. 'I'm not your servant! That's what Charles is for!'

Griselda cleared her throat pointedly, stopping Gretchen's rant mid-flow.

'I— Oh.' Her voice softened. 'Well, I suppose I could do it this once.' She grinned at her sister, evidently catching on to whatever unspoken message was being relayed between them. 'Don always preferred my tea anyway,' she muttered. She shuffled away to a little fireplace, over which a black kettle was hanging. With a click of her fingers, flames burst into life in the grate. Tanya watched her carefully as she set about fetching cups and saucers and collecting various pots and jars from the nearby shelves. Whatever concoction Gretchen was brewing, it certainly wasn't ordinary tea. She guessed that Don's suspicions were correct and that this would be something magical designed to keep them here. She would just have to find a way to get rid of it without the sisters seeing.

She turned back to the table. Griselda was peering through her eyeglass at a book, muttering to herself as she turned the pages. Don sat on the table before her, looking sorry for himself.

'It could just take something as simple as a Revelation spell,' Griselda said eventually. She clicked her fingers at Turpin. 'Fetch me the following ingredients: a baby's first cry; deer's eyes; dragon scales; a good boy's tooth; a twist of rainbow; a wishbone from a stewed chicken.'

Turpin stared at her insolently. It was clear she did not like taking orders.

'Well, what are you waiting for?' Griselda snapped. 'Do you want him turned back or not? Everything's in alphabetical order on the shelves and there's a ladder if you can't reach; it's not difficult!'

Turpin set off grumbling, as Griselda continued to read through the spell. 'You, girl,' she said to Tanya. 'Bring me that wooden bowl. And that magnifying glass hanging up over there. The silver scales, too.'

Tanya duly set about doing as she was told.

'Oh, Griselda,' Gretchen called from over by the fireplace. 'Could you come here a moment, dearest?'

'Can't you see I'm busy?' Griselda growled, plucking the stopper from the first bottle that Turpin had collected. At first glance, the bottle appeared to hold nothing, but as she tilted it over the wooden bowl a shimmering silver substance trickled out and the room was suddenly alive with the sound of a baby crying.

'I wouldn't ask if it wasn't important!' Gretchen trilled.

Griselda slammed down her eyeglass and stalked over to her sister. Out of the corner of her eye Tanya noticed Gretchen glance at Don before she pulled her sister closer and began to whisper. There was something decidedly underhand about it all. Tanya moved closer, hoping to catch the gist of whatever it was they were saying, but before she was even past the table Griselda turned round with a sickly-sweet smile.

'What are you looking for?'

'The scales,' Tanya said stupidly, pointing to a brass set over by the fire.

'I said the silver ones, my dear. They're over there, near the table.'

Tanya slunk away in defeat, with no choice but to let the sisters go back to their huddling. She collected the scales and stood by the table, pretending to polish them with her sleeve, while waiting for Turpin. Eventually, the fairy returned with two more jars of disgusting ingredients: one full of teeth and the other glistening with fat, round eye-balls. Don hopped closer, inspecting the jars in disgust, and covering his ears to drown out the sound of the baby crying, which was still going strong.

'Turpin,' Tanya whispered. 'They're up to something – something to do with Don. I just tried to listen in, but they were on to me. Can you get close enough to hear what they're talking about?'

'Tricksy pair,' said Turpin, her eyes narrowing to slits. She nodded. 'Well, Turpin can be just as tricksy.' She watched the sisters out of the corner of her eye. 'If you create a distraction, I can get close. Very close. Wait for my signal.'

Tanya nodded, moving away from the table to collect the

magnifying glass. She spotted a silver tray nearby and picked that up, too, watching Turpin closely. The fairy browsed the shelves, scratching her chin convincingly, all the while creeping closer. When she had reached the end of the shelves of ingredients, she turned and gave Tanya a small nod.

Tanya dropped the tray. It landed on the floor with a loud clatter, making the two sisters jump and causing the baby's cry to escalate into even louder wails.

'Sorry,' she called, bending down to pick it up. When she stood up again, Turpin had vanished.

'Did she make it?' Don whispered.

'Yes,' Tanya whispered back, catching sight of the fairy. 'She's right next to them, hiding behind a cauldron.'

'What do you suppose they could be plotting?' Don asked.

'I don't know, but I think you're right about them wanting to keep us here a little longer. Whatever it is, Turpin is bound to hear them.'

It was not long before Turpin skulked back to the table, unseen by the sisters who were still deep in conversation. As she approached, Tanya detected a look of worry in her eyes.

'What is it?' she said in a low voice. 'What are they whispering about?'

'Don,' Turpin replied. 'Gretchen says they should make the spell go wrong on purpose, so he stays as a toad.'

Don looked furious. 'She said what?'

'Whatever for?' Tanya asked.

'Because now he is ugly, like them,' Turpin said. 'And she

thinks, if he stays ugly, he is bound to love one of them back sooner or later.'

'That's absurd!' Don spluttered. 'And what does Griselda say?'

Turpin glanced over her shoulder. 'She likes the idea, but doesn't think Don will believe that they won't be able to break the spell.'

'Too right I wouldn't believe it!' said Don. 'I can't stay like this. I just can't!' he shuddered. 'Besides, no matter how ugly I was, it wouldn't make a difference. I could never love either of them. Just look what they've done to each other!'

'Gruesome and grisly,' said Turpin, nodding in disgust.

'Exactly,' said Don. 'And I don't even mean how they look. I mean the very fact that they did this to each other and would be willing to leave me like this. They're completely nuts, the pair of them!'

'Then I'll have to make sure the spell goes right,' said Tanya. 'They can only cheat if they think we don't know what they're doing.' She leaned across the table, skimming the spell's ingredients and instructions in the open book. 'In a silver bowl, blend a child's first cry to a smooth paste with the eye of an innocent,' she said under her breath. 'Add seven dragon's scales, crushed to a powder with a tooth from the mouth of a good boy who always tells the truth. Fold in gently with a twist of rainbow, then, using the wishbone from a stewed chicken, stir with a good gob of spit from the afflicted. Weigh the mixture into equal parts and discard half before generously applying to the skin. This spell is best

224

performed by someone left-handed, but, if not, then any time between Monday and Thursday is the next best solution.' She reread it several times and shook her head. 'What a weird spell.'

Shortly after, the sisters finished their huddling. Gretchen resumed making the tea and Griselda returned to the table and set about measuring out the ingredients Turpin had collected. She pulled out an eyeball and plopped it into the silver bowl with the baby's cry, then took to it with an implement like a potato masher. There was a soft popping sound and the baby's cries eased to a soft snuffling, then a gurgle as Griselda puréed them both together. Tanya watched carefully. Griselda was definitely right-handed, but luckily it didn't matter, for today was a Tuesday. She just hoped the normal days of the week still counted in an inbetween.

When the contents of the bowl were a paste, Griselda stopped and leaned over the book. 'What's next?' she muttered.

'Seven dragon's scales,' Tanya said, offering her the jar.

'Oh.' Griselda looked taken aback. 'How, um, helpful.'

Tanya smiled. 'I just find magic so interesting. You're very clever to be able to work it.'

Griselda gave a little snort and looked away. 'Yes, well,' she muttered a little guiltily. 'It's just a matter of following the instructions. And, of course, it helps if you have magic in your blood.'

'So I wouldn't be able to do it myself then?' Tanya said.

Even though she had only been playing along, she couldn't help feel a hint of disappointment. She had experienced plenty of magic at the hands of the fairies, but never had the chance to see it being made like this before.

'Well, of course you would,' Griselda said. 'You have the second sight, don't you? There's magic in your blood all right.'

'There is?'

'Indeed.' Griselda eyed her appraisingly. 'Everyone with the fairy sight has magic in their blood. And coupled with an interest in it, well. That's a perfect combination. You'd need a natural talent, too, of course, but I think, given some time, I could make a proper little witch of you.'

At this, Don's eyes widened. Behind Griselda's back, he made several warning motions.

'Er, maybe when I'm a little bit older,' said Tanya hurriedly. 'I still have to finish school first. And my mother would miss me if I didn't come back.'

'Oh.' Griselda looked disappointed. 'Well, the offer's there if you change your mind. I can deal with schools and mothers easily enough. Little bit of this and a little bit of that in the cauldron and POOF!' She clapped her hands. 'They all go away!'

Tanya forced a smile. 'I'll let you know if I change my mind.'

'Good, good,' said Griselda, patting her on the head.

Thankfully, Gretchen chose that moment to return to the table with a large tray. 'Tea time!' she trilled, setting cups out before each of them. A curl of steam rose from the spout of the black teapot. Tanya sniffed dubiously. Though it smelled fairly ordinary, the length of time it had taken to make warned her that this was definitely not the stuff you dunked your biscuits in. She waited until Gretchen had poured, then stirred in some milk.

Turpin prodded a sugar lump in the bowl. 'There are ants stuck to these.'

'They won't hurt you,' said Gretchen. 'They're dead.'

Turpin pushed the bowl away. Don looked at the ants longingly, but managed to keep his tongue in his mouth.

'So, where were we?' Griselda said. 'Ah, yes. Dragon's scales. Seven, to be precise.' She took the lid off the jar and began picking out the iridescent scales, placing them in a stone mortar. 'One, two, three, four ...' She paused and coughed delicately. 'Six, seven.'

'You missed out number five,' Tanya said quickly.

'I don't think I did,' Griselda said, reaching for the pestle.

'You did, my dear,' said Don. He batted his eyelids. 'Please check again. For me? It's very important.'

'Of course,' Griselda simpered. She peered into the mortar. 'You're quite right. There are only six.' She reached into the jar and took out another scale. There was a thud from under the table and she gave a small squeak. Tanya looked at Gretchen, who was glowering at her sister, and guessed she had kicked her for admitting her deliberate mistake.

One by one the rest of the ingredients were added and,

despite Griselda's best efforts to get the quantities or order wrong, Tanya's sharp eyes caught every mistake and she corrected her every time. By the time it came to the weighing, Gretchen's face was like thunder and Griselda had been on the receiving end of several more none too subtle kicks.

'Now spit,' said Griselda, holding the bowl towards Don. Dutifully, he obeyed, and she stirred the mixture again with the chicken bone. Slowly, it became a slimy, yellowish-green in colour, much like Don himself. 'Good,' Griselda nodded. 'That means it's working.' She spooned out a stiff lump of the sludge and dolloped it on one side of the scales. They remained equally balanced.

'Are those scales working?' Tanya asked. 'Only normally the heavier side goes down.'

Griselda scooped up the rest of the mixture and put it on the other side of the scales. Even though one side clearly contained more, they still didn't move. 'Of course they're working. You think I'd be using them if they didn't?'

'But—'

'Listen, clever clogs,' Gretchen snapped. 'They always look perfectly balanced. We're in an inbetween, remember? The scales will always be perfectly balanced, and that's a good thing where spells like these are concerned. It means less waste.' She glared at Tanya. 'You haven't touched your tea. Drink up.'

Tanya lifted the cup to her lips and pretended to take a sip before replacing it quickly back in the saucer. Gretchen looked away, her scowl replaced by a small smirk.

'Right,' said Griselda. 'I think we're ready.' She spooned up some of the sludge from the larger pile on the scales and splatted it on Don's head.

'Oooh,' he said with a shiver.

'Now just relax,' Griselda cooed, her voice suddenly much lower. 'Let me rub this in for you.' She grabbed Don's clammy toad fingers and began massaging them between her own. 'How does that feel?'

'Oooh,' said Don again.

Griselda's snout twitched out a little snort of happiness. 'I know,' she whispered. 'Sensuous . . .'

'Um, not exactly,' Don said. 'It's rather cold, that's all.'

'Let me do it,' said Gretchen jealously. 'Sensuous, my beard. I'm more sensuous when I'm basting a turkey!' She took Don's other leg and began working the sludge over the mottled, green skin.

'We'll both do it!' Griselda screeched, pulling back on her side and rubbing vigorously. Tanya and Turpin watched, helpless, as poor Don was yanked this way and that in a gloopy tug of war.

'Ha! Ha! That tickles! Oh . . . um, I don't think you should . . . I mean, maybe I should do that part? It's just—CRIPES! Not there, woman! Let go! LET GO!' he yelped. 'I'll do it myself!' Somehow, he managed to extract himself and backed away, continuing to rub the horrible slushy mixture over himself.

'Now look what you've done,' Griselda hissed at her sister. 'You always have to take things too far, don't you?'

'Me?' Gretchen whined. 'You started it!'

'Ladies, please!' Don said wearily. He blinked out of the gungy mess like a small swamp monster. 'How long should this take?'

Griselda peered at him. 'Are you sure you're completely covered?'

'Completely,' said Don, looking very sorry for himself.

'Oh.' Griselda blinked. 'Then it hasn't worked.'

'What? But it has to,' Don protested. 'Are you sure you did it right?'

'Yes,' said Griselda.

Gretchen muttered something. It sounded like 'Unfortunately'.

Tanya watched Griselda closely. She was positive the spell had been followed correctly, and Griselda's disappointment seemed genuine. She took pride in her spells, Tanya realised. She didn't like to fail, even if it meant not keeping Don for a while longer – or permanently.

Gretchen wrung her hands. 'Then I'm afraid there's nothing to be done. Dearest Donald will have to remain a toad. And it's so dangerous for magical creatures, back in the human world. But here with us you'd be safe. We'd look after you ...'

Don shook his head, his eyes wide with horror. 'No!' He crawled over to Griselda, tugging at her sleeve. 'There has to be something else you could try! You said you could undo it!'

Griselda hesitated. 'It's very dark magic. Much stronger

than I thought. And there's something . . . familiar about it.'

'Please,' Don croaked. 'It's not just for me. My son's life is at stake – I must return to my true form before I get to him.'

Griselda wiped her snout and sighed. 'There is something. A spell to undo darker magic.'

'No,' said Gretchen. 'No, there's no such spell!'

'Quiet,' her sister snapped. 'You know quite well that there's the Moon spell.' She took a cloth and began wiping the sludge from Don's skin. 'The moon is a powerful symbol of trickery and lies. To cast them out, the timing of this spell is crucial. I can prepare the potion for you, but it must only be drunk when the moon is visible.'

'Is there anything that would work faster?' Tanya asked.

'Not of this strength,' Griselda replied. 'And, if the Revelation spell failed, I believe this has the best chance.'

'We'll take it,' Don said. 'As soon as it's ready, and then we should be on our way.'

'Oh, but you must stay until it's time to drink it,' Gretchen implored. 'We have to make sure it works after all.'

'I'm afraid we can't,' Don said firmly. 'We must get back. There are preparations to make. And if you say it's the best chance then I'll take your word for it. Now, I have very little fey money to pay you with, but I do have some four-leaf clovers which I understand you can make use of?'

Griselda's eyes lit up, but she waved her hand. 'No charge for old friends,' she said.

'No, really,' said Don. 'I insist.' He nodded at Tanya and

she rummaged in the rucksack for the red envelope and pulled out the clovers. Griselda swooped on them greedily, nudging her sister.

'Fetch a jar, Gretchen,' she urged. 'Let's keep these beauties fresh! Gretchen?'

Gretchen hadn't moved. She was sitting very still, watching her sister with an expression like that of a bulldog chewing a wasp. Her eyes were pinched tight, her jaw was grinding, and even her beard looked fiercer. Her face grew steadily red, then purple. Without warning, her fist smashed down on the table, jogging the teacups and sending the mice in her hair into a frenzy of squeaks.

'You've ruined everything!' she bellowed at Griselda. Her nails scratched the table like claws, and little white sparks flew out from her fingertips. 'This was our chance, don't you see? We could have kept him, forever! But you're so selfish you had to show off and do it right!'

'You're the selfish one!' Griselda roared. 'Willing to deny us his beauty just to keep him here!' She turned to Don, her eyes blazing. 'Wanted to keep you as a toad, she did! Thought you'd be too unhappy to go back and would stay with us for good!'

'Um . . .' said Don, but for the first time the two sisters were too caught up in their angry exchange to listen to him.

'Well, I've got news for you, Gretchen,' Griselda declared. 'True love isn't all one-sided. Sometimes it's about making sacrifices. And if that means letting him go in order to be happy then so be it!'

'Oh, and here comes the Goody-Two-Shoes act!' Gretchen jumped up from the table. 'Not that it matters with a face like yours!'

Griselda stood up with a snort. Red sparks flew from her snout. 'You and me both, dear sister!'

'Uh-oh,' said Turpin.

Tanya sat frozen between the pair of them, unsure of what to do or what was about to happen.

'Ladies, please calm yourselves,' Don said. 'It's so ugly when sisters fight.'

'You said it, mister!' Gretchen shrieked. 'And it's going to get uglier still!'

'Is that a threat?' Griselda said, her voice dangerously low.

Gretchen cackled. 'It's a promise, dearie!'

'Then bring it on!' Griselda blew into her hands and rubbed them together. Blue smoke rose from her palms and, as she pulled her hands apart, a swirling, cloudy ball was suspended between them in mid-air.

'Yikes,' said Turpin.

'Fancy some new teeth?' Griselda said wickedly. 'To fit that big mouth?' She flung the smoky ball in her sister's direction. It exploded on impact with Gretchen's head and, as the smoke cleared, two huge tusks were visible protruding from her mouth.

'Fiend!' Gretchen ran to the fireplace, scooping out a ball of flame with her bare hands. 'How about some dead man's fingernails?' she lisped through the tusks. 'Nice and

233

hard and crispy, to help you scratch those fleas of yours?' She hurled the ball of flame back across the room.

'Duck!' shouted Turpin, grabbing Tanya and pulling her down as Gretchen's triumphant laughter filled the air. They crouched under the table. 'Stay here,' said Turpin. 'Turpin must get Don!' She scrambled back on to the table amidst the shouted curses of the two sisters, returning a moment later with the toad in her arms.

'Now what?' Tanya asked. 'How do we make them stop all this?'

A second ball of blue smoke flew over their heads and a pungent stench of strong cheese filled the air. 'Have some cheddar breath!' Griselda yelled. 'That'll keep your mice happy!'

Don shook his head. 'I was afraid it would come to this. I always seem to bring out the worst in them. Once they start, there's no stopping them.'

'But we have to,' said Tanya. 'We can't leave with you still as a toad! We have to get them to perform that spell.'

'Don is right,' said Turpin. 'Have seen this many times before. We must leave, now, before one of us ends up in the firing line.'

A second ball of flame ripped over their heads, blasting across the table and shattering the teacups into smithereens.

'At least we don't have to worry about drinking the tea,' Don said gloomily.

Turpin pointed to the door they had been shown in through. 'Get ready to run,' she said.

'No,' Tanya said. 'We came here for help and I'm not leaving until we get it.'

'Are you blind?' Turpin demanded. 'These two are stark raving mad! They'll be at it all night now – we'll never get them to do the spell!'

'Then I'll do it myself,' said Tanya.

Don gaped. 'But . . .'

'You heard Griselda. She said I have magic in my blood. That means I can perform the spell. We just have to know what to do and what to use.' She waited for the next missile from Griselda to fly across the table, then reached up and heaved the heavy spell book down on to her lap. 'Griselda said it was a Moon spell,' she said, thumbing through the pages. 'If we can find it, then it'll tell us the ingredients . . .'

'Crow's feet!' Gretchen yelled above them.

'Then hurry,' said Don. 'Every moment we stay here we're putting ourselves in danger.' Before he had even finished speaking, the table shattered into splinters, sending them scrambling in opposite directions. Turpin took cover behind a huge cauldron, while Tanya and Don hid behind a moth-eaten armchair.

'Moon, moon, moon,' Tanya said to herself, flicking through the pages of the book. 'Moon Mischief and Muddles . . . Moon Mayhem, Murder by Moonlight . . . None of these say anything about undoing a curse!'

'Try "lunar",' Don suggested.

'Oh.' Tanya flicked back a section. 'Lunar Love . . . Lunar Labyrinth . . . wait, I think this is it – Lunar Lies and False

Disguise!' She ran her finger over the crabbed words. 'It's some sort of spell to alter a person's appearance, but under that there's an antidote to change someone back to their true form.' She read quickly. 'To be performed in sight of the moon. This must be it.' She looked up cautiously, but needn't have worried. The sisters' war was still in full flow, and above their screams there was no way the delicate tear of the page could be heard as Tanya ripped it out of the book.

'Turpin!' she hissed. 'Can you get me these ingredients? Moon dust, a liar's tongue, a caterpillar, a fox's whisker, a thread from a hangman's rope, powdered chameleon . . .' She paused. 'We also need an egg, a mirror and a playing card, but I can get those back at the cottage.' She looked up again, gesturing to the shelves. 'Go, quickly, and be careful!'

Turpin zipped off in the direction of the shelves, grabbing jars and piling them up in her arms. One by one, ducking and diving through the sisters' shrieked curses, she rolled the jars and bottles to Tanya, who checked them off the list and bundled them into her waiting rucksack. Between the snatches of cargo, she and Don watched – Don through his fingers – as the sisters threw every hex they could think of at each other.

Griselda was now struggling to walk, forced to teeter unsteadily on two great crow's feet that snagged her dress and caught in its hem, while Gretchen was also clumsy on two cloven hooves, not helped by the fact that her beard was now three times longer and wrapped round her legs.

Two more jars rolled towards Tanya and she snatched them up. 'That's almost everything. Well done, Turpin!' she called. 'Now all we need is the liar's tongue.' She watched anxiously as Turpin ran up the ladder like a rat into a pantry, gathering up several more jars. 'What is she doing?' she asked Don in confusion. 'We only need one more thing on the list – she's carrying at least three!'

Don watched, wide-eyed and as bewildered as Tanya was. 'Turpin, hurry!' he croaked.

'Am hurrying!' Turpin panted. 'Just need one ... more ... thing!'

'Leave it!' Don cried as a shelf of jars just an arm's length from the fairy toppled over and smashed. 'Whatever it is, just leave it!'

Whether Turpin chose to ignore him or simply couldn't hear him over the din, she continued to climb up the ladder, reaching out for something on the topmost shelf. As she did so, Gretchen hurled another curse.

'You're as stubborn as a goat,' she yelled. 'So you may as well look like one!' She flung a fireball, but at the moment of release one of her hooves tangled in her beard and the curse flew askew.

'Turpin, watch out!' cried Tanya.

Turpin reacted swiftly and almost managed to dodge – but not quite. The curse caught the very tip of her wing, knocking her off the ladder. At the same time, Griselda's counter-curse flew the other way, catching Turpin's leg on her way down. She emitted a pained squeak, but managed to snatch whatever it was she had wanted from the shelf before tumbling to the floor and scurrying back to Tanya, her wing tip smoking. Two small, pointed horns poked up through her hair and from under the back of her waistcoat a long, thin tail with a bushy end flicked like an agitated cat's.

'Oh, Turpin!' Don said in horror. 'Look what they've done to you!'

'What?' Turpin said, oblivious.

Tanya reached out for a shard of glass from a cabinet that had been shattered nearby and held it up for Turpin to see her reflection. 'Maybe there's another spell,' she said. 'If we take the rest of the book, perhaps we can undo it . . .'

But a wide grin had spread across Turpin's face as she peered into the shard. 'Turpin does not want it undone,' she breathed, stroking the little horns and swinging the tail in wonder. 'Turpin *loves* them!'

'That's settled then,' Don said hastily. 'Now, if you're sure you don't mind, let's move!'

Tanya nodded, stuffing the rest of the jars and Don into the rucksack, and prepared to run. 'On the count of three, head for the door,' she told Turpin. 'Ready? One, two, three!' The two of them sprinted for the door, skidding on broken china and spilled tea, and narrowly avoiding another ball of smoke headed in Gretchen's direction. Tanya grabbed the door handle, but, before she could even twist it, another fireball from Gretchen blew it apart and they fell into the tiled hall where the ghostly butler was hovering with a resigned expression.

'Run!' Tanya gasped and, with no time to dodge the butler, whipped straight through him.

'Well, really,' he huffed. 'No manners at all!'

'Sorry!' Tanya yelled, hurtling towards the front door. She flung it open, and then she and Turpin bolted into the empty street, leaving the madness of the bearded sisters behind as they fled under the bruised sky of the inbetween.

19

The Sleep of the Dead

THE CART SPED ALONG THE TRACK, whipping away from the potting shed and leaving Tanya breathless.

'Do you think they'll come after us?' she said. A glance over her shoulder told her nothing; her hair was flying everywhere and everything beyond it was a blur.

'I doubt it,' said Don. 'They probably haven't even realised we've left.'

Tanya clung to the sides of the cart, wincing as it jerked and jolted. She would be sure to have bruises later, although for now there was something else that worried her far more. 'How long have we been gone? It feels like we were there for hours and hours. My mother must be wondering where I've got to . . . and poor Oberon has been waiting all this time!'

'Worry not,' said Turpin. 'Was an inbetween, remember? When passing from here to there and back again, time is nothing. Like the clock got stuck.'

'Are you sure?' Tanya asked doubtfully, but even as she did so she became aware of the distant sounds of chiming.

240

The cart slowed and the air grew warmer and stuffy. The sugary sweetness of candyfloss filled her nose. There was a mechanical clunk as the track they were on shifted ... and then they were back on the seaside ride once more, surrounded by waxwork mermaids and with the chiming of the clock still striking midnight. It was as though they had never left the ride at all.

The cart veered to the right, bursting through a set of double doors into bright sunshine before swooping down a slope and into another door. Behind this one was a makeshift graveyard with spectres floating overhead and bony hands reaching up through burial mounds. 'You are now in limbo,' a voice announced with an eerie chuckle. 'The land in between the living and the dead.'

'Oh,' said Tanya, slumping back in the seat as a wave of nausea rushed over her. 'I feel ...'

'Dizzy? Sick?' said Turpin.

'Yes,' Tanya said weakly. 'How did you know?'

'Is normal for a human going into an inbetween for the first time. Not what you are used to.' She reached up and rubbed Tanya's head. 'But it will pass very soon.'

The cart bumped its way through one final set of doors and then, thankfully, came to a final stop. Tanya clambered out shakily, hauling the rucksack with the heavy ingredients over her shoulder, and headed for the exit. She took a few deep breaths, trying to gulp away the sickness she was feeling, but the seaside smells only made things worse. She managed to reach the ticket booth where

Oberon was waiting patiently, then leaned against it and closed her eyes.

A throaty chuckle caused her to open them again and she found the strange little man who had sold her the ticket staring at her. 'First time in an inbetween?' he said knowingly.

She waited for him to offer some kind of advice, but none was forthcoming. Instead, he motioned at Oberon and gave Turpin a curt nod.

'Well, best be on your way,' he said in a low voice. 'Can't have you hanging around here looking green, never know who might be watching. I don't need any unwelcome attention.'

Tanya took the hint, calling to Oberon. He stuck his wet nose in her hand in greeting, then trotted alongside her as she made her way back through the other funfair rides. To her great relief, Turpin was right. Within a couple of minutes, the sick feeling had passed and she was almost back to normal, though her knees still felt a bit wobbly.

By the time she reached the carousel, her thoughts turned to the contents of her rucksack and a tremor of excitement went through her. She had a spell in her bag. An actual magical spell and the ingredients to perform it. Yesterday she would not have believed that such a thing was even possible.

As the carousel whirled next to her, a dark figure standing among the brightly-painted wooden horses caught her eye within the rainbow of colours. Tanya slowed a little. Unlike the other people on the ride, the figure was not on a horse. Nor was it laughing or shouting – or even moving for that matter. It was standing motionless amongst the rising and falling horses, and there was something odd about its face. It vanished from view as the carousel continued its circuit, reappearing a moment later, not having moved. Tanya looked harder, realising with a jolt that the face was a painted mask rather like that of an unhappy clown.

'What's the matter?' Don asked, his voice muffled by the pocket of the rucksack. 'Why have we stopped?'

'Nothing's the matter,' Tanya answered. 'I just spotted someone standing on the carousel. They seemed like they didn't fit for some reason.' She gave a little laugh. 'But then I saw the mask – it must be another waxwork. Funny, I never noticed it earlier.' She shook her head and was about to continue walking on when something happened that made her freeze where she was. The figure had moved. She watched as it lifted a gloved hand to one of the poles and held it to steady itself. What was most disturbing was that, even though Tanya could not tell exactly where the figure was looking from behind the mask, she got a strong feeling that it was watching her. And, more than that, the suspicion that she had seen it before.

'Keep going,' Don croaked. She looked down and saw that he had risked a quick peek out of the pocket.

'What is it?' she asked, moving off into a crowd of people. 'You look . . . worried.'

'How can you tell what I look like?' Don snapped. 'How many worried toads have you ever seen?'

'Well, none,' Tanya admitted. 'Until now. But I'm getting pretty good at reading your expression.'

'Just keep moving,' said Don. He shot an anxious look at Turpin. 'Keep to the crowds, where it's busy.'

His words sent a chill creeping over Tanya's skin. 'What's going on?' she asked. 'Are we in danger? Who was that in the mask?'

But Don either did not hear or was pretending not to for she got no answer. She continued onwards, making her way through the crowds of fun-seekers, eventually reaching the exit on to the street. A quick look back reassured her somewhat; the masked figure was not in sight. Still she stuck closely to groups or families as she headed back towards Hawthorn Cottage, remembering at the last minute to stop by a little shop on the way for the groceries she had promised her mother.

The sun had burned through the clouds by the time they returned to the cottage. Her mother was reading on the porch once more, and looked up from her book as Tanya approached.

'Fancy a stroll down to the funfair this afternoon?' she asked.

'Um,' said Tanya, trying to think of an excuse.

'No.' Turpin pinched her leg, causing her to wince. Her mother looked at her strangely. 'No meddling mothers botching things up this afternoon. Is work to be done! Must keep her away.'

'Maybe later,' Tanya said, not meeting her mother's eyes. 'I've arranged to, er . . . meet Ratty on the pier.'

Her mother pursed her lips. 'Oh. That Ratty again. I see. Well, make sure you stay on the pier and don't go gallivanting off by that lonely river again.'

'I won't.' Tanya went into the cottage and offloaded the groceries in the kitchen before shutting herself in the bedroom. She heaved the heavy rucksack off her back and flopped down on the bed with a sigh, unzipping the pocket so that Don could climb out. Turpin immediately leaped on to the dressing table, admiring her new horns and tail and pulling gruesome faces at herself in the mirror.

'So now what?' Tanya asked. She lay back on the bed and let her head sink into the pillow, suddenly exhausted. The inbetween appeared to have sapped her strength.

'Now we must prepare everything,' said Don. 'There's no time to waste – you have to get the spell ready for tonight.'

'And what about my mother?' Tanya asked. 'We can't have her snooping around while I'm trying to do it.'

'No,' said Don, thoughtful. 'And we also need to take care of her when we set off to find Henry. She can't know you're missing.'

'No, she can't,' Tanya agreed. 'Turpin, you said you had some tricks we could use?'

'Turpin always has tricks,' the fairy announced, baring her teeth at herself in the mirror.

'Then can you stop preening for a moment and tell us about them?' said Don.

Reluctantly, Turpin dragged herself away from her reflection and came to sit on the bed by Don. She delved into the rucksack, removing the stolen jars one by one and setting them into two piles. Tanya sat up and hurriedly began hiding the jars she recognised beneath her pillow, fearful that her mother could walk in. When the last one was concealed, she studied the others, realising as she did that in one of them something was moving.

'What did you bring him for?' she asked, staring at the red-faced Cornish brownie, who was eyeing his new surroundings with contempt.

'Bargaining with,' said Turpin. She tapped on the glass, enraging the brownie further. 'Always good bargains to be made when it comes to a fairy's freedom.' She grinned slyly. 'Magical bargains that could help us.'

'That seems a bit ... cruel,' said Tanya. 'Perhaps we should just release him.'

Turpin made a disgusted noise. 'Shan't! Not yet anyway. He could come in useful. And anyway borrowing a bit of his magic is nothing to what the bearded sisters would have done.'

'What would they have done?' Tanya asked. The brownie's eyes flicked from side to side, glaring at each of them in turn. He pressed his ear against the glass.

'Depends.' Turpin delved into the bag again, removing a clear glass jar containing a shimmering substance. It looked a little like the baby's cry, except thicker, and within it fine strands were visible. 'A stew, maybe, or fried up with liver and onions. Or dipped in chocolate.'

Don nodded. 'Chocolate brownie.'

Inside the jar, the brownie was not looking quite so angry now. In fact, he had begun to tremble.

Tanya was horrified. 'They would have eaten him?'

'Oh, yes,' said Turpin. 'Is a good way to absorb more magic. The best way probably. So, you see? He should be thanking us.'

This time, Tanya didn't disagree. 'So back to my mother,' she said at last. 'What can we do?'

'Plenty,' said Turpin. 'How easy do you want it to be?'

'As easy as possible,' said Tanya.

Turpin held up the shimmering jar. 'Then this is the answer.'

'What is it?'

'Spidertwine.' Turpin unscrewed the lid and pulled out a shimmering, silver strand between her fingers. It was so fine it was almost invisible. 'Is magical, very strong. Unbreakable by mortals.'

Tanya frowned. 'Yes, I remember. But how can this help us?'

Turpin looked at her as if she were simple. 'We wait until she's asleep, then tie her up, silly!'

'I hope you're joking.'

'Is perfect!' Turpin insisted. She gave a wicked laugh. 'She won't be able to move at all! And we could even sew her lips up so she can't shout. Hey presto.'

'I am not tying my mother up!' Tanya said in exasperation. 'Or sewing her lips together. Good grief!'

Turpin scowled. 'You said you wanted it to be easy.'

'Yes, but I thought . . . oh, never mind.' Tanya rubbed her eyes tiredly. 'Do you have any sensible ideas?'

'We knock her out cold,' Turpin said sulkily. 'With a sleeping potion.'

'Now that has potential,' Don said.

'Go on,' Tanya said. 'How long would it last? And how would we make it?'

'Can last between a day and a week,' said Turpin. 'Depends how strong you brew it.'

'It takes the form of a tea, I believe,' said Don.

Turpin nodded.

'Does it taste like normal tea, though?' Tanya asked.

Turpin made a face. 'Oh, no. Tastes nasty.'

'Then she'll never drink it,' Tanya said. 'Isn't there another way? Sleep would be the best solution – she'd never know I was gone.'

A crafty look crept into Turpin's eyes. 'There is another way. A much simpler way, used by thieves and robbers in the night. The Sleep of the Dead.'

'I'm not sure I like the sound of that, either,' said Tanya.

Turpin rolled another jar into Tanya's lap. Tanya lifted it and examined the contents. It was filled with something dark and powdery. 'What is this stuff?'

'Graveyard dirt,' said Turpin proudly.

Tanya squeaked and tossed it away.

'Careful, stupid girl!' Turpin pounced on the jar and hugged it to her. 'You could have broken it!'

'Well, it's a horrible thing to be carrying around!'

'Is a very clever old trick,' said Turpin, clutching the jar protectively. 'Throw a handful of this at a house in the night and POOF! Everyone inside falls into a deep, deep sleep until the spell caster chooses to wake them. Is perfect.'

Tanya stared at the jar. Though she was repulsed by its contents, it certainly seemed a simple solution. 'That's all you have to do? Throw a handful at a house?'

'Easy-peasy,' said Turpin.

Tanya narrowed her eyes. 'Then why didn't you just tell me about this first?'

Turpin shrugged. 'Because humans are so squeamish.'

Tanya snorted. 'Because you wanted it for your thieving supplies more like.'

Turpin nodded, not embarrassed in the least.

'Fine,' said Tanya. 'The Sleep of the Dead it is then. Now we'd best get on.' She delved into the rucksack and took out the page from the spell book. It was a little rumpled from being bumped about, but otherwise undamaged. She smoothed it out on the bed. 'We have everything except for three things: a playing card, a mirror and an egg.' She got up and removed the mirror from the wall above the dressing table. 'That takes care of one. I'll find the other two, then as soon as my mother comes back into the cottage we'll sneak outside and throw the graveyard dirt to put her to sleep before I make the potion.'

'Excellent,' Don said brightly. 'All under control.'

But that was about to change, for, as Tanya left the room

in search of the playing cards her mother had brought, she became aware of voices from outside the cottage. There were several, one of which was her mother's, and there was something oddly familiar about the others. Curious, she crept closer to the door and listened.

'Are you quite sure it was my daughter you saw?' her mother was saying.

'Quite sure,' a smooth female voice confirmed.

Tanya's breath caught in her throat. She knew that voice! But how was it even possible . . .?

'Wait here.' Her mother sounded cross now. 'I'll go and get her.'

Tanya flung open the cottage door, making her mother jump.

'Oh. I was just coming to get you.' She gestured to three figures standing on the porch. 'These people have just told me something rather worrying about you, and I'd like you to tell me if it's true.'

Tanya stared into the eyes of the three people standing behind her mother and felt the blood draining from her face. At first glance, they could almost be taken for strangers, for indeed even she had never seen them like this before. But she knew them all right. The woman who had spoken was tall and pale, with long, black hair and an even longer black coat. There was a feathered trim at the collar and cuffs, and sitting by her side was the ugliest, scruffiest brown mongrel of a dog that Tanya had ever seen. Its fur was full of fleas and it wore a scruffy green collar.

Next to her were two men. The younger one was dark-skinned and wore a smart, green suit and a tie with a leafy pattern. His golden eyes watched her fiercely, yet there was a hint of a smile on his lips. The other man was dressed in an old-fashioned tweed suit and a hat a little like the one her grandfather had owned, with a telltale feather lodged in the band.

Tanya eyed the three fairies in horror. Never, ever had they allowed themselves to be seen by either of her parents before or appeared to her like this. Though overdressed and out of place, their wings and pointed ears were hidden and, no matter how unusual they looked, they still passed for human. Oddballs, perhaps, but definitely human. She had expected a punishment from the moment she had broken their rules about speaking to Ratty, but this? This was completely unexpected and meant only one thing: big trouble.

'W-what is it they're saying about me?' she asked.

'They're saying that they saw you jumping into the river,' said her mother, a little crease of worry forming over her eyebrows. 'Playing dares with a boy. Is it true?'

'Of course not!' Tanya gazed at her mother desperately. 'I told you – I fell in when the bridge collapsed!'

'But it only collapsed after it had been set fire to, didn't it, young lady?' said Feathercap.

Mrs Fairchild's mouth dropped open. 'You didn't say anything about a fire. Is that true?'

'Well, yes, but ' Tanya stammered.

'But she didn't want you to know that she and the boy

were the ones who started the fire in the first place,' Gredin said, giving her a hard look.

'But I didn't!' Tanya protested. 'We didn't! That's a rotten lie!'

'Did you know you have your T-shirt on inside out?' Raven said suddenly.

'I'm sure I don't,' said Tanya, her voice icy cold.

Her mother frowned. 'Yes, you do. There's the label. Go inside and put it on the right way, please.'

Tanya lost her temper. 'Well, what does it matter?' she shouted. 'These people are standing here telling lies about me and all you care about is whether my stupid T-shirt is on inside out?'

Her mother gripped her arm, hard. 'I care about whether you're dressed properly, not wandering around like a little scruff! You'll go and change it now. And then you'll come back here at once.'

Tanya wrenched her arm out of her mother's grasp and went into the cottage, slamming the door behind her. Tears pricked at the corners of her eyes as she tugged off the T-shirt and turned it in the right way. But she was not going to surrender her protection that easily. Perhaps she could slip an iron nail into her pocket out of the fairies' sight – and her mother's – or even turn her socks inside out. But what would they resort to, she wondered, if they couldn't use magic? She paused as a mad idea struck her. It would mean she had to play along, at least for a few moments, but it just might work.

She dashed into the bedroom. 'The graveyard dirt, where is it? I need it, quickly!'

'It's in there,' said Don, nodding to Turpin's sack. 'Whatever's wrong?'

'Everything.' Tanya snatched the bag and upended it. Its contents fell out in a jumble.

'Hey!' Turpin began. 'That's not yours!'

'And I bet half of it isn't yours, either,' Tanya retorted, spying the jar and grabbing it. 'Does this stuff work on fairies?'

Turpin folded her arms, suspicion twisting her mouth. 'Works on anyone who's inside the house. Why?'

'No time to explain.' Tanya scooped out a handful of dirt and shook it into her pocket. 'Just get out of the cottage, both of you, right now. Use the window and wait outside. Turpin, do you think you can hide near to the front of the cottage until I get everyone inside?'

'Of course,' Turpin said a little scornfully.

'Good. When you're sure we're all in, wait a minute or two, then knock at the door and hide. Got it?'

Turpin and Don nodded mutely. Tanya left the room and gently coaxed Oberon out of his snoozing spot under the table. She needed to make sure he was outside, too. 'Come on, boy, walk,' she lied, feeling only a little guilty. Oberon shot up immediately, scrabbling to get out of the door before she had even opened it.

At the sight of the fairies on the porch, he stopped dead, and would have retreated back inside had Tanya not shut the door quickly behind herself. Cautious, he approached the mongrelly Mizhog, sniffing it curiously. The Mizhog sniffed back and gave a little mew, obviously forgetting it was supposed to be posing as a dog. Oberon backed away, his tail firmly between his legs, and hid behind Tanya.

Mrs Fairchild regarded the Mizhog strangely. 'I've never heard a dog make that noise before. What kind is it?'

'Oh,' Raven said dismissively. 'No one really knows.'

'Are you sure it's all right?' Tanya's mother asked. 'Only it appears to be eating a slug.'

Raven gave a little laugh and nudged the Mizhog with her toe. 'Exotic tastes.'

Mrs Fairchild wrinkled her nose. 'Hmm.' She shook her head and turned to Tanya, examining her T-shirt. 'So, what do you have to say about all this?'

Tanya hung her head, doing her best to look gloomy. Her adrenalin began to race. 'Perhaps we should go inside.'

Her mother pursed her lips. 'Very well.' She turned on her heel and went in, holding the door open for the three visitors. One by one they went in. Tanya hung back, keeping her fingers on Oberon's collar. When the three fairies were inside, she slipped in after them, just managing to push Oberon's long, brown nose out of the way as she shut him on the porch.

As soon as she closed the door, a strange sensation came over her. Her mouth felt tingly, like little electrical pulses had taken over her tongue. It did not feel quite her own any more. She stared at the fairies in dread, knowing that some sort of spell had just been cast.

'Well?' her mother asked. 'This boy you were with. Do I even need to ask who it was?'

Next to her mother, and safely out of her eyeline, Gredin's lips moved silently.

'It was Ratty,' said Tanya's mouth, without any control of her own.

'Oooh,' said a familiar voice hidden nearby. 'Ooooooh. A tricksy spell! Thingy approves, oh, yes!'

'I thought as much. And the bridge?' Her mother's expression already registered disappointment, as though she knew what she was going to hear, yet there was still a faint glimmer of hope. 'Did you ... did either of you have anything to do with it catching fire?'

Of course not, Tanya tried to say, but her lips would not form the words. Instead, Gredin's lips moved again and a completely different sentence came out of Tanya's mouth. 'Ratty did it. I just watched. It was such fun seeing it go up in smoke!'

'Tanya!' Her mother's voice was stricken. 'How could you say something like that? Someone could have been seriously hurt!'

Tanya clenched her fists. She was powerless to defend herself, and the worst of it was that her mother now believed something of her that was completely untrue. It was just one of many, many things the fairies had done over the years, but each one had chipped away a little bit of the real Tanya in her mother's eyes and presented her with a version of her daughter that was untrue. A problematic, troublesome girl who revelled in mischief and went out of her way to cause it. It was so, so unfair.

'You're not to see that boy again,' said Mrs Fairchild.

'Can't stop me,' said Tanya. She pressed her hands to her mouth, but it was too late. The words were out and her mother's fury was growing by the second.

'We'll see about that,' her mother snapped.

Feathercap coughed politely. 'If you like, I could have a word with the boy's father?' he said. 'To let him know what's happened. It's only fair that the boy should be punished also.'

'Thank you, Mr . . .?'

'Feathercap.' Feathercap docked his hat and gave a little bow. 'Happy to oblige.'

'Mr Feathercap,' Tanya's mother repeated slowly, eyeing the fairy's cap. A look of doubt entered her eyes, but then vanished as Gredin delivered the final blow.

'Thank you, Mr Feathercap,' Tanya mimicked sarcastically. 'You nosy, interfering old troll!'

From under the floorboards, Thingy let out a delighted cackle.

A tear leaked from Tanya's eye and she swiped at it angrily. After what they had done this time, she no longer cared if the fairies were protecting her, or about their stupid rules. If this was what it took to save Ratty, then the rules had to be broken. *Hurry up, Turpin!* she thought. *Where are you?*

'Tanya, go and pack your things.' Her mother's voice was cold. 'We're leaving immediately.'

'Hurrah!' Thingy crowed. 'Finally! And good riddance!'

Three loud raps at the door silenced them all.

'Who on earth could that be?' said Mrs Fairchild. She started towards the door, but Tanya marched ahead of her, her heart pounding. This was it. It *had* to work.

She threw open the door. Already Turpin had vanished out of sight. Slowly, as though puzzled, she stepped out on to the porch, as if to look for whoever had knocked. The door swung shut with a creak, leaving her alone outside.

Quick as a fox, she darted off the porch and delved into her pocket, filling her fist with earth. Then she flung it at the cottage with all her might. It hit the walls and windows, coating it with a scattering of brown freckles. A fine powdery dust hung in the air for a few seconds before dissolving on the breeze . . .

. . . and a deathly stillness settled over Hawthorn Cottage.

20

The Missing Ingredient

TANYA STARED AT THE FRONT DOOR, terrified it was going to open at any moment. It remained closed, but a movement at the side of the cottage startled her. Turpin, Oberon and Don emerged from behind a thorny hedgerow.

'Did it work?' Don asked in a whisper.

'I don't know,' Tanya mouthed. Then she realised something. 'Oh, thank goodness! I can talk again!'

Don and Turpin looked sideways at each other.

'Never mind,' said Tanya. 'But it means it must have worked!' Otherwise, it stood to reason that Gredin would still be controlling her.

'Of course it worked,' said Turpin, strolling up the steps to the door. 'Turpin's tricks always work! Can't you smell it?' She sniffed the air. 'Magic!'

'No, but I can feel it,' Tanya answered. And she could. The bizarre stillness in the air surrounding the cottage remained. She followed Turpin to the door and opened it tentatively.

A peculiar sight awaited them. Tanya entered the

cottage, unable to tear her eyes away from the four figures – plus the Mizhog. She had expected to find them
slumped in the chairs or even on the floor, but instead they
were frozen almost in the positions she had left them in;
Gredin, Raven and Feathercap huddled together, the
Mizhog-dog halfway through scratching its fleas, and her
mother almost at the door, her hand outstretched. Yet
every one of them was in a deep slumber where they stood,
eyes closed and breathing deeply and peacefully.

'Who are these people?' Don asked, hopping into the
cottage.

'Fairies,' said Tanya. 'Though they're not usually as big as
this. They must be using glamour. They've visited me since
I was young.'

'Guardians then,' said Don.

She nodded. 'That's what Ratty said. They came to me
before, a few days ago, warning me not to talk to Ratty –
about fairies anyway.'

'Given what's happened, I suppose you wish you'd
listened,' Don said dryly.

Tanya didn't answer. It was too late for regrets now;
besides, Ratty needed her. She walked round the sleeping
figures. She had never imagined that she might be the one
to cast a spell over the fairies, or her mother for that matter.
It didn't seem real to see them like this, so vulnerable and
helpless.

'Should we ... move them?' she asked. 'What if they
topple over?'

'Even then they wouldn't wake up.' Turpin leaped on to the table and began picking over the contents of the fruit bowl. 'They'll only wake up when you tell them to.'

'Then let's get on with the spell,' said Don.

'Right.' Tanya finally managed to drag her eyes away from the sleeping statues and forced herself to concentrate. 'Those playing cards must be around here somewhere.' She poked around in her mother's handbag and checked the chair on the porch where her mother had been sitting, eventually finding them on a pile of board games at the side of the sofa. She pulled a joker from the pack and put the rest back in the box. Next, she took a smooth, brown egg from the fridge.

'That's everything,' she said, suddenly nervous. 'We're ready to start.' She gathered the rest of the ingredients and the page with the spell, and set them out on the table. 'Lay the mirror flat,' she read. 'Release the caterpillar and allow to crawl over the mirror.' She shook a caterpillar out on to the mirror, then lifted Don on to the table. 'Don, make sure it doesn't wriggle off. And don't you dare eat it – I can see you licking your lips.'

She turned back to the spell. 'Crack the egg into two halves, keeping the yolk in one and discarding the white.' She took the egg to the sink and cracked it. Luckily, she'd baked enough cakes with her mother to be able to keep the yolk successfully and allow the slimy white to slide down the plughole. Once accomplished, she returned to the table, where Don was gazing at the caterpillar longingly.

'Pierce the yolk with the fox's whisker. Add a shake of moon dust and a pinch of powdered chameleon. Stir well and leave to brew in the shell.' She found an egg cup in the kitchen cupboard and rested the shell in it. 'Oh,' she said, shuddering. 'I'm not looking forward to the next bit.'

Turpin peered at the spell and sniggered.

'Take the liar's tongue (take heed not to listen to its protestations or promises, for they are all untrue) and silence it by tying a knot around it with a thread of hangman's rope.' Tanya stared at the tongue in the jar. There was a smear of blood where it had been cut out, but it still looked fresh and pink. 'I don't suppose you want to do this bit, Turps?' she pleaded.

'Yikes!' Turpin shook her head. 'Turpin does not want to! Things like this make her glad she can no longer do magic.'

'Oh.' Tanya willed her churning stomach to be still and prised the lid off the jar. She paused. 'How exactly did you lose your magic anyway?'

Turpin stared at the caterpillar, her face solemn all of a sudden. 'Can't remember,' she muttered. Tanya watched her for a moment, certain that the fairy was not being truthful. The tip of her wing appeared to be trembling slightly and her eyes were far away, as though she were lost in some distant and troubling memory. It was clear she was not going to answer further and so, uncomfortable, Tanya continued with the spell.

'Wrap the tongue in the playing card and place on the mirror, then burn.' Grimacing, she reached into the jar and

261

took the tongue between her thumb and forefinger. It was warm and wet and, as soon as she touched it, it began to wriggle.

'It's not going to work, you know!' the tongue said in a whiny voice. 'It's all nonsense, a waste of a perfectly good tongue! If you take me back to my owner, I'll make you rich, I swear!'

'Quiet,' Tanya told it, giving it a shake. 'I'm trying to concentrate. Turpin, fetch me the matches from the kitchen.'

'No! No matches,' the tongue hissed. 'Come on, I'm telling the truth! Honest I am! I can take you to a stash of fairy silver . . .'

With her other hand, Tanya hooked out a thread of hangman's rope and looped it round the squirming tongue. With a flick of her fingers, she knotted the rope and, to her relief, the tongue fell still. She placed it in the playing card and rolled it tightly, then struck one of the matches. It seemed unlikely that the tongue would burn as it was wet, but as she held the match to the playing card the entire thing went up in a fierce, orange flame. Within seconds, it had burned away to thick, grey ash.

'When it is reduced to ash, add this to the egg mixture and stir again. Carefully transfer the mix into a clean glass vessel and drop the caterpillar into it.' Using one of the empty jars, Tanya carried out the instructions and picked up the caterpillar. 'Sorry about this,' she told it, dropping it into the eggy-ashy gunk. 'Secure and wait until the moon is visible in the sky. By this time, the caterpillar should have drunk the entire mixture. By the light of the moon, the afflicted should swallow the caterpillar without chewing. Transformation will occur when the first star appears in the night sky.' The three of them observed in silence as the caterpillar floundered in the nasty-looking mixture.

'It'll drown surely,' Tanya murmured, but the caterpillar bobbed happily on the surface, wriggling like a tiny eel. Tanya replaced the lid on the jar. 'Now we just have to wait until the moon is out.'

'Which gives us time to gather what we need for what's to come,' Don said gravely, 'and to collect the memory from its hiding place.'

'And when the memory is given back?' Tanya asked. 'You said . . . you said something terrible could happen.'

Don nodded. 'Yes. It could. But I don't plan on giving the memory back, or at least I won't allow it to be used. It's simply to be used as bait to get Henry returned to us.'

'But how do you plan on not letting it be used?' Tanya persisted.

'I'm still working on that.' Don looked up at her, then at Turpin. His blue eyes were watery. 'The important thing is that, when the time comes, the two of you must do what I tell you. *Exactly* what I tell you. Do you understand? Do you promise?'

'Turpin does not like promising,' said Turpin.

'But you will if it means getting Henry back,' Don said sternly.

'For Ratty, yes,' Turpin agreed.

'Good,' said Don. 'That's settled then.' He looked to Tanya. 'And you?'

She hesitated, uneasy, but there did not seem to be any other choice. 'I promise I'll do as you say,' she said at last. 'What do we need to take with us?'

'Protection,' Don replied. 'Everything you have that will defend yourself against fairies. Fetch whatever you can now.'

Tanya went into her room and collected the iron nail Ratty had given her. She slipped it into her pocket. In her mother's room, she found a red shawl which she stuffed into the rucksack along with a tub of salt from the kitchen cupboards.

'I think that's it,' she said, poking around in the rucksack. 'But I've still got the torch, too.'

'Keep it,' Don instructed. 'The torch could come in useful.' He went silent.

'What is it?' Tanya asked.

Don glanced at Turpin and sighed. 'I have reason to believe that we have another enemy. Someone, or rather something, that is also searching for the memory. Something that isn't fey.'

'Then what is it?' Tanya asked. 'Human?'

'Not exactly.' Don's voice was soft. 'Though it was created by one. By Henry, to be precise.'

'I don't understand,' said Tanya. 'If it's not human, and not fey, then what is it? And how . . . how could Ratty have created it?'

Don sighed again. 'I suggest you take a seat. It's time you knew the truth about the memory Henry stole.'

Silently, Tanya perched on a chair at the table, waiting for Don to collect his thoughts.

'Tell me,' Don said eventually. 'Were you especially imaginative as a young child?'

Tanya frowned, wondering where this was leading. 'My parents always thought so. They said I had an extraordinary imagination.' She cast a look at her mother, frozen in sleep by the cottage door. 'When I used to try to tell them about the fairies, that is. I haven't done that for a long time.'

'And did you have an outlet for your imagination?' Don asked. 'What I mean by that is did you tell a lot of lies or create especially inventive games?'

'I lied a lot to cover up for the fairies,' said Tanya, puzzled. 'But only because I had to, not because I wanted to.'

'No,' said Don. 'That's not quite what I meant. How about pictures? Did you draw much, or did you tell stories perhaps?'

'I made up stories,' said Tanya. 'Lots of stories. My parents encouraged me to write them down. At first, it was an easy way of describing the fairies and the things they did, but when the fairies found out they didn't like it. So I started to hide those stories and not show them to anyone, and I started writing different stories instead.' She paused. 'I'm not sure what any of this has to do with Ratty.'

Don gave a sad little smile. 'Rather a lot actually. You see, what I'm getting at is this: children with the second sight tend to be creative and have very powerful imaginations, often much more powerful than the average child who is unable to see fairies. Can you think of why that might be?'

'Well,' said Tanya, 'I suppose because we don't just want to believe in magic, like other children do. We know it exists because we see it all around us when others don't. And if we know fairies can exist then it makes it easier to believe in other sorts of magic . . . and to imagine it, too.'

'Precisely,' said Don. 'Well, like you, Henry was an imaginative child. Perhaps even more so. Though he had Turpin, his ability made it difficult to be friends with other children, as I'm sure you understand. Having the second sight can often be very lonely, and the thing Henry longed for more than anything was a little brother or sister. But, after his mother died, I never met anyone else. And so Henry invented one.'

'Invented one? You mean like an imaginary friend?'

'Yes,' Don replied. 'An imaginary friend. Lots of children have them. He named this friend . . .' He paused and took a shaky, almost fearful breath. 'Morghul.'

As he uttered the word, Turpin let out a little moan.

'Morghul,' Tanya repeated. It was the name the fairy had whispered when the shape-shifting creature had attacked them on the bridge, and again in the castle dungeons.

'It all began well enough,' Don continued. 'Whatever Henry did, Morghul did, too. I became so used to it that Morghul was talked about like it – he – was a real person.

Henry even insisted on having a place set for him at every meal. It seemed to keep Henry happy, for a while, and so I was happy, too. Well, Turpin was jealous, of course.'

Turpin sniffed, but said nothing.

'Anyway, we both thought it was something Henry would grow out of, in time,' said Don. 'And perhaps he would have, had it not gone on for so long, and if Henry were an ordinary boy. But ... but because we had allowed it and encouraged it, this, mixed with his belief, well ... it had unlocked something in his imagination. And, with Henry's imagination being so powerful, Morghul, too, took on some of that power.' Don's voice lowered to a whisper. 'And he became real.'

'Real?' Tanya repeated. 'Real enough for others to see, too?'

'Not at first.' Don's eyes were filled with guilt. 'Only Henry was able to see him. But, with the power of Henry's imagination, slowly but surely, he grew stronger. It was only when the time came that Henry outgrew Morghul and decided he didn't want him around any longer that everyone, including Henry, discovered just how strong Morghul had grown. Because he wouldn't go away, and Henry didn't know how to make him.'

'So Ratty's imagination not only created Morghul, but brought him to life,' said Tanya.

'Yes,' said Don. 'And now that Morghul was outgrown and unneeded, he grew angry and resentful. Instead of Henry being the one in control, things began to change.

Morghul's anger not only fed his power, it also made him cruel. He began to do things, things that got Henry into trouble. At first, it was put down to mischief on Henry's part, but, as the incidents grew more unpleasant, it was plain that Henry was afraid. And, in turn, that fear of Morghul lent him further strength still.'

'Like the fear of a bully,' Tanya murmured.

'I only realised the truth one day when Morghul turned his anger towards Turpin. Henry was now about six years old, and he and Turpin had been playing in the garden. One minute there was laughter and the next a terrible scream.' Don cast an apologetic look at Turpin.

'When I arrived outside, Henry was crying and Turpin was simply shaking. There was a horrid smell of . . . burnt flesh. Somehow or other, they had managed to unearth an old key in the garden. It was made of iron. At first, I thought that Turpin had accidentally dug it up, but then I saw the impression on the back of her hand. It had been pressed into her skin. Henry was hysterical by now. He said that Morghul had made him do it, and that, if he refused, Morghul would feed the key to Turpin in her sleep.' Don paused. 'If a fairy swallows iron, it will kill them.

'I was furious. Henry was ordered to his room with strict instructions to never speak of Morghul again. But as he was walking away . . . it was Turpin who saw it.'

'Saw what?' Tanya asked. She glanced at Turpin, but the fairy's face was stony, giving nothing away.

'Henry's shadow. It was sort of . . . separate from him. Still joined, but not quite mirroring his actions. Like it was something else. Once it knew we had noticed, it tried its best to mimic Henry's movements, but though it came close it was still out of step. And that's when I knew that Henry had been telling the truth, and that Morghul had become more than just a figment of Henry's imagination. I knew then that something had to be done, and that Morghul had to be sent back to wherever he had come from before he took over Henry completely. The problem was, neither Turpin nor I knew how. Because how do you get rid of something that's been created by the power of someone else's imagination?'

'You can't,' said Tanya. 'I mean . . . I guess only the person who imagined it in the first place has the power to un-imagine it.'

'Exactly,' said Don. 'And trying to convince a small boy to do such a thing – that he was even capable of doing such a thing – when Morghul was so real and so powerful . . . well. It was impossible. Henry's fear made it impossible, unless he learned to conquer it at least, and there was no telling how long that might take. So we began to try and think of another solution. And that's . . . that's when I remembered Solomon.'

'Solomon? That's the fey man you mentioned before,' Tanya realised. 'Whose memory Ratty stole.'

Don bowed his head. 'Yes. I'd known him since I was a boy. He lived next door—'

'Wait,' said Tanya. All this had started to sound familiar. 'Gretchen and Griselda lived next door to you . . .'

Don nodded and gave a weary sigh. 'Solomon is their brother. Like them, he not only had magic in his blood, but a great gift for it, too. He was focused and determined, always reaching towards the next level of greatness. He became a success; in both his secret practice of fey magic and his outward appearance as a doctor.' Don paused. 'A very, very good doctor, who could heal all kinds of ailments. Of course, those who knew him realised that magic was involved. And where was the harm in that? If it healed, what did it matter if it was magic or medicine? Over the years I lost touch with him, especially since everything that occurred with Gretchen and Griselda, but I heard that he had suffered a personal tragedy. He had fallen in love with a human woman, a dying patient whom he vowed to save. But though he tried everything he could, with both magic and medicine, the illness was just too strong. She died, leaving him devastated.

'Then, about six months before we sought his help with Henry, I bumped into Solomon by chance. He invited me for tea, so of course I went. We reminisced for a while, but I noticed he seemed distant, like something was troubling him. When pressed, he confessed that he had ambitions for a particular spell which he was sure was possible, only he hadn't quite figured it out yet. This spell, he said, would have the power to change lives, for, in essence, the spell was a life form itself. His aim, he told me, was to undo the suffering brought about by death – not only by preventing it, but by bringing loved ones back from the dead.'

'But that's a wonderful idea, isn't it?' Tanya said. She thought of her Nana Ivy, who had died two years ago and whom she missed terribly.

'Is it?' Don answered. 'Think about it a little more. We all have people we miss, and for whom we'd do anything to spend another day with them, or even another minute. But life isn't like that, and it's not meant to be. However difficult death is for us to accept, we must, because the alternative is far worse. The world would become crowded. The sick would cling to life, even if their illness meant no real life at all. And how would we learn to appreciate each moment if it were not precious? If life were forever?'

Tanya fell silent, digesting Don's words. Reluctantly, she had to admit that what he said was true.

'When I told Solomon my thoughts, he was angry,' Don went on. 'He said if I'd seen the suffering he had, I'd think differently. I didn't agree, but to spare further argument I said nothing else. When we parted, I thought no more about it or him, until we came to ask for his help in ridding us of Morghul. But when I saw him again I was shocked.'

'Why?' asked Tanya.

'He was thin and haggard, clearly not eating or sleeping properly, and was on the verge of losing his job. I felt uncomfortable, for he was rambling to himself about this elusive spell, and how if he could only figure it out then all would be well again. I almost left right then, for it was obvious he'd driven himself half mad in pursuit of this spell, whatever it was, and I didn't want to trouble him further.

Yet a spark of the old Solomon remained and he saw that I, too, was in distress and insisted I tell him what was wrong.

'When I explained, a feverish look came into his eyes. He became excited and said he was convinced he knew of a way to rid us of Morghul.' Don shook his head. 'Foolishly, I thought his enthusiasm came from the thought of helping Henry. Little did I know the truth.'

'Which was?' Tanya asked.

'That he had just found the answer to what he was looking for. The missing ingredient that would finally complete his spell.' Don closed his eyes and took a deep, shaky breath. 'Morghul.'

21
The Hidden Memory

'ORGHUL WAS THE INGREDIENT
Solomon needed to make the spell work?' Tanya
asked.

'Yes,' Don replied. 'As soon as Solomon heard about Morghul, he knew it was the key to unlocking the entire thing. For a spell so ambitious, he needed a vital ingredient to make it work: a life force. Up until then he had worked out that to undo death would take the cost of a life, but he could not bring himself to kill. After all, it was the opposite of what he wanted to achieve.' He paused. 'Given time, though, I often wondered if his desperation would have led him there, had we not brought him the solution. And what a perfect solution it was. A life form created entirely from the power of a child's imagination.'

'So what happened next?' said Tanya. 'Did he manage to free Ratty from Morghul?'

'He did,' said Don. 'But at great cost to us all.'

'What do you mean?' she asked, but Turpin's fist hit the table, snapping her back to the present.

'Enough talking,' the fairy said fiercely. Her face was scowling and red. 'Is growing later and later. Time for us to leave.'

'Yes,' Don said, shaking his head a little as though to free himself from the past. 'Turpin is right, we must go. It's time to collect the memory.'

Tanya rose from the table, placing the spell jar in the bag. Already the liquid inside had diminished a little; clearly, the caterpillar had been busy. 'I think we have everything,' she said.

'Not everything,' said Turpin. She hopped off the table and disappeared into the bedroom.

Tanya and Don waited expectantly, saying nothing. Sleeping noises filled the air and Tanya turned to watch the statue-like figures with a pang of guilt. It was the first time since her parents' divorce that she had seen her mother look peaceful. The little worried crease between her eyebrows was gone, and her lips moved softly, as though she were singing or speaking within her dreams.

Raven's and Feathercap's faces were blank and unreadable, but Gredin's wore a slight smirk. *Probably dreaming up some horrible punishment for me as payback for this*, Tanya thought dismally. A rumbling snore drew her attention to the Mizhog, but, though it was drooling heavily, the sound was coming from elsewhere. It was only then she remembered that someone else had been in the cottage when she had thrown the graveyard dirt: someone unseen.

'Thingy,' she whispered. She dropped to her knees, ears

straining to follow the noise. Oberon trotted over to her, his claws clicking softly. 'Where is it, boy?' she said. 'Where's it coming from?' Another snore, softer this time, sounded nearby. Oberon snuffled along the floorboards near to the coffee table. Tanya caught sight of a small section of wood lifting slightly under his paw. Using her nails, she prised the section of floorboard out and peered into the cavity below. An underground draught whistled out of the space.

'What are you doing?'

Turpin had appeared next to her, clutching two jars. One contained the shimmering Spidertwine and the other held the Cornish brownie.

'I think we just found our resident grudge-keeper,' Tanya answered. They stared into the space below the floorboards. There, amongst years of thick, grey dust and dirt, lay a pitiful figure, about half Turpin's size. He wore ragged, patched-up clothes, but his feet were bare. Matted hair stood out in a cloud from his head and his face was deeply lined. His mouth was open to display the broken, yellow teeth Tanya had glimpsed through the floorboards when she'd first arrived at the cottage. She remembered the anger and dread she had felt, but found that now all she felt was pity. Thingy snored again, then shivered in his sleep. Tanya reached out and touched his arm. It was painfully cold.

She reached into the cavity and gently lifted the little figure out, trying not to flinch as her hand broke through thick cobwebs. With her other hand, she replaced the floorboard. Then she got up and took the pathetic creature into her room and placed him in the bed, wrapping the covers round the cold little body.

'You sleep now, Thingy,' she told him. 'Sleep in the warm.' She leaned closer. 'I forgive you.'

The snoring paused and the faintest of smiles tweaked the corners of the fairy's mouth. Tanya left the room, brushing dust and cobwebs from her hands. Turpin was on the table, stuffing the Spidertwine and the brownie into the rucksack.

'Let's go,' said Tanya. She led the way, past the sleeping figures and out of the cottage. The stillness outside remained; it seemed even the birds were reluctant to sing. Her footsteps sounded loud and unwelcome on the path. 'Where is it we're going to anyway?'

'You know the place,' said Turpin.

'I do?'

'The place where you first met Ratty.'

Tanya thought back to her first encounter with Ratty, only days ago. It already felt much longer. 'The Wishing Tree,' she said.

The fairies along the wooded path to the meadow were strangely quiet as they trampled over the grass. Perhaps, Tanya thought, they were aware of the deterrents, or even the captive brownie, she carried with her, unless it was the presence of Turpin – one of their own – that explained the lack of sniggers and whispering she had encountered before. Either way, she welcomed their silence, for they were a distraction she did not need. Already she could feel a tight

276

little knot of fear in her stomach, but it was mixed with a curiosity to know more.

'You were telling me about Solomon,' she said in a low voice, watching as Turpin marched ahead with Oberon closely at her heel. She dropped back a little, to make sure the fairy was out of earshot. 'Before Turpin got upset.'

'That's right,' said Don, from the pocket of the rucksack. 'Where was I?'

'You said he managed to free Ratty from Morghul, but at a great cost. What did you mean by that?'

Don nudged the zip back a little further and pushed his head out into the open. 'When we took Henry to Solomon, we had no idea what he had in mind to resolve the problem. It turned out that Solomon had been researching ways to draw Morghul away from Henry and trap him, and he'd discovered an ancient ritual which he believed would work. Immediately, I was uneasy. The ritual was very dark magic and not something Solomon had performed before, though he assured us he could do it. And so, against my better judgement, I allowed myself to be convinced and for the ritual to go ahead.

'Henry was put into a trance. Solomon promised that he would have no memory of the events – or of Morghul – once the ritual was complete. He started to draw Morghul out, and for the first time we were able to see what Henry had created.' He shuddered. 'His fear had made it monstrous, a mix of creatures from every nightmare. As the separation progressed, Morghul started to lose his form. He became like a figure of melting wax, with no proper features, no proper face. Solomon assured us that this meant the ritual was working, for it was only Henry's imagination that gave Morghul his strength – and his form. But we had all underestimated Morghul's power. He didn't *want* to be separated from Henry. He clung on with every ounce of his strength.

'It was clear that even Solomon's power was not enough. He was out of his depth. I begged him to stop the ritual, to find another spell, but he refused. He screamed that this was the only way, and that he needed Morghul if his life's work were ever to be achieved. Then I realised the truth: that Henry was of little importance to him – he was just a means of getting Solomon's final ingredient for that wretched spell of his. And that's when Turpin – dear, loyal little Turpin – stepped in.

'She attacked Morghul with everything, all her physical and magical strength. It was terrible to behold. Poor Henry was caught between them like a piece of meat between lions. Morghul ripped away Turpin's wing. Physically, she was no match for him and it seemed all was lost. But perhaps it was her love for Henry which tipped the balance. Something in her overpowered him, and Morghul finally released his hold and fell aside, weakened.'

'Morghul is the reason Turpin lost her wing?' Tanya asked, stunned.

'And her power,' said Don. 'She used it all to sever him from Henry. She's never performed a single act of magic since. Afterwards, Henry woke from the trance, seemingly as he was before except that he showed no fear – nor any memory even – of Morghul, just as Solomon had promised. But I knew we had a problem. Solomon wanted Morghul for his spell – but Morghul was not Solomon's to keep. That was never part of the deal. And for the first time I saw a problem with what we had done, for, if Morghul had been created by Henry and was part of him, then what would happen if that part were used in Solomon's spell?'

'What are you two whispering about?' Turpin said suddenly.

Don stopped speaking abruptly and Tanya lowered her eyes, unable to meet the fairy's gaze. She had been so caught up in Don's tale she had not noticed Turpin had slowed down to allow them to catch up.

'Oh, nothing much,' Don said cheerfully. 'Just how I'm looking forward to not being a blasted toad any more.' His tongue shot past Tanya's ear, snaring a midge out of the air. 'See what I mean? It really is an embarrassment.'

'Hmm,' Turpin said, her tone disbelieving.

'We're nearly there,' said Tanya, eager to change the subject. Now she knew the truth about the loss of Turpin's magic, she could understand why the fairy was so reluctant to speak of it. 'Look, there's the tree.'

Up ahead, the Wishing Tree sparkled in the sunlight. Its beauty still took Tanya's breath away. Behind it, the castle paled in comparison, just a grey shape on the horizon.

'This is where you hid the memory?' Tanya asked. She

gazed around them into the vast area of grass and trees. Between the tree and the castle, there was nothing else. 'Did you bury it somewhere?'

'You'll see when we get there,' said Don. 'Keep going.'

They walked the rest of the way in silence, shattered only by a fit of sneezing from Oberon as he disturbed a dandelion clock. The tree was asleep when they approached, or was pretending to be. Tanya caught sight of it peeking out of one eye before quickly snapping it shut.

'Young lady, fetch me down, would you?' Don said.

Tanya took the toad out of the rucksack and set him on the ground. He hopped closer to the tree and cleared his throat. The tree opened its eyes and yawned lazily, looking straight past Don and fixing Tanya with a bored look.

'Back again to be a pest?' it asked. 'Or at last with a request?'

'Um, actually,' Tanya began, 'it's not me who . . .'

'I really haven't got all day.' The tree looked snooty now. 'Make your wish or go away.'

'There's no need to be rude,' Tanya retorted.

'Ahem,' said Don. 'I have some business to attend to, if you don't mind.'

The tree blinked, noticing Don for the first time.

'Wishes are for human folk,' it said. 'Not animals who talk and croak.'

'I am a human,' Don said haughtily. 'Or at least I will be again, by tonight.' He puffed out his chest. 'Anyway, it's quite obvious you don't remember me. I was here one night, several years ago. I made a very particular wish and I've now come to collect.'

'If that's the case, then you must know a special phrase to prove it's so,' the tree answered.

'Of course,' said Don. 'The password is forget-me-not.'

'How curious. I don't recall your wish or special phrase at all.'

Don stared at the tree, stricken. 'B-but ... that is the phrase. That's the password! I know it is!' He shook a fist at the tree. 'You crook! I trusted you with my wish and you've lost it! Do you know what this means? What you've cost us?'

'Temper, temper! Do stay calm,' said the tree. 'There's really no cause for alarm. I see my little joke fell flat; I shouldn't have attempted that.'

'Joke?' Don growled. 'You mean to say—?'

'No wish made here has been forgotten – even if it's really rotten. Each wish that's made, both great and small, I can immediately recall.'

Don glared at the tree. 'I really don't find that amusing. Now kindly give me what I asked for.'

The tree smirked and winked at Tanya. 'No sense of humour, what a bore. Oh, well, I shan't joke any more.' Two of the tree's branches spread out overhead – a little like arms, Tanya thought – sending coloured ribbons and wish bottles swaying in the air. One of the branches came lower and lower, until it was almost touching Don's nose. Then a curious thing happened.

A knot in the end of the branch began to untwist and

widen, much like the tree's eyes and twig-toothed mouth. But this was no facial feature. Instead, the knot grew wider and larger until it was in the distinctive shape of a keyhole and about the size of a dinner plate.

'You wished for this to stay concealed,' the tree said, solemn now, 'and only on your word revealed. I kept your secret hidden well, but now it's time to break the spell. So reach inside the hidey-hole; it's time to take back what you stole. And, once retrieved, that's it, my friend. Your one wish is at its end.'

'Tanya, you'll have to do it,' said Don. 'It'll be too heavy for me.' He nodded at the nook in the tree. Tanya stepped closer and knelt down, then plunged her hand into the dark knot within the branch. Her fingers slid over something cool and smooth. Carefully, she lifted it out and, with a rustle, the branch withdrew, leaving her staring at the object in her hand.

It was an hourglass, beautifully crafted into the form of two golden hands. Within the palms sat two gleaming glass globes, joined by a thin flute of glass in the middle. The lower of the two was filled with fine, gold sand. It seemed to warm in her hands, and a faint whispering sound floated up from it, reminding Tanya of the objects in Ratty's jar.

'This is it,' she said. 'The hidden memory?'

'Yes,' said Don. 'It belonged . . . belongs to Solomon.'

'All the time it's been hidden here,' Tanya said in wonder. 'Within the tree itself.'

Don's chest puffed with pride. 'I needed a hiding place

that, even if it were ever discovered, could never be breached by anyone other than me. I'd heard about the Wishing Tree several years before, but had never known whether to believe it was true. After that night, I knew I needed a hiding place and decided to take a chance. And what better way than to use my wish? Like I said before, it was a stroke of genius.'

The tree chortled. 'Genius? That's pushing it! Though it was clever, I'll admit.'

Don ignored it. 'I knew that as long as the tree remained here, the memory was safe. It was the perfect way to check without being obvious; I only had to see the tree, never the hourglass itself, to know it was safe. The magic of the wish was enough to protect it.'

'And with the tree being such an important part of Spinney Wicket's history there was little chance it would ever be cut down,' Tanya said. She was finding it hard to concentrate now, for the whispering sound was growing louder and more insistent, like it *wanted* to be listened to. She remembered when she had discovered Ratty burying the jar of objects; how the memories had stirred and began whispering at her fingertips.

'Cut down? No way, I'm a VIP!' said the tree. 'A superstar celebrity! I'm Spinney Wicket's number one. The top, the best, second to none!'

'All right, we get the picture,' Don cut in. 'You're in no danger of being cut down any time soon.'

'But there's always lightning,' Turpin said wickedly. 'And

gales and hurricanes that blow up and dig out trees by their roots . . .' She grinned at the tree's horrified face.

'Turpin,' Don said sternly. 'Stop tormenting it.'

'Well, it needed taking down a peg or two,' said Turpin. 'Turpin has met many trees, but never one so vain as this.'

'Call me proud or vain or haughty,' the tree said, 'at least I'm not a thief who's naughty.'

Turpin began to protest, but her voice sounded far away. The hourglass in Tanya's hand felt warmer still, and the whispers grew into fully-fledged voices, some of which she recognised and some she didn't. An image danced briefly before her eyes: the hourglass in someone else's hands. A child this time, with familiar blue eyes and black hair. *Ratty.*

Unable to resist, she closed her eyes and succumbed to the memory. It came in flashes, just the way Don had described. In a darkened room, almost like a hollowed-out cave, a thin man with grey hair and thick glasses stood hunched over a huge, black cauldron, chanting frenziedly in words Tanya could not understand. She recognised him immediately as the man who had taken Ratty from the clearing. At the side of the room, Don and Turpin watched tensely, their eyes fixed upon the small boy.

Ratty's own eyes were glazed, his expression completely blank. In his hands, he held the hourglass. Inside, the globe at the top was full, with the thinnest trickle of sand escaping into the bottom half.

The vision was interrupted by Turpin's voice in the

present, unleashing a string of insults directed at the tree. Tanya caught a few choice words, but the pull of the memory was stronger. This time, when she returned to it, half of the sand had escaped into the bottom of the hourglass and Ratty, still in his trance, was caught between two figures in a savage tug of war. Turpin fought like a feral cat, her teeth bared and her hair wild. Against the pale, melted-wax figure of Morghul, it seemed all was lost. There was a terrible scream as her wing was ripped away, floating to Don's feet.

'Turpin!' he yelled, then turned to Solomon. 'Make it stop! You *have* to stop it, he'll kill them both!'

'No,' screamed Solomon. 'I'm so close! The creature is mine!'

Don's face drained of colour as Solomon's intentions became clear. He wanted Morghul, *needed* him for the spell he'd spent so long working on.

'Solomon, I beg of you . . .' Don whispered.

Stop, Tanya felt herself pleading. *Please, stop!*

But Solomon was not listening. A wild look entered his eyes and he continued to chant. His bespectacled eyes slid over the hourglass. The sand was almost gone.

A blinding flash of light lit the cavern. Solomon was thrown back. He hit the wall with a horrid crack, then lay motionless, his spectacles shattered. Morghul let out a roar, releasing Ratty from his clutches. A gilded cage sprung up around him and he gripped the bars, howling with rage. At the same moment, a golden key appeared on a chain around Ratty's neck. Turpin clung to him, sobbing and shaking.

285

Glittering, fiery embers ebbed away from her, vanishing into the darkness. Her magic, Tanya realised.

Ratty blinked, as if awaking from a deep sleep. 'What happened?' He stared at the hourglass in confusion, then at Solomon. 'That man . . . he took something from me.'

Don rushed to his side. 'Yes. You . . . you were sick, remember? The man made you better.'

'Is he all right?' Ratty asked. 'He looks hurt.'

Don did not answer. He cast a glance at the cage, where Morghul's howls had faded into confused whimpers.

'What's in the cage?' Ratty asked.

'Nothing,' Don muttered. 'It used to be a monster, but it can't hurt anyone now.' He drew Ratty into his arms. 'We have to leave,' he told Turpin urgently. 'Before Solomon wakes. And we . . . we have to take Morghul with us. We can't leave him here, not for Solomon to use.'

'What will we do with it?' Turpin said weakly.

'I don't know,' Don muttered. 'But I'll think of something.'

'We're taking the monster with us?' Ratty asked. 'Why?'

'Because . . . because the man wants to do a spell on him,' said Don. 'A bad spell. And we can't let that happen. But you don't need to be afraid. The monster won't be with us for long.'

'Solomon will come after us,' Turpin hissed. 'He will never rest until he finds what he's looking for!'

'He'll have to find us first, though, won't he?' said Don. 'Anyway, what other choice do we have?'

'What if I make him forget?' said Ratty.

'Don't be silly, Henry,' Don began.

'I'm not,' Ratty said solemnly. 'I can make people forget things now.'

Don stared. 'What do you mean?'

Ratty rubbed his eyes with one hand, still clutching the hourglass with the other. 'I don't know. I just know that I can.'

Turpin and Don looked at each other.

'The spell,' Turpin whispered. 'When Solomon made him forget, it must have done something . . .' She gave a slight nod.

'You think you can make the man forget all about the monster?' Don placed his hands on Ratty's shoulders, searching his eyes. 'It's very important that he mustn't remember anything about it at all.'

Ratty nodded.

'Are you sure?'

'I'm sure.'

'All right then,' Don said.

Ratty turned the hourglass, releasing the sand. He closed his eyes, a look of intense concentration on his face. His lips moved soundlessly. Behind them, Solomon stirred and muttered, but did not wake.

'Turpin,' Don whispered. 'Gather Solomon's books, notes . . . everything you can find. He must never find out that Morghul is the missing ingredient to his spell. Quickly now, before he wakes.'

Turpin scurried around the room, collecting armfuls of books and scraps of paper.

Don reached out and took the key from around Ratty's neck. Warily, he approached the cage. Morghul stared through the bars, his expression unreadable.

'If you know what's good for you, you'll leave this place and never return,' Don warned. 'You'll go somewhere you can't be found, the fairy realm perhaps.' He jerked his head towards Solomon. 'Just be sure of this: if he ever finds you, finds out what you are, you'll cease to exist. He'll destroy you. And finally, wherever you go, you don't come anywhere near Henry ever again. Understand?'

Morghul bowed his head and nodded in defeat.

'Very well.' Don unlocked the cage and Morghul lumbered out of it, still sluggish from the effects of the ritual. 'Turpin, do you have everything? All the notes you can find on the spell?'

'All that can be found,' said Turpin, armed with books and papers. She stood over her wing, staring at it sadly. It was torn and trampled on the ground.

Don caught sight of her face. 'Perhaps we could save it. If we can get some Spidertwine—'

But Turpin shook her head. 'No. Is done now. Beyond repair.'

Don nodded and moved to Solomon's side. 'Now we just need to take care of Solomon to give ourselves a head start.' He stooped and lifted the sorcerer under the arms. 'Hold the cage door open for me . . .'

Slowly, and as Solomon began to stir, Don dragged him across the floor and bundled him into the cage, then locked it and pocketed the key.

'What . . .?' Solomon's eyes opened behind his shattered spectacles. 'What are you doing? Don? Why am I in this cage?'

Don didn't answer. Instead, he scooped Ratty into his arms. 'Put that down,' he said, trying to prise the hourglass from the little boy's hands, but Ratty held on.

'No, we have to take it with us or the man will remember,' he said in a small voice.

Don's fingers loosened on the hourglass. 'The memory is in this?'

Ratty nodded.

'We must hide it,' Turpin hissed. 'Somewhere it can never be found.'

'All right.' Don shooed Turpin in front of him, casting a fearful glance at Solomon, then at Morghul who had retreated to the shadows, still confused. 'Let's go.'

'Wait!' Solomon shouted. 'Where are you going? And what are you doing with my hourglass? Bring it back! Return it, I say!'

But his words went unheard, for he was alone.

The vision ended and Tanya blinked, dazed. She saw that Don was watching her closely. Turpin, however, was oblivious, still wrapped up in exchanging insults with the tree.

'Turpin could destroy you with a single match!' she was yelling.

289

'Huh! Says you, a measly flea,' the tree shot back. 'A squirt, a pest! No "match" for me!'

'You saw, didn't you?' Don asked. 'You saw the memory.'

'I didn't mean to,' said Tanya. 'It just . . .'

'It's all right,' said Don. 'I know. If you touch an object for too long, it overpowers you. Goodness knows I've done it myself enough times over the years, with things Henry left lying around.' He paused. 'You understand now, don't you? How he got his ability.'

'I think so,' said Tanya. 'It happened when Solomon did the ritual. When he took Ratty's memory of Morghul, somehow Ratty became able to take memories from other people.'

'Yes.' Don gazed at the hourglass. 'I think it was partly to do with being separated from Morghul, and being forced to forget him, when he was such a big part of Henry's imagination. But also I think . . .' He hesitated. 'I think it was partly to do with Turpin sacrificing her magic to sever the bond between them. I think some, or maybe even all, of her magic was absorbed by Henry. It did something to him and somehow he knew it instinctively.'

'And so it really did cost you all something,' Tanya realised. 'Turpin lost her magic, and you and Ratty lost your freedom. All these years you've been running and hiding.'

'And all these years I should have known that running and hiding would never solve the problem,' Don said. 'Now Henry's gone and it's all my fault.'

'But we'll get him back,' said Tanya. 'We'll find him . . .'

She trailed off. 'Wait, how do we even know where to go? Where Solomon is keeping him?'

'We don't,' said Don. 'Which is why we have to let Solomon come to us. And it's only a matter of time before he will.'

'Unless ...' said Tanya. She chewed her lip, thinking. 'Unless we bring Ratty here.'

Don shook his head. 'How?'

'Yes, how?' Turpin demanded, her argument with the tree forgotten.

'Because ...' Tanya stared at the tree. It raised a mossy eyebrow. 'I haven't used my wish yet.' Her mind raced, along with her heart. A lump had risen in her throat and she swallowed it away. 'I'm so silly. All this time, I could have used my wish to bring Ratty back to us, but I didn't think of it. I was too ... too selfish.' She fell silent, thinking of her parents, and her plan to wish them back together. Apart from wishing for the fairies to leave her alone, it was the only thing she had ever really wanted.

'No,' Don said sadly. 'Wishing Henry back to us wouldn't solve anything, not really. We'd still have to hide and live in fear. It's time that stopped and Solomon is dealt with once and for all. Besides, your wish should be your own. It's not selfish to want something for yourself. It would be wrong of me to let you, especially when you've already done so much.'

'That's just it, though,' said Tanya. 'It *is* a selfish wish. It's completely selfish and wouldn't change anything. I was going to wish for my dad to come home. But, even if he did, everything would be the same as before. The arguments, the unhappiness. None of that would change. So now I don't know what to wish any more. All I know is that I want to help Ratty.'

Don's eyes glistened with tears. 'Are you sure?'

'I'm sure,' she said. 'And if I can't wish him back to us then the only other way is to wish us to him.'

22

Tempus Fugit

THE WISHING TREE LOOKED FROM TANYA to Don and then back again.

'Finally, Miss Fussy. You have a wish for me?' it said. 'Then speak it loud or hang it up so I can make it be.'

'Just a minute,' said Tanya. 'There are a few things I'd like to check before I say the words.'

The tree rolled its eyes. 'Here we go. I might have known with you there'd be a snag. Rules and regulations – could there be a bigger drag?'

Tanya put her hands on her hips. 'You're the one who warned me to be careful what I wished for, so I'm doing just that. Firstly, I want to know if a return journey is possible. And secondly, can I decide exactly when we leave and when we come back?' She looked up at the sky. It was now late afternoon; Don would not be able to take the potion until the moon was visible, and that was several hours away. Worryingly, there were a number of dark clouds looming over the castle.

'A cheeky wish, but just this once I'll do a return ticket,' the tree replied. 'Though only if the final stop is here in Spinney Wicket.'

'That's fair enough,' said Tanya. 'What about the timings?'

'After wishing, take a twig and keep it safe with you. Once you're ready to depart, just snap it clean in two. When you want to come back here, you make those two twigs four, and Spinney Wicket is the place you'll find yourself once more.'

The tree lowered a branch towards her and Tanya took a twig in her fingers hesitantly. 'Are you sure this won't hurt?'

'If it does, let Turpin do it,' Turpin muttered under her breath.

'It's just a tickle, not a pain,' said the tree. 'I'm sure to grow it back again.'

Tanya broke off a twig that was around the size of her hand and carefully stashed it in the rucksack. 'One last thing. If it's a certain person we want to be taken to, rather than a place, how do we know you'll get it right?'

'It's not the tree who gets it wrong, but you who makes a mess,' said the tree. 'Do you have an object that this person once possessed?'

Tanya looked at Turpin. 'I don't have anything of Ratty's, apart from the iron nail he gave me which I don't really think counts. Do you?'

Turpin shook her head. It was no use asking Don, of course. He had no possessions with him at all.

'We could go to the van,' Don said. 'But it's a risk.

Solomon or Morghul could be lying in wait. If we want the element of surprise on our side, then we have to find them before they find us.'

'Wait ...' said Tanya. 'We have the hourglass. That belongs to Solomon and, even if he's not with Ratty when we arrive, he's bound to lead us to him.'

'Of course!' said Don. He looked relieved, then glum. 'I think this toad lark is addling my brain. I'm getting slower and stupider by the day.'

Turpin patted him on the head, with a look that said she plainly agreed.

Tanya took a step towards the tree. 'I'm ready to make my wish now.'

'About time, too,' the tree said lazily. 'I've never known someone to dawdle so. Make it quick, I'm due a nap. Now wish and off you go.'

'Charming,' said Tanya. She took a breath, setting the words out in her mind. 'I wish for us to be taken to the owner of this hourglass and brought back again, both at the moments I choose.'

'As you wished it will be done.' The tree yawned. 'I hope the next wish is more fun.'

'Well, sorry to disappoint you,' said Tanya. She put the hourglass in her rucksack, preparing to leave. 'But thank you, all the same.'

The tree's only response was a little snore.

Tanya looked at the sky again. The clouds had grown heavier over the castle and were reaching towards the sun.

295

'Come on,' she said to Turpin and Don. 'Let's go back to the cottage. All we can do now is wait for nightfall.'

Back at Hawthorn Cottage, the hours crawled by as they waited for sundown. While Don repeatedly checked on the caterpillar's progress in the spell jar, Tanya prepared a simple meal of pasta for herself and Turpin, and found some more creepy-crawlies for Don to eat. Thankfully, she told herself, this should be the last time.

Meanwhile, Turpin amused herself by ransacking Mrs Fairchild's make-up bag. By the time Tanya realised what she had done, Turpin had not only smeared her own face to resemble that of a clown's, but had also turned her attention to the sleeping figures. Not even the Mizhog had been spared.

'Wipe that off now!' Tanya scolded, collecting her mother's make-up and putting it out of reach. Turpin did as she was told, but smirked all the while.

Finally, darkness fell outside. Yet, as the three of them gathered by the window to watch for the moon, Tanya's fears were confirmed, for the sky was thick with cloud with only the faintest of glows hinting at where the moon lay hidden behind them.

'Now what?' said Turpin. She flicked the spell jar irritably. The caterpillar, which had been crawling up the side, fell to the bottom. Sure enough, the rest of the jar was empty with no trace of the mixture in sight.

Tanya pointed. 'Look. There's a break in the cloud over

there. It looks like it'll reach the moon in the next few minutes.'

They watched anxiously as the gap floated nearer. It was maddeningly slow, changing shape as it approached.

'It's getting narrower!' said Don. 'It's going to miss it!'

For a moment, Tanya feared he was right, but at the last second the break widened once more to reveal a brilliant sliver of silver in the sky. 'Quickly, open the jar,' she said. 'And remember not to chew!'

Turpin took off the lid with barely enough time to move her hand before Don's tongue shot out, so quickly that none of them saw the caterpillar disappear.

'Look for a star,' Tanya said, but it was too late. The moon vanished, swallowed by the cloud once more. She searched the sky in vain. 'I don't see any more gaps.'

'Then what shall we do?' Don asked. 'The potion's only good for one night. What if a star never appears?'

'One has to sooner or later,' said Tanya. 'We'll just have to keep watch for it. But until then I think we should just go.'

'Go?' Don croaked. 'Now? But what good am I as a toad? Solomon will laugh in my face.'

'Not if he doesn't see you at first,' said Tanya. She thought quickly. 'It could even give us an advantage, you being a toad.'

'How?'

'Because if it's just me and Turpin he'll be less worried. He doesn't know the three of us are together. Even if Morghul saw us at the fairground today, he would only have seen Turpin and me because you were hidden in the rucksack. And with you being that size it'll be easier for you to sneak away if you have to, until the right moment comes when you can transform.'

'Is a good plan,' said Turpin.

Don looked unconvinced, but did not argue. 'All right,' he said reluctantly.

Tanya helped Don into the pocket of the rucksack, then checked its contents one last time. The Cornish brownie must have tired itself out, for it lay sleeping in the bottom of its jar. Tanya slipped the iron nail into her pocket. Her pulse had begun to race. 'Oh, I almost forgot.' She sat down and took her shoes off, quickly turning her socks inside out. 'Right, I'm ready.'

'Remember that the protection will only work against fairies if they try to use magic,' Don warned. 'Solomon can still harm you in other ways and so can Morghul. And ...' He paused, glancing at Oberon. 'Must you bring the dog?'

'Of course,' said Tanya. 'Why wouldn't I?'

'Well, he's not exactly known for his bravery, is he?' Don scoffed. 'He was even afraid of the Wishing Tree.'

'He wasn't afraid,' Tanya bluffed. She rested a protective hand on Oberon's head. 'He was just ... confused. He's as brave as a lion when he needs to be.'

Don sniffed and began to say something else, but Tanya zipped the pocket shut and hoisted the rucksack on to her back a little more vigorously than usual. She knelt again and put a hand on Oberon's collar. 'Turpin, hold on to me,' she said. Turpin dutifully hopped up on to her shoulder. With her free hand, Tanya broke the twig in two. There was a crisp snap that sounded unnaturally loud, and a rush of freezing air whooshed past Tanya's face, forcing her eyes closed.

When she opened them again, the cottage was gone. Instead, she found herself on a busy street, where people jostled past, knocking into her and tutting. She toppled, caught off balance, then managed to right herself and darted quickly to the side of the pavement. Though it was dark, the street was more brightly lit than most and full of noise. She stared around, trying to get her bearings.

Across the street people queued outside a huge, grand theatre. Either side of it, restaurants and pubs heaved with people and noise. The air smelled stale and familiar, and then Tanya spotted something unmistakable: a red double-decker bus.

'What is this place?' Turpin said in obvious disgust. She gagged. 'Iron, iron everywhere. It stinks.'

'We're in London,' said Tanya. 'Though I'm not sure which part.'

'Well, it stinks!' Turpin lifted her foot and examined the underside of it in a temper. A stringy glob of chewing gum stretched from her sole to the pavement. 'London *stinks*!'

'London is my home,' said Tanya softly. 'And I happen to quite like it.'

There was a sharp prod through the rucksack as Don

poked her impatiently. 'Never mind that. Where's Solomon?'

'I don't know,' she said. 'There are so many people, it's hard to see them all.' She glanced up at the sky. 'And it's just as cloudy here as it was in Spinney Wicket.'

'Great. Wonderful,' Don retorted. 'I'm doomed to remain as a toad, and that blasted tree has muddled things up good and proper.'

Tanya leaned into the wall. Something must have gone wrong with her wish, it was the only explanation, and, to top it all off, she was attracting curious glances from some of the passers-by.

'You lost, kid?' a ruddy-faced man asked. He staggered slightly and a strong smell of beer wafted off his clothes.

'No, just waiting for my dad,' Tanya lied.

The man suppressed a burp and moved on, knocking into a harassed-looking figure carrying a battered suitcase who was coming in the opposite direction. Tanya was just on the verge of looking away when she spotted something: a glimpse of grizzled hair flying out from beneath the dark hood. The figure gave an angry growl at the man, then turned swiftly into a dark little side street.

Instinctively, Tanya began to follow.

'Where are we going?' Turpin asked, still trying to extract herself from the chewing gum.

'I think we just found Solomon,' Tanya said in a low voice.

There were fewer people on the side street, which consisted largely of shops interspersed with one or two late-night cafés. The figure stopped up ahead, fumbling in a shop entrance. Tanya slid into a nearby doorway, tugging Oberon and Turpin in with her. She listened hard and heard a creak as the door opened, then closed after the figure slipped through it.

Tanya emerged from her hiding place and approached the shop into which the figure had vanished. Through a small glass pane in the door she could just make out a dim light coming from the back of the shop, but the windows either side were dark, and a sign hanging up said CLOSED.

'*Tempus Fugit*,' Tanya read from the sign jutting out of the wall. 'What does that mean?'

'It's Latin,' Don announced. 'It means "time flies".'

'Time flies,' Tanya repeated. She peered into the window at a cluttered display of antique watches and an old grand-father clock. 'But why would Solomon come here?' she wondered. 'Perhaps I was mistaken and it wasn't him.' She went to move away, but a squeak from Turpin stopped her.

'Look,' the fairy hissed, her nose pressed to the glass of the second window. 'Look!'

In amongst an equally jumbled display of clocks and watches, a cluster of hourglasses sat in one corner of the window. They were various shapes, sizes and colours, some simply designed while others were more intricate.

'Hourglasses,' Tanya whispered. 'Of *course*. Solomon knew Ratty had taken the hourglass, so if he was trying to track it down this is exactly the sort of place he'd come looking for it.'

Don poked his head out of the pocket and examined the sky. It was still full of cloud, with no stars in sight. 'Be careful.'

Tanya tested the door, but it had shut firmly.

'I wonder if there's a back way,' she said.

'No need for a back way.' Turpin elbowed her aside and dug something out of her sleeve – a plastic hairpin, probably stolen from Tanya's mother's make-up bag. She inserted it into the lock. With a jiggle and a click, the door was open.

'You're far too good at that,' said Tanya, half admiringly and half appalled.

Turpin beamed.

Cautiously, Tanya pushed the door open, holding her breath as it creaked softly again. Beyond it, the shop lay in darkness except for a few small lights that had been left on in display cabinets. There was no sign of the dark figure, but another door at the back marked PRIVATE was ajar. She closed the front door quietly and headed towards the other one, listening.

A muttered voice drifted through it, so faint that Tanya could not make out the words. She pushed the door open soundlessly.

'Careful,' Turpin murmured.

Ahead of them were three more doors, the first of which opened on to a storeroom full of boxes and the second to a small kitchen. To Tanya's left was a set of stairs leading down. Yet another stack of boxes, empty this time, was piled up beside it. 'There must be a cellar,' she whispered. The third door was open a crack and, from there, the muttering could be heard. Tanya and Turpin crept closer, then Tanya felt a light nip on the back of her ankle. She bit her lip and turned round. Oberon sat by the stairs, his tail wagging gently.

'He's trying to tell us something,' Tanya mouthed. 'I think Ratty's down there!'

'We must go to him—' Turpin began, but a loud thump from the third room made them both freeze.

'No, no, NO!' Each word was punctuated with a smashing sound. 'None of these is it!'

Recovering herself, Tanya edged her way to the door and peered through the crack. The room beyond was crammed full of shelves of dusty or broken items, a few of which were clocks but the vast amount were hourglasses. Hundreds of them, lining the walls and stacked up in haphazard piles. In the corner of the room, a man with grey hair and thick glasses sat hunched over a table, glowering at a pile of smashed hourglasses.

Solomon.

With a sweep of his arm, he sent the fragments flying to the floor, where they shattered on a pile of previously discarded hourglasses.

Solomon leaned back, removing his spectacles to massage the bridge of his nose. 'It's out there somewhere,' he murmured to himself. 'Haunting me. Eluding me. I can *feel* it.'

And it's closer than you know, Tanya thought, dread creeping through her. She backed away, tugging Oberon and Turpin into the storeroom as Solomon got up and stomped to the door. They waited as the sound of his footfall faded down the cellar steps.

'What do we do now?' Tanya asked. She slipped the rucksack off her shoulders and turned it to look at Don. 'If Ratty is down those steps, Solomon is with him. And you're still a toad! Solomon's not going to bargain with me – if I go down there and hand him the hourglass, he'll take it off me and probably keep me prisoner with Ratty, too. We need to get you turned back.' She peered round a stack of boxes. 'Look, here's a window.' She thought quickly. 'If I put you on the window ledge, you can watch for a star. In the meantime, Turpin and I can create a diversion to find Ratty and get him out.'

'What kind of diversion?' Don asked. He looked hopefully at the window. A ribbon of navy sky was visible between the cloud, but no stars.

'By using this.' Tanya pulled the hourglass from the rucksack. 'If I can get Solomon to play a little game of hide-and-seek, Turpin can sneak into the cellar and free Ratty. By the time Solomon finds the hourglass, you'll hopefully be ... well, *you* again and you can tackle him.'

'And if I'm not?' Don said. 'If I'm still a blasted toad?'

'Then we grab the hourglass and run,' said Tanya, feeling far less brave than she sounded.

'Is dangerous,' said Turpin. 'Very risky.'

'There's no other way,' said Tanya. 'Unless we leave it another night and come back for Ratty—'

'No,' Don interrupted. 'We only got here because of your wish. If he's here, I can't go without him. If Solomon leaves this place and takes Henry, there's a chance we might not trace him again, not without giving up the hourglass. Even then I don't think Solomon would hand Henry over – his gift is too powerful.'

'Then we have to do it now,' said Tanya. 'Turpin, you wait by those boxes by the stairs. I'll sneak down and surprise Solomon. When he chases me back up the stairs, push the boxes into his path. That'll give me time to hide the hourglass.'

'What if he catches you?' Don whispered. 'What if he does something magical? You could be a toad in two seconds flat!'

'He won't catch me. I'm faster than he is and I'm protected. Whatever he does, he'll know there's a chance I could drop the hourglass and break it. I don't think he'll take that risk.'

'Where will you hide the hourglass?' Don looked around. 'What about in one of these boxes?'

'No.' Tanya shook her head. 'That'll probably be Solomon's first thought. I'm going to hide it in plain sight.'

'In the shop?' Don gasped.

Tanya nodded.

'By the time Solomon makes it up the stairs and past the

boxes, I'll have hidden the hourglass in amongst the others, then I can join Turpin and help get Ratty out.'

Don took a deep breath and nodded at the window ledge. 'All right. Let's do it. Put me up there.' He lowered his voice even further. 'And pray that I see a star.'

Tanya pulled out her mother's red shawl from the rucksack and threw it round Oberon, tucking the ends into his collar. Provided he stayed quiet, it should hide him from Solomon until she was ready. She placed Don on the sill, then took the hourglass, trying to steady her suddenly shaking hands. 'Turpin, get ready,' she whispered.

Turpin gave a fierce nod. Then the two of them crept out of the storeroom and towards the cellar steps. Turpin took up her position behind the stack of boxes.

'Wait until I've cleared the stairs and you've got a clean shot at Solomon,' Tanya whispered. 'Then shove as many boxes his way as you can.'

'It will be many,' Turpin promised. She reached up and gave her horns a little stroke as if for courage or luck.

Tanya readjusted her grip on the hourglass. Her fingers were damp with nervous sweat. Then she edged closer to the narrow stone steps and started down them as quietly as she could.

23
Captives

WITH EVERY STEP TANYA TOOK FURTHER down into the cellar, a musty, damp smell grew stronger. She paused, pinching her nose to press the tickle away, and felt Oberon's nose bump into the back of her leg. The hourglass in her other hand felt warm and, now she was touching it again, the whisperings of the memory had begun once more. She forced herself not to listen. She could not afford to be sucked into it this time.

At the bottom of the steps, an old wooden door was half open, hanging crookedly on its hinges. She crept nearer, trying to steady her breathing, and peered through the gap in the door into one side of a dimly-lit room. It looked very similar to the room she had seen in the memory, for there was all sorts of equipment and magical paraphernalia crammed everywhere. Dusty books teetered in piles, crates jammed with jars of nasty-looking ingredients were stacked up on top of one another, and a huge, black cauldron stood at the centre of it all. Exactly how long had Solomon been here? Tanya wondered. Several months at least, from the looks of things.

She drew back on to the staircase as heavy footsteps sounded on the other side of the room. Then Solomon's voice came in a low growl.

'Wake up, boy!'

Holding her breath, Tanya moved forward again and slunk to the edge of the door, looking round it on to the side of the room she had not yet seen. It was all she could do not to gasp, for there, just a short distance away, stood a large, silver cage. Inside it, shivering and sleepy-eyed, was Ratty.

Tanya pressed a hand over her mouth. Poor Ratty looked dreadful. He was thinner, and his brown skin had taken on a grey look. His eyes were sunken and dull and even from where Tanya stood she could see they had lost their sparkle.

Solomon stood on the other side of the cage bars, but he was not alone. A hulking figure lurked just beyond him in a shadowy alcove. It wore plain, dark clothes and its face was hidden by a gruesome mask that looked like it had been painted by a child. It had two black holes for eyes and a thin, red slash for a mouth. Though the mask was different to the one she had seen before, Tanya recognised the figure as the same one she had seen at the fairground. Confusion and panic swept through her. What was Morghul doing here, with Solomon? And, more importantly, how would Turpin get past him to uphold her part of the plan?

Solomon took the bars of the cage and rattled them. 'I said wake up!'

At the sound of his voice, Tanya felt Oberon's body go

rigid beside her. She looked down and saw that the fur on the back of his neck was standing up.

Ratty rubbed his eyes and glared.

Solomon eyed him nastily. 'Are you hungry enough to talk yet?'

'Hungry enough to eat a dead dog,' Ratty answered, coughing weakly. 'But I'll never talk to you.'

'Just tell me where the memory is hidden!' Solomon snapped. 'Where did your thieving father put it?'

Ratty's mouth set in a determined line. 'If I told you, would you let me go?'

'Of course.'

'I don't believe you.'

'You don't have much choice,' said Solomon. 'No one knows you're here. And your wretched father somehow escaped from where I left him, not that much good will come of it in his present form.'

'What do you mean?' Ratty asked. 'What have you done to my pa?'

Solomon gave a thin smile. 'Let's just say I've cut him down to size. Now, are you going to tell me what you know? Where is that hourglass?'

'I don't know,' Ratty said. Hatred burned in his eyes. 'And, even if I did, I'd never tell you.'

Tanya screwed up her courage and stepped beyond the door into the cellar room. 'You're asking the wrong person.'

Solomon spun round, his eyes wide with shock. '*You!*'

'Tanya?' Ratty gasped. He jumped to his feet. 'What are you doing here?'

Tanya swallowed, her knees suddenly wobbly. 'I've come to give Solomon what he wants,' she said. 'In exchange for you.'

Solomon stared at the hourglass, transfixed. 'That's it,' he whispered. He lifted his hand, taking a slow step towards her like she was a bird he was afraid to frighten away. 'That's the one. How . . . where did you . . .?' He shook himself slightly. 'Give it to me, girl. Give it to me and I'll release him.'

Morghul shifted in the shadows. Even though there was no face to read, Tanya sensed his longing. It was as strong and as greedy as Solomon's, and every bit as terrifying. Perhaps she could lure them both out of the cellar, leaving Turpin to release Ratty from the cage. She took a tiny step back, waiting. 'No. Let him go first.'

Solomon's lip curled back. He took another step towards her. 'Now listen, girl. Don't be stupid. Give me the hourglass or it will be taken from you. Forcibly.' He snapped his fingers and Morghul lurched out from his shadowy corner.

'No, *you* listen,' said Tanya. She brandished the hourglass, noticing how Solomon's outstretched hand shook. 'I know how this works. So if either you or that thing—' she jerked her head at Morghul, '—does anything that makes me nervous, and I happen to drop this, the memory will be lost forever. And I don't think you want that.' Beside her, Oberon gave a growl that sounded almost convincing.

Solomon blinked, noticing Oberon for the first time.

Then his face drained of colour. Tanya silently congratulated herself on putting him in his place, but it was only when he spoke next that she realised that what she had mistaken for fear was in fact rage.

'You *dare* threaten me? You've no idea who you're dealing with, girl! You're not leaving this place until you hand that over. And if it breaks you won't be leaving at all.' He gave a nod to Morghul. 'Get her. And remember the same goes for you, if you damage it.'

Morghul grunted and lunged towards Tanya.

'Run!' Ratty yelled.

Tanya turned and fled, flinging the cellar door wide. Behind her, she heard Oberon snap and snarl as he tried to block Morghul's way. 'Oberon!' she shouted, terrified he'd come to harm. His claws scraped the stone steps beside her and together they scrambled up them. She heard Morghul's heavy tread behind her, closer than expected, and fear spurred her on. The rucksack bounced against her back as she ran, and from somewhere inside she heard enraged squeaks as the Cornish brownie bounced with it. Finally, she reached the top of the stairs, with barely enough breath to speak.

'Turpin, now!' she gasped, hurtling past the pile of boxes. She caught a glimpse of two small hands giving a hard shove, and the mountain of boxes tumbled on to the staircase like falling dominoes. She heard rather than saw Morghul stumble backwards, losing his footing and crashing to the bottom. From the depths of the cellar, Solomon roared.

Tanya fled into the back room.

Heart thudding, she hurried over to the pile of discarded hourglasses on the floor by the table. She glanced at the real one in her hand, aware that she was about to take a terrible risk, but unable to think of another solution. Carefully, she placed it at the edge of the pile, scooping up smaller parts of some of the broken ones and placing them on top to hide it. Mixed in with the others, it was a good hiding place. With a final look to memorise the spot, she took another one of a similar size from the pile, then, checking the coast was clear, slipped out of the room.

Loud thuds sounded from the stairs as Morghul hurled the boxes out of the way. Tanya edged past into the storeroom, where, to her dismay, Don was very much still a toad.

'What's going on?' Don hissed. 'Did it work?'

'Not exactly,' said Tanya. 'Morghul is here. Solomon sent him after me and he'll be here any minute. With Solomon still in the cellar, I can't send Turpin down!'

'Morghul is *here?*' Turpin skidded into the room, her hair standing on end.

'Yes. And Ratty is locked up downstairs. Our only hope is for Solomon and Morghul to both come up here.'

Don blinked, his blue eyes huge in his warty face. 'I don't understand. What is Morghul doing here, with Solomon? I warned him what would happen if Solomon ever remembered what he was! Solomon would destroy him to get his spell to work.'

Tanya shook her head. 'But Morghul wants the hourglass just as badly as Solomon does.'

'Because the hourglass not only holds Solomon's memory of that night, but Ratty's memory of Morghul, too,' said Turpin. 'Without Ratty knowing what he is, Morghul has no power. Solomon can use glamour to change Morghul's shape, but just for a short while. Only Ratty can give him a lasting form. Without him Morghul lives a half-life. He needs Ratty to remember . . .' She trailed off as a tumult of noise sounded from the stairs. Boxes flew over the handrail, crashing every which way as the path from the cellar was cleared.

'They're coming,' Tanya whispered. She pushed Turpin towards a crate in the corner. 'Hide. I'll lead them to the front of the shop and then you go down and get Ratty out of the cage.'

'What about me?' Don hissed.

'Keep looking for that star,' Tanya said desperately. 'We're going to need it.' She darted out, shutting Oberon in the storeroom behind her, and slipped into the darkened front of the shop. A thought struck her and she approached the door. Perhaps she could fool Solomon into thinking she had left and lure him out of the building altogether. But as she touched the handle a white spark snapped off it, followed by the sound of a lock clicking into place.

'I told you that you couldn't leave, didn't I?' Solomon's voice rang up the stairs, high-pitched and triumphant. 'Every door and every window in this place is barred by magic. You're going nowhere, girl.'

A trickle of cold sweat snaked down Tanya's spine as she sought a hiding place. There were few options. With only seconds to spare, she dropped down and crawled under the counter, the sound of her own heartbeat thumping in her ears.

Overhead, the lights snapped on. Tanya squeezed her eyes shut, listening. Footsteps moved over the floorboards. Cupboard doors opened then banged shut. Display units were tossed aside, sending watches scattering over the floor. The footsteps came closer.

'There aren't many places to hide here.' Solomon's voice was taunting, sing-song, as he approached the counter. His shoes clipped into view, slowly and deliberately. Tanya considered running, but knew it was hopeless. There was nowhere to run, and nowhere else to hide. *Please*, she thought. *Please let Turpin get Ratty out.*

A second pair of legs appeared in front of her. The movement was soundless; the movement of someone or something that was used to creeping in shadows, unseen and unheard. Without warning, a pale, waxy hand reached under the counter and seized her by the shoulder, pulling her out painfully. She yelled and struggled, but to no avail. The hand shook her into stillness like she was no more than a rag doll being shaken by a dog, and then she found herself looking up into the hideous, masked face of Morghul. Up close, the melted-wax look of his pale skin could be seen at the sides of the mask and, horrible as the mask was, Tanya was glad it was still on.

Solomon snatched the hourglass from her hands, but his jubilant expression quickly twisted into one of anger. 'I don't have time for this!' he roared. His eyes were wide and crazed. He threw the hourglass across the room where it shattered against a wall. 'Where is it?'

'You just broke it,' Tanya lied, stalling desperately. 'It was disguised . . . with glamour.'

'You can't fool me,' Solomon sneered. He wrenched the rucksack from her, rifling through it, then threw it aside. 'I'd know that hourglass anywhere, disguised or not, and that wasn't it. It's still here somewhere. I can feel it. The memory is so close it's practically singing to me!' He grabbed Tanya roughly, shaking her out of Morghul's grip.

'The girl has hidden it somewhere. Find it! Search every room, check every hourglass.'

Tanya bit her lip.

'Yes, Master.' Behind the mask, Morghul's voice was muffled, yet still Tanya could make out a strange quality to it. Like there was more than one voice mixed in, as fluid and changeable as his face. He bowed his head and lumbered out of sight.

Solomon smiled thinly. 'Time for you to come downstairs. You can join the little friend you were so eager to see.'

Tanya struggled. Though Solomon was not as powerful as Morghul, he was still much too strong for her to escape. 'What are you going to do with me?' Her voice betrayed her fear.

'That depends.' Solomon scrutinised her. His eyes, now she

saw them close up, were grey, and curiously cold and blank, rather like a dead sea creature. 'On how difficult you plan on being. I have ways of dealing with difficult people. Ways of silencing them or making them disappear completely.'

Tanya stamped on his foot, hard. Even though she knew it wouldn't do much good, she certainly wasn't going to make it easy for him.

'I'm already getting tired of you,' Solomon growled, his eyes watering. He reached into his pocket and withdrew a tiny tin, from which he took a pinch of blue-grey dust between his finger and thumb.

'Sleep tight,' he whispered, then blew the dust straight into her face.

Tanya's eyes and throat itched and stung as the dust took hold. She coughed, her eyes streaming, then the unpleasant sensations faded, leaving Solomon looking even angrier.

'Protected, are we?' he hissed. 'Very well. We'll just do things the hard way then.' He dragged Tanya through the door at the back of the shop and forced her down the stairs into the cellar towards the cage where Ratty was imprisoned. With a click of his fingers, the cage door opened and Solomon threw her inside.

She landed on her knees with a painful bump and the cage door slammed behind her. Then a cold hand was on her arm, helping her to her feet. She looked up into Ratty's worried face.

'Heck,' he said miserably. 'So he got you, too.'

Tanya rubbed at her eyes, blinking away the gritty dust.

'He blew something into my face. Some kind of powder,' she said. 'Whatever it was, it didn't work – my socks are inside out.' She turned and stared through the bars of the cage into the dimly-lit cellar.

Solomon was leaning over a book, running his finger down the page. Before him was a large, black cauldron. Thick smoke rose from within it and a strange, herby smell filled the air. From a wooden beam above hung a lacy white dress, swaying gently like a cobweb.

'Where's the hourglass?' Ratty asked.

'I hid it, just before Solomon caught me,' Tanya whispered. 'But it's only a matter of time before that creature finds it and brings it to him.'

'How did you find it?' Ratty asked her. 'And how did you find me?'

'I didn't find it. Don did. He'd hidden it, in the most amazing place—'

'You've seen him? You've seen my pa?'

Tanya held a finger to her lips, afraid Solomon would hear. 'Yes. He's here, upstairs.'

Ratty's eyebrows knotted together. 'Then why doesn't he come down? Why isn't he helping us?'

'Because he can't.'

'Why not?'

'Because Solomon turned him into a toad.'

'*What?*'

'I don't have time to explain, except that hopefully he won't be a toad for much longer.' She looked past Ratty into

317

the dark corners of the cellar. 'Where's Turpin? I sent her down here to try and get you out after Solomon and Morghul followed me with the hourglass.'

'She tried,' said Ratty. 'But it wasn't as simple as picking the lock. It's protected by magic. She couldn't free us.' He scanned the cellar. 'She shot off somewhere when they came back down here; she must be hiding.'

Tanya leaned forward and gripped the bars. 'She's our only hope now, along with Don.' She bowed her head, knowing how useless it seemed. 'A fairy who can't do magic and a toad. What chance do we have?'

Ratty gave a sad little smile. 'There's always a chance,' he whispered. 'I still can't believe you found me. How is that even possible?'

'I—' Tanya began, but was cut off by a triumphant shout from upstairs.

Solomon's head snapped up from the book as heavy foot-steps thudded down the cellar steps. Then the door opened and Morghul stood silhouetted against the light. In his out-stretched hand, he held the hourglass.

Solomon stared at it, licking his lips like a thirsty man about to receive water. 'At last. After years of searching, I'm about to find the truth once more.' He turned to the wraith-like dress, his voice tender now. 'And finally I'll be able to bring her back. Morghul,' he said, his voice hoarse. 'Bring it to me.'

'That thing . . . Morghul,' Ratty whispered. 'I don't know what it is, but it gives me the creeps. It's like Solomon's pet the way it follows him around, doing everything he says.'

Tanya watched, uneasy. Despite what she knew, there was something not right about Morghul's being here with Solomon. What exactly was he planning?

Solomon edged round the simmering cauldron, reaching out towards Morghul. But Morghul continued to walk past him, approaching the cage.

'What are you doing?' Solomon demanded. 'Give that to me!'

Morghul seemed not to hear. Instead, he loomed before the cage, reaching towards Ratty with the hourglass in his hand. Inside it, the sand had begun to flow. And finally Tanya understood what was about to happen.

'Take it,' Morghul urged. Behind the mask, Tanya could hear his breathing, fast with excitement.

Ratty stared at the hourglass, mesmerised. 'I remember this. I saw it before, one night a long time ago ...'

'Take it,' Morghul repeated, thrusting it through the bars as Solomon charged towards the cage.

'Ratty, there's something I have to tell you ... about Morghul,' Tanya whispered. 'You mustn't touch that.'

'Pa said that Solomon must never have it,' Ratty murmured, reaching for the hourglass.

'No!' Tanya shouted, trying to knock Morghul's hand away. 'It's a trap!'

It was too late. Ratty's fingers closed round the hourglass and Tanya was powerless to do anything except watch as the lost memory flooded back.

24

The Sacrifice

RATTY RELEASED THE HOURGLASS AND backed away, pressing himself against the bars of the cage and as far as he could get from Morghul's terrifying, painted face.

'You . . .' His breath came in noisy gulps, and his already grey skin turned even paler. 'I remember now. I remember everything!'

Morghul stood motionless at the edge of the cage, still holding the hourglass and watching Ratty with his blank, black eyes. Solomon arrived next to him, his face screwed up in temper.

'What's going on here?' he demanded. 'Give that to me!' He grabbed Morghul's arm.

Tanya lunged for the hourglass, determined that Solomon shouldn't get it, but he was too quick. Morghul released it into his hand easily, and Solomon clutched it to himself. Horrified, Tanya moved to the back of the cage next to Ratty. He was trembling and wide-eyed, frozen to the spot and unable to look away from Morghul.

'Ratty,' she whispered desperately. 'You can't be afraid. You have to overcome your fear or he'll only grow more powerful!'

If Ratty heard her, he gave no sign of it.

He still hadn't moved and he was trembling even harder than she was. Solomon shuffled away, gazing at the hourglass. Slowly, he turned it in his hands and the sand began to trickle once more. He closed his eyes, his face twitching as the lost memory took hold.

'Aren't you going to do something?' Tanya hissed at Morghul. 'Don't you care what will happen when he remembers what you are?'

Morghul didn't answer. Instead, he reached up and slowly removed his mask. Tanya wanted to look away, but found she couldn't; the sight was so terrible she was helpless not to stare. The melted, misshapen face looked like bubbling porridge. It rippled and pulsed, as though an unseen hand were modelling it from clay. But Tanya knew there was no hand. Only one thing could shape Morghul's form and that was Ratty's imagination.

'Ratty,' she said urgently, tugging at her friend's arm. 'Please, listen to me. You have to stop being afraid!' Already she knew her words were wasted. Ratty was plainly terrified and, with every second that passed, Morghul seemed to swell in size.

A loud smash made her jump. Solomon was standing by the cauldron, the hourglass in pieces at his feet. He stared at Morghul, his face a strange mixture of delight and disbelief. 'You?' he whispered. 'All this time . . . *you* were the hidden memory, the secret ingredient? And yet you dared to seek me out, to hide under my very nose. Why?'

'You should know the answer to that,' Tanya said. She stepped away from Ratty to the edge of the cage. 'You took Ratty's memory of him and locked it into the hourglass. Without it, Ratty couldn't imagine him or fear him and, apart from your glamour, that was all he had to give him life. He wanted the hourglass just as much as you did, but knew that without you he'd never find it.'

Solomon smiled faintly. 'A risk you shouldn't have taken, my friend.' He made a circling motion with his hands. Silver chains appeared, binding Morghul's hands and feet. Solomon beckoned and Morghul was propelled towards him as if held by an invisible rope.

'I'm afraid it's into the cauldron with you,' Solomon said, with a contented sigh. 'A life in exchange for a life.' He reached up and stroked the faded, lacy dress, then lifted the lid of a small box on a table next to the cauldron. From it, he took something thin and white: a skeletal hand. A jewelled ring glinted on one finger. Tanya felt a scream rising in her throat and bit it back.

'We're almost there, my love,' Solomon crooned, placing the skeleton's hand back in the box. 'Bone of the beloved and the last garment worn.' He turned his attention back to Morghul. 'But first it's time for the sacrifice.'

'You can't do this,' Tanya said. 'If you destroy Morghul, you'll destroy part of Ratty's imagination – part of *him*! Do you really want to be responsible for that? For killing the part of him that's able to create and believe? The part that's able to listen to stories and bring them to life in his head? He'll never be the same!' Her voice rose to a shout. 'Never!'

Solomon hugged the box to his chest, his triumphant look replaced by one of sadness. He looked older suddenly. Tired and haggard. 'Imagination is overvalued,' he said bitterly, running his finger over the lid of the box. 'Memories, imagination . . . it's all the same. For years I've lived in mine and it's a lonely place. All that matters is what's real. And what's real is life, the here and now.'

'No,' said Tanya. 'You're wrong. Memories make us what we are, and imagination lets us dream of what's possible. What we can be. No one can put a value on that.'

And, just for a moment, Solomon hesitated. But it was only a moment and it was over too quickly. The cold eyes hardened, filling with feverish madness once more. 'No,' he whispered. 'I *will* bring her back! No matter what the cost.' He beckoned once more, eyeing Morghul greedily as the creature stumbled towards him.

Tanya shook the bars of the cage desperately, but it was useless. There was nothing, *nothing* she could do except watch as Morghul neared the cauldron. And then she froze, for Morghul had stopped. She glanced at Solomon. His face was blank with confusion and he gestured wildly, cursing under his breath at the unseen magic that was clearly failing him. And now Tanya could see why: Morghul was changing. The lumpy-porridge texture of his face was smoothing out like moulded wax, taking on new features. Features, she realised with horror, that encapsulated Ratty's worst nightmares. Rotting flesh peeled from the skull, while blackened tooth stumps gnashed behind the lips.

As Solomon looked on in horror, Morghul's lips drew back in a terrible smile and he lifted his hands, shattering the silver chains that bound them like they were no stronger than paper. A piece flew into Solomon's face, striking his cheek and leaving a huge welt there. He threw his hands up, staggering back. Next, Morghul kicked out, separating the bonds that held his legs.

'No!' Solomon cried, recovering himself. 'No, no, no!' He lunged at Morghul, his eyes burning bright with madness as he tried to drag him to the cauldron – but he was no match for Morghul's strength, not any more. Morghul seized him by the neck, squeezing hard with a rotting hand. Solomon's face turned red and terrible choking noises forced their way from his throat. He clawed at Morghul's face, forcing the monster to release his neck, but still Morghul grabbed at it.

Tanya turned to Ratty. His fear had paralysed him, leaving him unable to do anything but watch as the horrible scene unfolded.

'Make it stop, Ratty!' she begged. 'You have to!'

Ratty's head shook very slightly. 'I can't ... he's too powerful ...'

Tanya grabbed him and shook him hard. 'He's only powerful because you're letting him be! You're the only one who can stop this, don't you see? If you don't, you'll never be free of him and he'll grow and grow until he takes you over completely!'

'I can't,' Ratty repeated. 'I don't know how.'

His voice was empty, devoid of hope. Somehow, the sound of it terrified Tanya even more than the sight of Morghul. She glanced around the cellar, dimly aware that upstairs Oberon was barking from behind the closed storeroom door. She balled her hands into fists. Don must still be up there, trapped and in toad form. There was no hope of him coming to their rescue. And, even if he did, she did not know how he would stop what was in motion. She did not know how anyone could, even Ratty.

A sudden movement caught her eye. There, on the cellar steps, a shadow lurked in the beam of light coming from above. It loomed large, like a demon, with wild hair, pointed horns and a long tail swishing from side to side. Tanya felt the tiny hairs on the back of her arms rising, then realised what she was looking at. The beam of light widened and a small, fearful face peered round the door into the cellar. At the back of Tanya's mind, it triggered something, something Don had told her. A bold little idea began to tap in her head.

'Turpin!' Tanya mouthed. 'Here, quickly!'

Turpin hurried down the steps, moving swiftly through the shadows. With Solomon and Morghul still jostling for power, neither of them noticed as she slipped into the cage.

'He is changing,' she said, nodding at Morghul. She

sounded more afraid than Tanya had ever heard her. 'Ratty has remembered?'

'Yes,' Ratty said softly. 'I remembered.'

'Then hope is lost,' said Turpin. 'Whichever one of them wins.'

'Hope isn't lost,' said Tanya. 'Not yet. Listen, I have an idea, but we have to be quick. Can you go back upstairs and fetch the rucksack and sneak it to me without them seeing you?'

Turpin nodded. 'Yes. Turpin is good at sneaking.'

'Good,' said Tanya. 'Then hurry.'

Turpin squeezed through the bars again and scurried up the stairs. Morghul's grunts and Solomon's roars filled the cellar as they crashed around, each trying to gain the upper hand. Books and papers skidded across and littered the floor, and jars of ingredients and captive fairies smashed, with the fairies making hasty bids for freedom. It was clear that Solomon was losing, only hanging on out of the sheer will to survive, and that it could not last much longer.

Turpin reappeared, not only with the rucksack, but with Don in her arms and Oberon behind her.

'Pa!' Ratty exclaimed, as Don hopped on to his lap. 'Heck, what a mess you're in!'

Don hung his head miserably. 'I'm sorry, Henry. I was hoping you wouldn't have to see me like this.'

Tanya reached through the bars and dragged the rucksack to the cage. On the other side, Oberon scratched and whined, frustrated at not being able to join Tanya.

'I know, boy,' she said, unzipping the rucksack. 'But you just have to stay there for now.' From the rucksack, she pulled out the jar containing the Cornish brownie. 'Listen to me,' she told it through the air holes. 'If I set you free, will you promise to help us?'

The brownie scowled and nodded reluctantly. Tanya removed the lid from the jar. A wisp of blue smoke curled into the air as the magical seal was broken.

'I need you to use your magic,' said Tanya. She motioned for the others to lean in close as she quickly explained her idea. 'Everyone clear?' she asked. 'Ratty, can you do this?'

Ratty nodded. 'I'll try.'

'All right,' said Tanya. 'Get ready.' She nodded at Turpin, who slipped out of the cage once more and began to head for the cellar steps. A terrible choking noise stopped her in her tracks and startled them all.

Morghul had grabbed Solomon's neck once more and, this time, Solomon did not appear to have the strength to fight him off. His eyes bulged then closed, and his face was swiftly turning from red to purple as he gasped for air. His hands flailed uselessly, then dropped to his sides. Morghul gave one final squeeze, then released him. Solomon's eyes snapped open again, full of cunning. He seized a heavy candlestick, ready to strike, but his foot slid on a pile of books and he skidded off balance, thrown back against the large, bubbling cauldron. As his legs buckled against it, his mouth gaped in a terrible realisation of what was about to happen. He grabbed at the air, trying to regain his footing, but to no avail. He toppled backwards with a blood-curdling scream and vanished into the frothing, steaming contents of the cauldron.

Immediately, the cauldron started to bubble and hiss, and wisps of white steam began to rise up. Morghul turned back to the cage, his gruesome face flushed with victory. Solomon would not climb out of the cauldron alive. Of that Tanya was now certain.

As the cauldron gave a rumbling gurgle, several things happened: there came a sharp sound of a lock clicking and the cage door sprang open. Inside the cage, Don gave an enormous belch, which produced a large, silver moth, and promptly transformed back into his rightful shape. He stared at his hands, wiggling his fingers in disbelief.

Morghul fixed his blank eyes on Ratty, advancing slowly.

'Now!' Tanya hissed, giving Ratty a hard push.

Ratty stood up unsteadily, his knees shaking as he approached the side of the cage. 'It's time for you to go, Morghul,' he said. His voice was quiet and nervous. 'You don't belong here any more.'

Morghul threw back his head and laughed. Even since the defeat of Solomon, just moments ago, his features had become more defined. His eyes, still black, were now more human and glistened with life in place of the dead, empty pits that had been there before. 'I do belong,' he said in a deep, throaty voice. 'I belong with you. You made me. And, from you, my strength grows and grows.'

'You're not welcome or wanted any more,' said Ratty. 'You

became something else, something wrong. And now I'm going to unmake you.'

'And how do you think you'll do that?' Morghul mocked. 'You're not strong enough. Even Solomon wasn't powerful enough, with all his magic!'

'Because Solomon never created you,' said Ratty. 'I did. You only exist because of me.'

'And yet you're still not strong enough to defeat me.'

'Maybe not alone,' said Ratty. 'But you're forgetting something.'

'And what's that?'

'That if I made you I can make others, too. And I did.'

'You lie,' said Morghul, but doubt had crept into his voice.

Ratty squared his shoulders, standing a little taller. 'No, I don't. See for yourself.' He pointed to the cellar floor in front of him. Morghul looked down.

Behind Ratty, Tanya watched as the brownie, hidden from sight in his jar, began moving his hands in a furious working of magic. At the centre of his palms a tiny, golden ball glowed like a furnace and a beam of light fell before Ratty, creating a long, dark shadow on the stone floor. Yet, as Ratty stood unmoving, the shadow did not. It folded its arms and, before their eyes, began to change shape so that it did not resemble Ratty, but something else entirely. The hair grew wilder and stood away from the head in fierce tufts, and two pointed horns protruded either side of the head. Behind it, a cat-like tail swished aggressively.

'No,' said Morghul. 'It's not possible!'

'Of course it's possible,' said Ratty. He folded his arms, looking bolder by the second. 'I created you when I was only small.' His voice was scornful now. 'But now I'm capable of so much more. I made something else. Some*one* else. Another friend.'

At his words, Morghul's eyes lost their glistening appearance and took on a dull, empty look once more. Tanya peered closer. Was it her imagination or was he shrinking a little, too?

'It's working!' Don whispered beside her. 'He's starting to lose his form. Don't stop!'

'I made something bigger, stronger,' Ratty continued. 'Something that will crush you.'

The shadow on the floor began to pace, like a cat stalking its prey.

Morghul's clothes became a little larger, a little looser. 'You can't crush me,' he said, but his voice betrayed him. It was less clear, as though he were having to try harder to form the words.

Out of the corner of her eye, Tanya sneaked a look at the cellar steps. There, in the beam of light from above, Turpin pulled herself up to her full height, pacing from side to side and flicking her tail, watching as her shadow was magically projected before Ratty.

'Surely you can see how powerful it is already,' said Ratty. 'Even as a shadow, it has its own form. You never did. Your shadow was just a copy of me.'

The rotting skin on Morghul's face faded, and the skin began to take on the texture of lumpy porridge once more. In the jar, the brownie moved his hands apart and the ball of light split in two. At the same time, Ratty's shadow moved away from the cage, separating from him.

'I suggest you leave now,' said Ratty. 'My new friend is hungry.'

Turpin began stamping her feet on the steps, like a bull about to charge. The shadow between Ratty and Morghul did the same. Morghul shrank further still.

'Keep going, Ratty,' Tanya whispered. 'You're winning! Soon he'll be nothing!'

The shadow moved towards Morghul, forcing him to step back. He glanced about nervously, as if looking for a weapon, or a place to hide ... and then his gaze rested on the cellar steps as he caught sight of Turpin. The fairy saw him and tried to leap into the shadows, but too late. Recognition flared across his face and he began to smile once more.

'A trick,' he said, his voice deep and dark as treacle. 'Just a feeble illusion! You can't defeat me. With every second I grow more powerful.'

'No,' whispered Ratty, backing into the cage. 'Stay away ...'

Morghul advanced, grinning. His skin rippled, starting to take shape once more as Ratty's fear grew.

'Don't let him win, Ratty!' Tanya yelled. 'You were doing it! You were defeating him!'

331

'But now he knows,' Ratty moaned.

'It doesn't matter!' Don urged. 'It wasn't the trick that did it, it was the trick that made you believe you could do it, don't you see?'

But Ratty didn't see, for he backed away as Morghul approached the cage, swelling and growing with every step. He reached through the bars, grabbing Ratty by the arm.

'You're mine again now,' he chuckled. 'Mine to feed off. Mine to grow from. And soon I won't need you at all.'

'No!' The shout came from above. Turpin hurtled down the cellar steps, charging at her enemy. 'You can't have Ratty! You won't! Turpin won't let you!' She flung herself at Morghul's face, lashing out, biting and shrieking. With a growl, Oberon joined her, snapping at his legs.

Tanya grabbed Ratty from behind, pulling him in the opposite direction. Don joined her, tugging him hard.

'Fight!' Tanya yelled. 'You have to fight!'

Morghul released a howl of rage as his grip was broken. Tanya and Ratty landed in a heap beside Don, panting as the fight outside continued. Turpin clawed like a wildcat, but even with Oberon's help she was no match for Morghul.

One of Morghul's great legs kicked out, striking Oberon and flinging him away. He landed with a yelp, but struggled to his feet once more.

'Oberon!' Tanya yelled. She scrambled to the cage door. A piercing scream stopped her. Morghul had snatched Turpin in one of his enormous fists and was crushing her, squeezing the life out of her.

'Let her go!' Ratty yelled.

Morghul obeyed with a cruel smile. He threw Turpin aside with great force. Her little body flew across the cellar, smashing into the side of the cauldron then sprawling across the floor, unmoving.

'No!' Ratty yelled. He pushed past Tanya and ran out of the cage, collapsing at Turpin's side. He lifted her in his arms, hugging her to him, but Tanya could see that her body was lifeless. 'She's not breathing,' he choked. 'You killed her.' His head snapped up and his eyes filled with rage. '*You killed her!*'

Morghul watched him, gloating. Tanya stumbled out of the cage and went to Oberon, hugging him to her with tears streaming down her cheeks. Turpin? *Dead?* She couldn't be. But as she looked at the tiny, broken body in Ratty's arms she knew it was true.

Ratty lowered Turpin gently to the floor once more, then slowly stood up. His hands balled into fists at his sides. Don ran to his aid, pushing Ratty behind him to shield him from Morghul. But Ratty stepped round him.

'No, Pa,' he said through gritted teeth. 'You can't help me with this. No one can.' He took a step towards Morghul, his face flushed. 'Turpin was a true friend to me,' he said. 'But you?' His voice trembled, only this time it was not with fear, but rage. 'You're nothing. Only a figment, a nightmare, a thought.'

Morghul growled, his gruesome face rippling at Ratty's words. He took a step towards Ratty, but Ratty held firm.

'You're nothing,' Ratty repeated. 'And it's time for you to go back to where you came from.'

A low groan rumbled from Morghul's throat. Tanya watched in horror as his face and hands began to run like melted wax, dripping on to the floor. Ratty took another step forward.

'You're nothing,' he said again. 'Just a shadow.'

Morghul howled something, but his words were lost and shapeless. His clothes began to rumple as his body shrank. They sank into the pooling mass at his feet.

'You're nothing, nothing, *nothing*.'

Morghul was now only the same size as Ratty and shrinking faster than ever. He reached out a dripping hand, as if pleading, but Ratty simply stared, his face stony and grim. The hand was lowered into the pile of clothes, blistering and bubbling on the floor. By the time Morghul's face reached it, it was little more than a clay-like lump, spreading and gurgling into the melting mass until finally it was silent. The grisly pile darkened like a stain, then slowly, slowly, stretched out before Ratty into a long, thin shadow. Ratty took one last step forward and the shadow bled into his own.

'Just a shadow,' Ratty whispered. 'Gone.' He turned away, his eyes blurred with tears, and knelt by Turpin's body, cradling her in his arms. He bent his head, sobbing silently into her hair.

Don emerged from the cage, his own blue eyes, so like Ratty's, full of sadness.

'Come on, son,' he said quietly. 'It's over. We have to leave this place.'

Ratty didn't answer. The only sound in the silence was that of the cauldron, still bubbling gently.

'Wait,' said Tanya. She stared at the cauldron, then at the dress, still hanging from the beam. She wiped the tears from her face. 'Solomon had the spell all set up. He was trying to get Morghul into the cauldron as a sacrifice ... a life for a life, he said. But ...'

'But he fell into the cauldron himself,' Don finished. 'Someone can still be brought back.'

'But you said it was wrong, Pa,' said Ratty. 'Messing around with life and death. You said it shouldn't be meddled with.'

'Turpin shouldn't have died like this,' Don said. 'And it's not like any of us know how to repeat the spell. It would just be once. Just this once, to right a wrong.'

Ratty stood up, sniffing. He looked down at Turpin in his arms. 'A life for a life,' he said, lowering her into the frothing liquid.

Tanya pressed her hand to her mouth as Turpin's little body was swallowed into the cauldron. No sooner had it vanished than the liquid stopped bubbling and fell still and silent. They watched and waited, yet nothing happened.

'It hasn't worked,' said Ratty. His eyes filled with fresh tears and he wiped them away angrily. 'Solomon was wrong.'

'No,' said Don. 'Look!'

A faint ripple moved across the dark mixture. It was followed by a stream of bubbles, and then a spluttering figure broke the surface, covered from head to foot in brown goo.

'Yikes!' Turpin exclaimed in disgust. 'What is this stuff? It's stinkier than a hobgoblin's sock!'

'Turpin!' Ratty yelled. 'You're alive!' He swept her into his arms, covering himself in the cauldron's contents. Delighted laughter burst out of him.

'Well, of course she is, silly boy,' said Turpin. She nuzzled his neck, looking confused but happy all the same.

'And now it really is time to leave,' said Don, looking around at the cellar with a shiver.

Tanya nodded at the brownie. 'Thank you,' she told him. In response, he glared at her while unleashing an angry stream of Cornish words that none of them understood. Once finished, he kicked the jar that had imprisoned him and vanished, leaving nothing but a bad smell behind him.

Wearily, they climbed the steps and left the cellar. As they reached the door, something swooped past them on the way out: a large, silver moth. It streaked into London's night sky, silhouetted against the moon and a trail of blazing stars.

Don stared up at them, his blue eyes reflecting every twinkle. 'Typical,' he muttered. 'Just typical!'

Tanya smiled faintly and reached into her rucksack for the two twigs from the Wishing Tree. 'Is everybody ready?' she asked softly.

Three exhausted faces, plus Oberon's brown, hairy one, stared back at her wordlessly. Without further ado, Tanya snapped the two twigs into four.

25
Promises

THEY ARRIVED BACK IN THE SILENT, sleeping cottage. Nothing had changed; Mrs Fairchild and the fairies were still held in slumber like they were playing a game of musical statues.

'So, these are your fairies,' Ratty said quietly, after Tanya explained what had happened.

Tanya nodded glumly. 'They don't always look like this, though. They're using glamour.' She sighed. 'Now I'm really going to be in trouble when they wake up.'

'They won't know you put the snoozes on them,' said Turpin. She climbed up Feathercap's coat and twanged his moustache curiously. 'The Sleep of the Dead is very tricksy like that.'

'Maybe not, but I was already in trouble anyway,' said Tanya, with a scowl. 'I'm sure they'll just carry on where they left off.'

'Not if they don't remember what they're here for,' said Ratty, with a glint in his eye.

'You mean ... you can still do it?' Tanya asked. 'I thought

when the memory of Morghul returned that things might go back to the way they were before.'

Ratty shook his head. 'I don't feel any different.'

'The more I think about it, the more I'm convinced that you absorbed Turpin's magic that night,' said Don, with an apologetic glance at Turpin.

Turpin shrugged. 'Turpin does not mind. Ratty can always have what is hers. Besides, magic is more trouble than it's worth sometimes.'

'Oh, Turps,' Ratty said fondly. 'What are we going to do with you?' He reached out and tweaked one of her horns, then looked at Tanya. 'So, do you want me to? Make them forget, I mean?'

Tanya grinned.

Ratty grinned back. He approached each of the sleeping figures. From Tanya's mother he took her watch and from the Mizhog its dog collar. Then a button from Feathercap, a thread from Gredin's coat and a brooch pinned to Raven's dress. He closed his eyes briefly, then opened them. 'Done.'

'Not quite.' Don's voice was gentle.

'What do you mean?' asked Ratty.

'There's still one more memory left to take.' He nodded at Tanya, smiling sadly.

'What?' said Ratty. 'But why? I'm safe now! Solomon's gone and so is Morghul. We don't need to keep on hiding!'

'No,' said Don. 'Maybe not. But your ability still makes you special and vulnerable. And that we *do* need to hide.

338

Just because one threat has gone, it doesn't mean there won't be others who'd want to use it for themselves, and would do anything to get at you. If you were both older maybe . . . if Henry were more experienced perhaps . . .' He shook the thought away and touched Tanya's shoulder. 'So you see, it isn't safe for you to know about Henry, because it puts you in danger, too. So, for now at least, I really think it's best that Tanya forgets.'

'But Pa . . .'

'It's all right,' said Tanya. She lowered her eyes, not wanting to show that they were filling with tears. 'I understand.'

'I'll leave you to say your goodbyes.' Don paused. 'But first . . . thank you. For everything.'

Tanya swallowed and simply nodded. A lump had risen in her throat and she did not trust herself to speak. Don shuffled to the door and quietly went outside. A long silence followed, in which she fought to regain her composure. Ratty was the first to speak.

'You never did tell me how you found me.'

Tanya sniffed and wiped away a stray tear that had leaked down her cheek.

'My wish,' she said finally. 'From the Wishing Tree.'

'You gave up your wish? For me?'

She nodded. 'I . . . it was important.'

A strange smile twisted Ratty's lips.

'What's so funny?' she asked.

'Nothing,' he said. 'Just that I nearly used my wish for

339

something stupid and selfish. I . . . I nearly wished to find out how I got my ability.' He gave a bitter laugh. 'Turns out my wish came true anyway.'

'So what did you wish for instead?' Tanya asked.

'I didn't. After I met you, I never got around to making it. And . . . and I'm glad. You know why?'

'Why?'

Ratty reached out and took her hand. 'Because I'm going to save it,' he whispered. 'And one day, when I'm older, and I can look after myself and it's safe, I'll make the same wish you did. My wish will be to find you.'

Tanya stared at his grubby, brown hand in hers. Her eyes blurred with fresh tears. She gulped. 'Do you mean it? Do you promise?'

He squeezed her hand. 'I promise.'

She rubbed her eyes again. 'I'm glad I met you,' she said. 'And Turpin.' Her cheeks were wet now, and there was nothing she could do to stop the tears from falling. Turpin clambered up on to her shoulder, dabbing at them with the bushy end of her tail.

'There, there,' she said. 'Stop now, silly girl.'

Tanya gave a watery smile. 'I wish I could say I'll never forget you.'

'Well, we'll definitely never forget you,' said Ratty. 'That's another promise.'

Tanya looked down at herself. 'What should I give you? Another button? A shoelace?'

Ratty released her hand and reached into his pocket.

From it, he removed something silky and dark: her braid of hair. 'I still have this.'

'Will I remember anything about you?' she asked.

Ratty shook his head. 'Nothing. Not me or Turpin . . . or anything we did or spoke about.'

'Just . . . do one thing for me,' Tanya begged.

Ratty's blue eyes were soft. 'Anything.'

'Just . . . wait till the morning? Please? I want to remember it all. That I had a friend, a proper friend. Just for one night.'

Ratty nodded silently. With that, they knew there was nothing more to say. Slowly, they walked to the door and opened it to a cool waft of night air. Don stood on the path a short way off, watching and waiting.

Ratty knelt and gave Oberon a scratch round the neck. 'No more digging up memories,' he whispered. 'Only bones for you.'

Oberon wagged his tail and licked Ratty's nose. Ratty stood up, facing Tanya.

'Well, this is it,' she said. She wrapped her arms round herself, shivering against the light breeze. 'This is goodbye.'

'Only for now,' Ratty whispered. 'It's a goodbye for now.' He gave one last smile, then turned to walk down the path and away from Hawthorn Cottage, Turpin skipping along beside him. Tanya watched as their figures grew smaller and darker, eventually blending into shadows in the inky night.

She closed the door and leaned against it, staring at the waxwork figures. Gently, she took her mother's arm and led her to her room, guiding her into the soft sheets. In her own room, she lifted Thingy from her bed and placed him in a soft blanket beneath the bed. He stirred slightly and smiled in his sleep as he snuggled down further, all traces of nastiness and resentment gone from his face. She would wake them both in the morning.

She crept back out and peered into the living-room area, where the fairies remained. Taking a deep breath, she whispered, 'Wake up!' before tiptoeing back to her bed and climbing in, fully clothed. There she lay, heart pounding. Their low voices carried from nearby, drowsy and confused. Her eyelids twitched. They were coming closer. She squeezed her eyes shut.

The bedroom door opened and, though she did not hear them enter, she felt it. Smelled it; the earthy, outdoorsy, leaf-mulch smell that always accompanied them.

'But I'm sure we came here for a reason,' Feathercap was complaining. He stifled a yawn. 'Why are we dressed like this anyway?'

'I can't remember,' said Raven, sounding equally puzzled.

'Something's gone on here,' said Gredin. He sounded the most alert. 'Some sort of hoodwinkery. Something's foxed us.'

'Maybe we just came to check on her,' said Raven.

'Maybe,' said Gredin, still suspicious. 'In any case, she seems to be behaving ... for now.'

Feathercap snorted. 'I don't suppose it'll be long before she's meddling again, trying to poke her nose into things that don't concern her.'

'I don't suppose it will,' said Gredin. 'But when she does we'll be watching.'

For a long time after they left Tanya lay unmoving, wanting to make sure they really were gone. When the earthy smell no longer lingered and her eyes finally stopped twitching, she opened them, reaching down in the darkness for Oberon's soft, brown head. Above her, moonlight streamed in through the gap in the curtains, playing across the ceiling. Sleep tugged at her, but she resisted, wanting to lie there in the quiet and dark, lost in her memories of the time she'd had with Ratty and Turpin.

For by morning, she knew, they would be gone.

'What is this place?' her mother grumbled the next morning, swatting midges out of her way as Oberon ran ahead, snuffling in the long grass.

'You'll see in a minute,' said Tanya. 'It's my favourite thing about Spinney Wicket.'

'Better than the pier?' Mrs Fairchild asked in surprise. 'Or the castle?'

'Much better,' said Tanya. 'It's completely magical.'

'Aren't I a bit too old to believe in magic?'

'No one's too old for that,' Tanya teased. 'Not even you!'

She dodged out of the way as her mother aimed a good-natured swipe at her, and they continued trampling along the wooded path, until finally the tree shimmered before them.

'Here it is,' said Tanya, marvelling at the rainbow flashes

of light bouncing off the bottles. 'The Wishing Tree.'

Her mother stood before it, a look of admiration on her face. 'Well, it's very pretty,' she said. 'A real grand old thing. I suppose we could make a wish, just for fun.'

The tree opened its eyes, beaming at the compliment. 'Very pretty, very grand,' it said. 'The finest tree in all the land!' It looked at Tanya critically. 'Your wish is made, my work is done. Don't ask for another one.'

Tanya frowned. She had the nagging feeling that she *had* made a wish, only she couldn't recall what it was. Yet somehow it was all right.

'Just you, Mum,' she said. 'I've already made my wish.'

Her mother went quiet for a moment. 'And would that wish have anything to do with your father and I getting back together?' Her voice was gentle. 'Because things don't work that way, love—'

'I know,' Tanya interrupted. 'I know that now. And you're right, I almost did wish for Dad to come back. But I knew it wouldn't change anything, and that things would still be the same. And I want you to be happy. I want us all to be happy. So I wished for something else.'

Her mother gave a wry smile. 'So, what do I have to do?'

Tanya took out the green glass bottle she had been saving for her own wish and handed it to her mother. 'You write it down and then hang it up. Or you can say it aloud, it's up to you.'

'I'll write it down,' said Mrs Fairchild, taking the bottle. 'It doesn't feel right to wish aloud. It might spoil the magic.'